the
new
girl

s. l. grey

CORVUS

Published in paperback in Great
Britain in 2013 by Corvus, an imprint
of Atlantic Books Ltd.

10 9 8 7 6 5 4 3

A CIP catalogue record for this book
is available from the British Library.

Paperback ISBN: 978 0 85789 592 9
E-book ISBN: 978 0 85789 591 2

Printed and bound by CPI Group (UK)
Ltd, Croydon, CR0 4YY

Corvus
An imprint of Atlantic Books Ltd
Ormond House
26-27 Boswell Street
London
WC1N 3JZ

www.corvus-books.co.uk

the
new
girl

S.L. Grey is a collaboration between Sarah Lotz and Louis Greenberg. Based in Cape Town, Sarah writes crime novels and thrillers under her own name, and as Lily Herne she and her daughter Savannah Lotz write the *Deadlands* series of zombie novels for young adults. Louis is a Johannesburg-based fiction writer and editor who worked in the book trade for many years. He has a Master's degree in vampire fiction and a doctorate in post-religious apocalyptic fiction.

Also by S.L. Grey

The Mall
The Ward

ACKNOWLEDGMENTS

S.L. Grey thanks: Lauren Beukes, Adam Greenberg, Sam Greenberg, Bronwyn Harris, Sarah Holtshausen, Alan Kelly, Savannah Lotz, Charlie Martins, Helen Moffett, Oli Munson, Sara O'Keeffe, Laura Palmer, Lucy Ridout, Alan and Carol Walters, Maddie West, Naomi Wicks and Corinna Zifko.

Chapter 1

RYAN

Ryan slices his hand on a loose snarl of guttering. He jerks his arm away and the light bulb slips out of his hand.

'Look out!'

The ladder judders and he braces himself against the aluminium rungs, watching the kids below him scattering backwards, tripping over their feet, bumping into each other in their urgency to move. All but one. A new girl he's never seen before drifts there, under the ladder, as if she hasn't heard him shout, as if she doesn't see the other children scurrying. The girl's hair is pale – a strawy yellow that looks artificial. The space around her is a void. The other kids don't look at her. The light bulb whistles an inch from her face and smashes at her feet with a hollow plock. She stops moving, but doesn't even look up.

The flexible frame of the ladder still bucks, and Ryan grips on tighter. Even though he's only two nouveau-kitsch, architect-designed, concrete-and-veneer high-school storeys above the ground, he imagines himself shattering on the walkway like that fragile glass orb.

'Mr Devlin,' calls out a voice from below. 'Mr Devlin!'

It's the headmaster, totally overdressed in a dark suit. 'Yes, Mr Duvenhage.'

'Are you all right up there?'

'Yes, sir.' There was a time when Ryan would never have said 'sir' to a man like this, but now he knows what greases the wheels, what makes life easier.

'Do try to be careful, would you?'

'Yes, sir,' Ryan says cheerfully. One good thing about becoming a blue-collar worker at the age of thirty-eight is that he feels a righteous resentment towards the managing classes. Solidarity with the workers. He now understands what lies behind those blank, passive-aggressive looks he got from labourers on the side of the road, or in the backs of trucks he used to trail in his car. It's hatred; a blanket, undifferentiated loathing. The same way he feels towards this little jerk barking orders below him. Their mistake, the reason they're still at the side of the road, on the back of that truck, is that they show it.

'And Mr Devlin...'

'Yes, sir?'

'You're dripping.' The man grimaces and steps backwards daintily before turning around and scuttling off.

Ryan looks at his slashed palm, clasps his hands together in an effort to staunch the flow, but watches with perverse fascination as the blood oozes its way between his palms and snakes down his forearm. Blood always finds a way out.

The flow gathers at his elbow, clotting with the late-summer sweat on his skin, collecting into a syrupy gout before reluctantly letting go and falling slickly. The kids have moved off along their lines like bees in an intricate dance. Except, right below him – he almost didn't notice; she is half obscured by his body – the new girl. She's like nobody he's ever seen before. She looks so thoroughly disconnected from the school kids around her. She doesn't move like other people. Most move along their predestined tracks just as they should, react to stimuli and repulsion just like idealised bodies in a science experiment. Occasionally they shunt off their path just a little – you can notice it in their lost expressions – but then they always correct their own course. Ryan sizes people up quickly, he knows where they fit. But this girl... she magnetises him like no other girl has before.

As he watches her, his hands clasped, noticing how she exerts no gravitational pull or push on the other kids passing by, a clotty drop of his blood hits her on the head, staining the long, straight, yellow hair like a stabbed duckling. Anyone else would look up, but she doesn't. She looks at her reflection in the ground-floor window. She calmly slides a middle finger over the blood on her head, then brings her hand down to look at it. She smears her thumb over the blood on the tip of her middle finger intently. Curiously.

Then, way after she should have, she tilts her head backwards and looks up at Ryan, clamped against the ladder's stilled struts. She stares at him, expressionless, causing Ryan to feel something very wrong. Then she lowers her head mechanically and continues to drift her void through the web of relationships in the yard below.

Ryan washes and disinfects his hand in the sink in the maintenance quarters, takes a pull of Three Ships from the bottle in his locker and breathes the fumes out tremulously, bracing himself against the clammy metal of the lockers.

'Eita, Ryan.' Thulani Duma, the school's chief groundsman, essentially Ryan's direct superior, comes in, the blue hibiscus of his Hawaiian shirt showing through his buttoned-down overalls. He taps his watch and shakes his head microscopically. 'Mr Duvenhage wants to see you.'

'Hmm, what now?'

Thulani shrugs.

Ryan rinses with the Listerine in his locker, knowing as he does it that the reek of mouthwash is more damning than any waft of whisky. He wonders why it matters. When he was a scholar at his dark, faux-Gothic government-funded boys' school, all the senior teachers were drunk half the time. It's the same at Alice's expensive Catholic private school... It's all about the show, of course. They can behave how they want as long as they look right doing it. Ryan can picture men like Duvenhage going home and beating his wife and kid – something Ryan never did, even in the worst of it – then cruising the streets in his tame sedan and raping some street child. He beams that sort of malice from those tiny eyes of his, tucked away behind that unctuous rubber smile and that fussy haircut.

Ryan's aware, as he announces himself to the school's 'executive secretary', that the 'Crossley College' stitched across the back of his blue overalls brands him. Property of the school. And since when did schools start needing 'executive secretaries' in the first place? This is apparently one of the innovations Duvenhage brought in when he joined the school at the beginning of the year, one of the wave of school administrators who take more pride in their MBAs than their teaching diplomas. Sybil Fontein is a fifty-something, thin-lipped, uptight bitch who reeks of her failure to land a job as a corporate PA. She treats her position as a portal to Duvenhage's petty majesty like some sort of holy penance. One day, having cleansed herself sufficiently, she might climb a rung and become – what? – a vestal sacrifice at the monthly meeting of the school governing body?

Ryan shakes off the image before it becomes too deeply lodged in his mind. Graphic images are at the root of his problems, this urge to actuate what he sees in his mind. He's never quite been able to separate the real world from the pictures in his mind.

He sits nonchalantly on the hard wooden bench outside the principal's office while, in the alcove opposite, Sybil Fontein makes a huffy show of filing papers and clattering on her keyboard. She looks up at him with distaste – the grubby help occupying her space – but then he smiles and she blushes and quickly looks down again. He knows she'll look at him again. Three, two, one – there we go – and this time the look on her face is more inviting. Ryan knows what works.

At length Duvenhage pokes his head around his door. 'Mr Devlin. Come inside, please.'

Like the rest of the school, the office is decorated in pale earth tones, with broad plate-glass windows, stone tiles and blond-wood furnishings. It's expensive and new – just eight years old, as its shammy coat of arms with the 'Est.' date below it proclaims – and not what Ryan imagines when he thinks of school. It's more like one of those corporate office parks. But as much as the rich parents are prepared to pay to keep their children out of the over-crowded, underfunded, directionless mess of South African state education, it's still fraying at the edges, and that, Ryan supposes, is why he has a job. The ceiling boards in this office are sagging and there's an invasion of rising damp and mildew eating through the wall where it abuts the picture window. Hurried architecture and shoddy work. Ryan goes to the corner to inspect the damp more closely.

But Duvenhage indicates a chair at his desk. 'Sit, please, Mr Devlin.'

Duvenhage sits and faces him across the desk, his smooth-skinned, pudgy face sheened, that oily smile. Ryan sits across from him, all casual deference calculated to placate the petty bureaucrat. Duvenhage shifts a pink folder across his desk and clasps his hands above it. 'As you know, Mr Devlin, Crossley College is concerned that the... ethos of the institution is pervasively and consistently upheld by each one of its members, whether that be student body, teaching staff or support services.'

Ryan lets him talk, nodding at the right times. The ethos. He's heard a lot about that. From what he can see, it's the same ethos as at his own high school: bullying, repression and conformism. Couching it in corporate cant doesn't change it. Ryan keeps his mouth shut. He needs this job.

'To that end,' your... uh, contract of employment states that all personal belongings brought onto the campus by... contract staff... are subject to regular inspection to ensure that the... said, ethos is upheld. At eleven fifteen this morning, I carried out a routine examination of the lockers in the maintenance staff changing room and found... uhm... certain items on the list of items banned from campus which was appended to your contract, namely... uhm... two bottles of alcohol and... uhm... one pocket knife—'

'Oh, that. Don't worry, I can—'

'A minute, Mr Devlin,' Duvenhage says. The smile is gone and there's something cold behind his eyes. The man's not used to being interrupted; he's surrounded by sycophants. 'You will have your chance to explain. Two bottles of alcohol, one pocket knife, and a book by a banned author. Let's see...' He takes out his phone and makes a show of flicking through a series of photos he has taken of Ryan's things. 'Yes, here. J. K. Rowling. *The Deathly Hallows.*'

'It's for my daughter.' The mild irritation Ryan's been feeling at this man's constipated tone and mindless bureaucracy shifts up a gear into anger. He wills himself to keep calm. He has to keep a lid on it.

Duvenhage pales and shakes his head, then finds solace inside the folder, opening it and shuffling through it as if to confirm to himself that the rules were laid down in ink. He finds what he's looking for and holds it up to Ryan. 'The list of banned authors is distributed to all staff on a weekly basis, Mr Devlin, and it is staff's responsibility to familiarise themselves with the contents. There is really no excuse for this... book, or any of the other undesirable items, to be brought onto campus. What's more, I can smell that you have been drinking alcohol, which is a gross contravention. I'm issuing a final, written warning which will go into your file. Hiring you in the first place was an act of kindness on the part of Mr Grindley – a misguided one in my opinion, since the security of our student body is the...'

Duvenhage's words have been dissolving as the anger simmers, and now they disappear. A familiar feeling wakes up and twitches inside Ryan, a painful itch that needs to be scratched. He's successfully kept the compulsion at bay for months now. The psychiatrist said that what he called Ryan's transient kleptomania was a dislocated symptom of the unresolved anger about the circumstances of his family's dissolution, and treating the rage with antidepressants had apparently all but put an end to the episodes. The last time he had given into it was during his last job, a short stint as a hospital porter at New Hope Hospital. He had no use for any of the items he stole from the staff and patients and he left the job before his petty thefts were discovered. But, now, being treated like a child by this pasty bureaucrat, the urge is back, as strong as ever. He fidgets in his seat, clenches his leaking palms.

'Are you even listening, Mr Devlin?'

He makes himself speak. 'Yes, Mr Duvenhage.'

'I need you to countersign this official notification of warning.' Duvenhage pages through the documents in the pink folder again, his face growing redder, his brow creasing.

'Mrs Fontein!' he bellows.

No answer.

'Mrs Fontein!'

He gets up from behind his desk, muttering, 'Where is...? Wait here,' he says to Ryan and leaves the office, closing the door behind him.

Now's his chance. Ryan springs up, locks the office door and moves to Duvenhage's side of the desk. There has to be something here. His lower belly thrums with the thrill of being caught. He's forgotten how powerful the feeling is, how seductive; it's almost sexual. He opens the desk's top drawer, knowing that Duvenhage is just across the hall and will be back as soon as he's found his document. Ryan's got to hurry. He scratches through the drawer. A sheaf of letters and documents he wouldn't mind reading sometime; a silver pen and pencil set, a stapler.

The second drawer. A Bible, some thin manuals, a box of tissues. Uh-uh.

He forces himself to slow down. The door handle rattles. 'Mr Devlin? What the...?'

Ah. There, there.

'Devlin! Open the door. What are you...?'

Duvenhage's briefcase, resting against the side of the bookcase. It's unlocked. Click, click. More papers, fuck it, but, yes, underneath, here we go. A tiny flash drive, shaped like a stylised dove. That'll do. It's something that Duvenhage will just think he's misplaced.

He shuts the briefcase, leans it back where it was, pockets the drive and rushes to the door, unlocks it.

'Devlin, what the... on Earth... are you doing?' Duvenhage is red in the face.

'Sorry, Mr Duvenhage, I noticed that a screw in the deadbolt was loose. I was just... If I'd had my... my pocket knife, I could've...'

'Don't try your luck, Mr Devlin. We have a complete inventory of maintenance equipment, which, school regulations state, must be kept under lock and key in the designated storage compartments, not, regardless, in contract staff's personal lockers.'

'Yes. I'm sorry.'

'Well, sign this, please, as acknowledgement of our discussion and of your warning. Note that this is a final warning, and contraband – and especially drinking during hours of service – will not be tolerated. Do you understand, Mr Devlin?' Duvenhage holds up a pen.

'Yes, I do, sir. It won't happen again.' He smiles his disarming smile, takes the pen and signs the paper.

'Good. Now get that stuff off my campus.'

Ryan nods and makes towards the door.

'And, Mr Devlin...'

'Yes, sir?'

'See to this rising damp tomorrow, would you? I'm sure it's unhealthy to work in this office. I believe there are spores breeding there.'

'Of course, sir.' The anger he was feeling just minutes ago is a distant memory. Now he just feels empty.

At four o'clock, Ryan changes into his jeans and T-shirt, stashes the knife, book and bottle in his backpack and heads towards the school's main gate. The elaborate boom system with a security booth in the middle is not designed for pedestrians and he has to take his chances against the polished 4x4s that choke the school's parking ground as parents idle, like sharks in a tank, waiting to pick their children up from sports.

Ryan crosses the main entrance road, scrapes past the security boom and out onto the street. It's hot for March; the summer rain is drying up but the sun still blazes. There's a steep hill up and over to his cheap room in Malvern; he's one of the immigrants now, who overcrowd the run-down houses in that buffer suburb. Since he lost his licence – and his car, for that matter – walking has become easier. He gets into a rhythm as he walks and he manages to quiet his mind. He's a lot fitter than when he used to drive to work, park near the lifts and ping out in his air-conditioned office. Not having a car is restrictive in Johannesburg, though, and he's had to limit his orbit to the Eastgate and Bedford malls, the crummy shops on Langermann Drive, his rented room and the school.

An image of that new girl flashes into his mind, the way she fingered the blood. It was intimate. She just looked at him, and there was no panic or disgust in her eyes. He couldn't read what those eyes held, and that's unusual for him. She must have just started at the school; it's not possible that he wouldn't have seen her before: he's spent the last two months up ladders, washing windows, nailing guttering, looking into classrooms and down on school thoroughfares. There are not that many kids at the school, something like five hundred. The way she looked at the blood on her fingers. Curiously.

'Ryan!' An engine guns next to him. 'Hi, Ryan!'

An olive-green Land Rover is matching his pace up the hill, window wound down and a smell of expensive car and expensive perfume and cigarette smoke billowing out of the window. Julie Katopodis. She's in good shape, fortyish, petite and buffed, straight black hair and manicured nails. Gold bracelets.

Ryan smiles and approaches the door. Julie stops the car.

'Hi to you,' he says.

'Hello again, Mr Maintenance Man,' she says.

Ryan smiles, knowing the effect his two-day stubble has on her.

'Listen, do you want a lift?'

Does he? Is he in the mood today? He supposes he is. What else is there to do? 'Sure, thanks.' He opens the passenger door as she dumps her handbag into the footwell.

'I came to pick Artie up from hockey, but he messaged me to say he's gone to his friend's for supper. Would have been nice if he'd told me, like, before. I don't like a wasted journey.'

She lights up another Dunhill with a slim gold lighter. The gold suits her tan. She offers the plush pack to him, heavy on the finger contact.

'No, thanks.' He stares out at the flats across the road.

'I wasn't following you, you know,' the woman's saying, sighing her first drag out into the air. 'Artie has practice every Tuesday and Thursday. Matches every Wednesday. Cricket and hockey.'

Ryan turns back to her. 'Hey, I believe you. You're bona fide.'

'So here's me... come all this way with nobody to pick up.'

Chapter 2

TARA

The library door slams, making Tara jump. She's been daydreaming, lulled by the drone of Skye's voice as he works his way through *Tina and Kevin Go to the Zoo*.

She looks up, expecting to see Clara van der Spuy, the school's head librarian, but a girl Tara's never seen before is staring into the room, her back pressed against the door. Tara's first thought is that the kid's mother should be shot – poor mite is asking to be bullied; Tara's almost certain her hair is dyed. It's that peculiar bile shade that results when wannabe-platinum brunettes get the peroxide mix wrong. And there's something off about her school uniform, her frayed blazer is a darker shade than Crossley's regulation baby-shit colour, and her skirt is too large for her small frame; the stitching showing in the seams as if it's homemade. Could she be one of the outreach kids, the small quota of less-privileged students Crossley College subsidises each year? As Tara stares at her she steps forward tentatively, then drops to her knees in front of the shelf of starter readers closest to the door. She grabs a book from the shelf, starts paging through it.

Tara glances over at Malika, the other library volunteer on

duty. Malika's supposed to be supervising the quiet-time kids, but she's smirking down at her iPhone and toying with her hair. It doesn't look like she's noticed the new arrival; either that or she's pretending not to see her. And none of the other kids seems to have registered the girl's presence. Tara would've expected at least a few of them to point and snigger, but perhaps they can't see her from where they're sitting. Unlike the rest of the school – a modern glass-and-wood structure with such crisp edges it looks like a giant Scandinavian architect's model – the library is cramped, dingy and ill designed, full of useless corners and pointless pillars; plenty of places to obscure the view of the door.

'Carry on,' Tara says to Skye. 'I'll just be a minute.'

Tara finds herself approaching the girl cautiously, as if she's a wild animal that might dart off at any second. It's only when Tara's right next to her that she realises the book she's paging through is upside down.

'Hello,' she says to the girl's back, putting on her I'm-your-buddy voice. 'Can I help you? Are you lost?' No reaction. Tara gently touches the girl's shoulder. 'Hey.'

The girl freezes, and then slowly turns her head and stares up at Tara through grey, unblinking eyes.

'Hi. I'm Tara. What's your name?'

She whispers a word that Tara doesn't catch.

'Say again? Sorry, sweetie, must be getting old, I didn't hear you properly.' Tara's used to her American accent breaking the ice with the shyer children, but it's not working with this kid. The girl isn't pretty – those eyes are way too large for her face – but there's something charmingly old-fashioned and serious about her, as if she's stepped out of an old sepia photograph. Tara crouches down next to her, notices a dark-red substance clotting strands of that strange hair together – and there's more on her fingers. She can't see any sign of an actual wound, but it certainly looks like blood. Paint, maybe?

'Hey, are you hurt?' The girl finally blinks and follows Tara's gaze to her hand. Her tongue darts out of her mouth and for a second Tara's convinced she's going to bring her fingers to her lips and lick them. 'Can I see, sweetie?'

The girl bares her teeth at Tara, then throws the book to the floor, leaps up and darts through the door, body listing to one side as if one leg is shorter than the other.

'Hey!' Tara calls after her, her knees popping as she scrambles to her feet. She pokes her head out into the corridor, but there's no sign of the girl. Could she have scuttled into one of the bathrooms? Maybe, but what the hell was she doing wandering around the school willy-nilly in the first place?

Bemused, Tara returns to where Skye is still doggedly working his way towards the book's predictable climax. 'You know that girl?' Tara asks.

'What girl?'

'The girl I was just talking to. She new?'

Skye shrugs. 'Ja. I s'pose.'

'She in your class?'

Skye looks at her blankly. Tara knows that he isn't the sharpest tool in the box, but it's hardly a challenging question.

'You know her name?' she tries again.

'Can't remember,' Skye mumbles, bending one of the book's pages into a triangle. Tara would usually discourage this, but in her opinion the only fit place for a book as stultifying as *Tina and Kevin Go to the Zoo* is the recycling bin.

The end-of-class siren whoops, making Tara jump as usual, and there's the screech of chair legs scraping on wood as the kids stand up quietly and file out.

'Hey,' Tara says to Malika, who's busily rummaging through her Louboutin bag. 'You see that weird-looking kid who came in here just now?'

Malika shrugs. 'They're all weird at that age, aren't they?' She yawns, drags her fingers through her hair. 'God, library duty is so boring. I can't believe you signed up for another year. How on earth do you put up with this every day, Tara?'

Tara shrugs. She started volunteering at the library last year to demonstrate to Stephen that she was at least trying to be involved in his son's life (pointless, really, as the little snot couldn't care less if she was here or not). Maybe she does it to get out of the house, as a tenuous link to her former profession, or to prove to herself that at least she's doing something useful while she waits for her permanent residency to come through. Although helping privileged Joburg kids with their remedial reading isn't exactly on the same level as, say, counselling AIDS orphans in the townships. Anyway, if all goes to plan – if her business takes off – she won't have time to volunteer here, will she?

But she isn't about to go into this with Malika, a member of that tribe of primped, alien women who waft in to fill in at the library and tuck shop, their bodies sculpted by Zumba classes and Botox, clouds of expensive scent trailing behind them as they clack through the corridors. Sure, they're friendly enough to her, but Tara's never managed to penetrate the clique, or make anything approximating a friend. Plus, she hasn't missed the contemptuous glances Malika tends to direct at her old Levi's and battered sneakers.

Malika makes a show of glancing at her phone. 'Do you mind packing up? I've got to meet my personal trainer at three.'

'Sure,' Tara says. She doesn't really mind. She's still got an hour or so to kill before Martin finishes rugby practice. Besides, she wants some time alone on the library computer. Her cellphone network is down again and she hasn't been able to check her emails on her BlackBerry all day.

It doesn't take more than a couple of minutes to re-shelve the books; the class today was small and in any case there aren't that many books to choose from. Most are dull, storyless starter readers along the lines of *Tina and Kevin Go to the Zoo*, but since Mr Duvenhage became head other, more disturbing, books have appeared on the shelves. Sinister self-published morality tales with amateurish illustrations, most of which involve a child getting his or her comeuppance in ways that pretty much amount to child abuse. Titles include such gems as *Lying Means Crying* and *Malicious Molly Makes a Monstrous Mistake*. At the beginning of the year, she'd enthusiastically brought in a selection of *Winnie the Witch* and Roald Dahl books, but Clara van der Spuy had nipped that in the bud: 'We try not to encourage this kind of distorted thinking, Mrs Marais. It's not really in line with the school ethos.'

Tara slips into Clara's small office at the back of the library, trying to ignore the saccharine baby-animal posters, complete with captions, that are tacked up all over the walls. Since she was last in here, Clara's added a glossy image of a pair of terrified-looking kittens ('I can haz friend') and a soft-focus photograph of a traumatised baby gorilla ('Needz a hug? Try me') to her collection. Tara fires up Clara's computer and quickly logs on to her website. It's only been up and running for a month, and she still feels a thrill when she scrolls through the photographs. She checks to see if her clients have posted their promised recommendations on her feedback page (they haven't), then clicks onto the Gmail account she uses solely for her work (her *hobby*, Stephen insists on calling it).

There are two messages – not bad. She opens the first, which is from a Susannah Ferguson, subject line: 'I Love Baby Paul!!!!!'

'Hi Tara! My name is Susannah and I am interested in adopting Baby Paul. He is soooooo beautiful. Please how much is he? I will pay anything!!!! Is 900 rand enough? Do you do lay-byes too?'

Tara smiles to herself. She knows most people can't afford her rates, and while she's tempted to cut the price, it's a fraction of what they go for in the States or the UK. She keeps telling herself she's not in it for the money, but since Stephen started whinge-ing about cutting back, she decided to do what the self-help books encourage and 'turn her passion into profit'. She takes her time crafting a gentle, encouraging response, providing the link to the rates section on her website.

Disappointingly, the second message looks like it's probably spam. It's from a Yahoo account, the sender's name listed as 'varder batiss'. No message in the subject line. She opens it anyway. 'We require baby,' is all it says.

Tara snorts. Don't we all, she thinks, pressing delete.

A cough makes her jump again, and she looks up to see Clara van der Spuy standing in front of the desk, smiling fixedly at her.

Tara feels guilty colour flushing her cheeks. It's not as if she's doing anything wrong – volunteers are allowed to use the library's computer – but Clara's perennial self-righteous expression always makes her feel as if she's nine years old again. Tara has no idea how old Clara is – she could be anywhere from fifty to seventy – and she appears to have an inexhaustible supply of high-necked sensible blouses and tweed skirts. According to Malika – the font of all school gossip – before she joined Crossley College, Clara spent years teaching English at one of those old South African colonial institutions. Tara has no problem imagining Clara happily teaching apartheid dogma and stamping the word 'Banned' on any slightly controversial book that came her way.

'Sorry about this, Clara,' Tara says, trying to smile. 'Just killing time before I fetch Martin.'

'It's *fine*, Mrs Marais. I was just popping in to add the new books to the catalogue. But I can wait until you are finished.'

Taking the hint, Tara quickly clears her browsing history and gathers her stuff together. She pauses, remembering that strange new kid. 'Hey, Clara, what's up with that new girl?'

'I'm sorry?'

'She came into the library earlier. Could be one of the outreach kids. Weird hair colour, might be slightly disabled.'

Clara squishes her lips in disapproval. 'You mean *physically challenged*, Mrs Marais?'

Jesus, Tara thinks. Excuse me for breathing. 'Yeah. She told me her name but I couldn't quite catch it.'

'I can't say I have a clue who you mean, Mrs Marais.'

'Really? I was worried she might have hurt herself.' She shrugs. 'Hey, maybe I just imagined her.'

Clara doesn't crack a smile. 'I don't think that's likely, Mrs Marais.'

'Please, call me Tara.'

'Best not to,' Clara says. 'It's good to keep on formal terms. It confuses the learners otherwise.'

'Well, I guess I'll see you tomorrow.'

Clara relaxes; her smile actually reaches her eyes this time. 'Yes. We do appreciate all the good work you do here for us, Mrs Marais.'

Tara steps out into the corridor. With the children gone now, the building feels more soulless and utilitarian than usual, as if it shrugs off the kids' energy every day like a dog shaking fleas off its back. Not that there's all that much energy to shake off. Even in the heart of the school morning, the kids who attend Crossley College are more subdued than the kids who inhabited the smelly chaos of the schools she's taught at over the years.

She heads out into the sunlight, sneakered feet crunching on the raked gravel. The grounds are similarly deserted and silent, just the distant buzz of a whistle and muffled yells from the sports fields. Ahead of her, a rangy figure emerges out of one of the maintenance sheds. Tara hesitates. If she carries on walking, their paths will cross. She pretends to fumble in her bag as an excuse to stop. She's seen him before, of course. Well, she could hardly miss him; his appearance is so totally at odds with the rest of the staff. According to Malika (who imparted the information in a slightly breathy fashion) he's the new maintenance man. He's swarthy-skinned, wild-haired, always looks dishevelled, but in a cool way like the hard-eyed alternative kids who used to hang out on the fringes of her own high school. Dangerous. *Sexy* dangerous. Like a gypsy; maybe a pirate.

But he doesn't even turn his head in her direction. Feeling like a fool, she hurries towards the parking lot.

Martin's waiting by the car, kicking at the back tyre. 'Where were you?' he whines. 'I've been waiting for ages.'

Tara knows this isn't true. She's five minutes late, if that. 'Sorry,' she says anyway. 'Hey, how was school?'

He shrugs.

'What would you like for supper?' she asks brightly as he straps himself into the back seat. 'How about chicken?'

'I hate chicken,' Martin mumbles.

'Okay. Steak and fries, then.'

'Whatever. Oh, and by the way, in *South Africa* we call them *chips*.'

'Not at McDonalds,' she says, trying to make a joke of it. 'You order fries there, don't you?'

Martin mumbles something that sounds like 'totally lame'.

She zoots down the driveway, pausing to let a Land Rover with tinted windows pull out in front of her. The driver sticks her hand out of the window, waves her thanks with a flick of her cigarette. Tara squeaks into the traffic, which, as soon as they reach the first intersection, slows to a crawl.

Martin's phone beeps out a gangsta-rap riff. 'Ja?' He sighs and kicks the back of her seat. 'It's Dad. Says he's been trying to get hold of you.'

She reaches back for the phone, which is slick with Martin's palm sweat. 'Hey, honey,' she says into the handset, automatically checking the mirrors for cops.

'Where've you been?' Stephen says. 'I've been trying to get you all day.'

'Sorry. Problem with the network again. What's up?'

Stephen huffs as if the vagaries of her cell provider are her fault. 'One of Olivia's clients needs her to go to Cape Town.'

'What? When?'

'Tomorrow.'

'*Tomorrow*? And she's only just told you?'

'It's not her fault. They sprung it on her.'

Bullshit, Tara thinks, smothering a bitter response. She hates it when Stephen defends Olivia, which he seems to do more and more these days, but she can't let Martin hear her bitching about his mother. 'Right. So that means...?'

'We've got Martin for another week.'

Goddammit, Tara thinks. Just what I need. 'Okay,' she says, hating herself for giving in so easily. 'No problem.'

'You okay to man the fort? I'm going to the gym after work, might be back a bit late.'

'I was hoping to get some work done tonight, Stephen.' At least when Stephen's around Martin is forced to be civil to her.

A pause. 'So? Martin's hardly a baby. He can look after himself, can't he?'

'I guess.'

'See you later.'

'Love you.' But he's already hung up. In the rear-view mirror she sees Martin miming vomiting. She has to slam on the brakes as the taxi in front of her screeches to a halt, feels the bite of the seat belt digging into her breasts.

'Don't you know how to drive?' Martin says. 'I could have *died*.'

Good, Tara thinks, furiously flicking on the radio and turning it up too loud. She does her best to concentrate on the Katy Perry track filling the car with perky good cheer, but her palms are aching from gripping the steering wheel.

Martin pushes past her the second she unlocks the security gate, making a beeline for the kitchen. Tara hesitates in the corridor. All she wants to do is lock herself into her sanctuary, but she forces herself to follow in Martin's wake, stepping over the shoes he's kicked off, the discarded backpack that's vomited pencil shavings, an apple core and textbooks over the tiles. Whenever she's alone with him, her insides feel like stretched rubber, a twanging anxiety that's grinding her down. Sometimes she fantasises about secretly dosing him with Ritalin, or even better, tranquilisers. Occasionally these fantasies turn darker – a swift plane or bus crash perhaps (instant and painless; she's not a monster).

Martin's already foraging in the fridge. She knows that the glass of milk he's pouring will sit, untouched, next to the couch until it grows a skin, until *she* clears it up.

'Don't forget to do your homework before you watch TV, Martin.'

'Ja, ja.'

'You need any help with it?'

'Course I don't. What are you? Stupid?'

That's *exactly* what she is, she thinks. Putting up with this crap. She can almost hear her mother's voice: 'You made your bed, Tara. This is what you get when you steal another woman's man.' It still rankles that her mother didn't come to the wedding last year. Stephen offered to buy her a plane ticket, but she didn't even respond to their emails until three weeks after the event.

And anyway, her mother's right. She *did* steal him, didn't she?

She's done her best to connect with Martin; tried to imagine how she would have felt if her father had left her mother and married someone else. For the first six months after she moved in, Stephen had been supportive, sympathetic. 'Don't worry, my baby,' he'd say when he caught her crying after Martin had called her a bitch, or refused to eat the lasagne she'd spent hours making from scratch. 'It won't be long before he accepts you.' Deep-fried bullshit with a side order of crap, she thinks. And Stephen's no longer quite as supportive; she knows he thinks she's not trying hard enough, although God knows what he expects her to do. It's not as if Martin treats only her with contempt. She's lost count of the number of times Stephen was called into the school last year to discuss Martin's 'anti-social tendencies' with the counsellor. The kid's a spoilt brat and a bully. Plain and simple.

She knows she should make Martin apologise to her for his rudeness, but she can't be bothered. Leaving him to paw through the fridge, she hurries up the stairs to the only place she can really call her own – the smallest of the four bedrooms at the top of the house.

She slips inside it, locks the door behind her and breathes in the comforting scent of Johnson's baby shampoo and talcum powder. She buys the essence bottled, it lasts longer that way on the babies' skin, and every day she adds a drop to the carpet so that it's the first thing she smells when she enters the room.

She opens the drawer where she keeps Baby Paul, all snuggled up in the monogrammed blanket she cross-stitched herself. She's not a fan of sewing, but Paul is special – he's her fourth baby, but her first boy. She's only sold two of her babies so far, and both times it's been a wrench. She doesn't know how she'll cope when Baby Paul is adopted, but if she wants to make this a success then she has to learn to let go. But, God, he's so beautiful; that perfect blush of health on his cheeks, his little fists scrunched to his chest. For a second she can almost imagine he's breathing. She gently strokes the fine hair that coats the shallow dip of his fontanel. There's no doubt about it, she's getting better. Really, she has every right to call herself a professional.

She fires up her laptop, clicks onto the Gmail account again. Nothing from Susannah, but there's another email from the weird, spammy account, this one saying: 'Perhaps we were being unclarified. Be assured we are serious beyond belief. We necessitate a forespecial baby now. Can you dispense?'

Could the sender be foreign? That would explain the odd syntax. And if so, she thinks, feeling a flicker of excitement, could this be a commission? God, that would be a real challenge. It would mean sculpting at least the head from scratch, rather than working from a kit, something she's never done before. She knows that some of the more skilled Reborners work from photographs, and she's well aware of the sad history many of the women who desire to own Reborns share. Women who can't have children of their own; women who have suffered terrible tragedies – a cot death or premature death – and who long to hold a facsimile of their lost baby in their arms.

People like her, she thinks, although she doesn't allow herself to dwell on this. She's only thirty-eight, there's time to try again. She gazes down at Baby Paul, lifts him out of his drawer, gently supporting his head. She still can't believe how quickly she caught the Reborn bug, remembers the exact moment when the desire to own one of these hyper-realistic infant dolls had swamped her. It had been during a holiday in Cape Town, a trip Stephen had organised a few weeks after their hasty wedding. They'd visited a toy shop in a sprawling mall to buy Martin a present, and she'd stopped dead, hardly able to breathe, when she spotted the Reborn section in the corner of the store. At first she'd been repelled, almost nauseated by the sight of the lifelike dolls displayed in their own little incubators, several complete with feeding tubes and heart monitors, a sign above the section reading 'Shhhh, babies sleeping'. As she stood there, she felt her initial revulsion turning to fascination, and when a sales girl offered to let her hold one, she felt something inside her shift as she cradled its little body in her arms. The next day she'd made an excuse to return to the mall and, using her US credit card, she bought Baby Lulu, a preemie baby with darling curled eyelashes. Stephen had been horrified but she blocked out his reaction, and when she discovered that with the right materials pretty much anyone could learn how to Reborn a doll, she decided to purchase her first starter kit. She found that she had a talent for it – an artistic side she never knew she had.

She writes a response before she loses her nerve: 'Hi! Thanks for your email. Sorry for not responding earlier. Are you interested in commissioning a baby? I would be very happy to help you, if so. Reborning is my passion! I think you should know, though, that the rates for me to create your own special baby will be slightly higher than those for adopting my existing babies.' How much? Five thousand? Should she dare? Why not? 'R5000, with a fifty per cent deposit required.'

Heart in her throat, she presses send.

She gets on with unpacking the parcels that arrived from the States yesterday – a selection of rooting needles, a fresh paint kit and a new torso that she purchased at a bargain price (and, again, bought with her American credit card so that Stephen won't be able to gripe about the expense). Her latest baby – Baby Gabby – is almost complete, and she carefully removes the infant's parts from her work-in-progress drawer. She finished mottling Baby Gabby's limbs at the weekend, using a new technique she learnt from a step-by-step tutorial on the internet, so all she has to do is make a decision about the baby's hair.

Something makes her turn back to her computer. That was quick – a response!

'This is primo news! We will supply mimeograph exemplar forthwith. The rate expressed meets our yearnings. Send remuneration details.'

A mimeograph? Strange use of language. This Batiss person *must* be foreign; probably uses Google Translate to write the emails. She feels another thrill of excitement as she taps in a response, remembering to include her bank account number. This could be it. If she can't go back to teaching, well, there's no reason why she can't make a success of her other passion, is there?

'Tara!' Stephen's voice floats up from the hallway downstairs. She checks the time. God, it's past eight already. She should have taken the steak out of the freezer hours ago.

She rushes out of the room, pausing to lock the door behind her. She doesn't dare leave it open for even a second. Months ago she'd made the mistake of showing Baby Lulu to Martin in an attempt to connect with the little shit. That had resulted in weeks of snide comments. She doesn't want to imagine what destruction he would wreak if he found his way in here.

She finds Stephen slumped in his La-Z-Boy in the lounge, flicking through the DStv channels. Martin's stretched out on the opposite couch, laptop on his chest, earphones in place. She tries not to look at the detritus from his after-school snack scattered on the rug.

'There you are,' Stephen says.

She bends for a kiss. He doesn't smell as if he's been to the gym. Perhaps he showered afterwards; he does that sometimes.

'How was your day?' she asks.

'Hard. Yours?'

'Usual. Hey, guess what?'

'What?'

'Looks like I might have a commission.'

'A what?'

'A commission for a baby. They're sending through a photograph for me to work from.'

His eyes flick back to the reality show on the screen. 'That's great. We going to eat soon?'

'Won't be long,' she says, fighting to keep the disappointment out of her voice.

In the time she's been holed up in her sanctuary, the kitchen has turned into a bomb site; the expensive Lurpak butter melting on the counter top, bread crumbs and empty Lay's crisp packets scattered around it. And guess who'll have to clean it up? Stephen refuses to hire a maid – he's paranoid about security, says that letting a stranger into the house is asking for trouble, even though they live on a security estate with more razor-wired fences than Rikers Island. Tara often feels guilty about not providing employment for one of the desperate women she sees begging at the traffic lights; it's not as if they can't afford to hire someone, labour is cheap here.

Tara hauls the steak and bag of fries – the *chips*, goddammit – out of the freezer. She chucks the steak in the microwave, presses the defrost button.

'I'm starving,' she hears Martin whine. 'Can't we get take-out, Dad? Her cooking tastes like crap.'

'Martin,' she hears Stephen say.

'But, *Daaad*.'

'Enough!'

She puts the oil on the stove for the fries, then rests her head on her hands and watches the steak as it whirls round and round on its plate in the microwave.

If she's quick, she'll have time to scoot upstairs to see if there's another message from Batiss. Maybe this time he – or she, who knows? – will have attached the photograph. She flies up the stairs, unlocks her room, her heart leaping as she sees the '1' next to the Gmail icon on her email.

It *is* from Batiss, and even better, there's an attachment! 'This is what we require' is all the message says. At first the attachment doesn't want to open, and she's forced to reboot her computer, then a tiny photograph about the size of a thumbnail appears on the screen. How is she expected to work from this?

'Tara!' she hears Stephen shouting. '*Tara!*'

She clicks on the zoom icon, and the photograph instantly increases in size, although it's too pixellated to see clearly. She experiments with the size settings, and gradually it begins to resolve; she's never seen an attachment behave like this before.

She leans closer. Is that…? There's a leg, the chubby shape of a baby's arm…

'Tara! Something's burning!'

It's a photograph of a baby all right, but there's something wrong with its face.

Her stomach tips over when she realises what it is.

The baby's eyes and mouth are sewn up, the flesh of its eyelids and lips scored with coarse, black thread.

Chapter 3

PENTER

The thought-seep this morning is even more noticeable than yesterday. She can't shake the feeling that she's being disregardful, even
though she knows she's on assignment and has special dispensa-
tion from the Ministry. Up here she can't get her regular penetration
renewal; they can't haul an entire clinic into the field with them.
When you're upside on a special project you're on your own;
you've got to monitor yourself. The drones warned her about the
thought-seep. They said it would be disconcerting, and it is. She
lies in bed, on the dark south side of the house, and tries to keep
her mind quiet.

She grabs her gelphone and hides under the blankets with it.
She reads the proclamation ticker for comfort, to make herself feel
closer to home. 'Victuals are precious. The meat tree is a fable. Use
your tokens appropriately.' 'Apparel does not auto-generate. Wash
sparingly.' 'Energy is scarce and opulent. Save energy for essential
tasks and services only.' Everyone knows that resources are scarce,
she finds herself commenting, you don't have to repeat yourself.
She tries to block out the disregardful thoughts.

She remembers talking to a now-depreciated member of her

grouping. He was old. He used to tell stories about when the world didn't know about the upside. She'd never been upside, nor had anyone she knew, and though there were plenty of mimeographs and artefacts and browns wandering around like off-course ants, sometimes she just couldn't believe it existed.

There were fewer people then, the old man said, and they got by. They burnt peat for warmth and light and ate what produce lived in the walls. Then when whoever it was discovered the upside, apparently all glare and ether, people flocked to the nodes like starving leeches to a wound. The first ones became blind, so the story went, their lungs grew weak and their skins became dry and sore with seeping cracks and strange moulds.

You'd think that would have been enough to keep them away from the nodes, but what they found up there was a temptation too great. Colour, radiance unimagined. Victuals of such strange variety and with flavours that first burnt their mouths with their intensity but then became addictive. Soon the traditional victuals were forgotten and people started copying the style of upside victuals. Which meant that upside supplies had to be gathered. The browns crowded at the upside of the nodes in numbers that bewildered the explorers. They swarmed like a mindless colony, but they had remarkable technologies: self-generating light and heat, machines for every conceivable purpose, and they exuded such energy themselves, a thin, light energy which was good for floating objects in ether – not much call for that in Penter's world – and a darker, heavier energy which permeated the walls.

The upside people were willing to trade; there were always many upside leaders clustered around a node who would sell their resources in exchange for their crude symbolic tokens, for numbers on a gelscreen.

That's when people started calling their own world *the downside*, trapping it forever after into an unbalanced relationship with the ants up in the ether. Then the world became what it is, what she's always known, a place of generated glare and colour and flavour to which her people are addicted. They have created an energy-sapping facsimile of the upside, even though there are no resources to maintain it. She can sometimes understand the argument of the Moles, those who believe people should cut their ties to the upside, stop living like slaves to the foreign influence of the upside and become self-sufficient again.

Just allowing the Moles to enter her head like this is treasonous disregard. While the Players and the Scrupulists battle over the best way to exploit upside relationships, some Moles threaten to destroy the facsimile altogether. It's a relief to remember that when this assignment is over she will have her penetration renewed and all thoughts of the Moles will be erased. Politics is not in her purview.

The Moles would never manage. There are too few of them, and besides, who would support them? They have darkness and scrabbling around in mud and eating root porridge to offer, while the status quo, always running critically low on energy and labour and parts though it is, is a pleasureland of tastes and styles in the Mall. There is good inculcation at the Academy, solid justice, a primo bureaucracy, and excellent modification and termination at the Wards. There's no way the world would go back to its primitive roots.

It was all a fable anyway, just like the meat tree. The old man would sit by his fire and stare at the flashing neon as he told the story. It was just a whimsical myth to describe the way the world is now.

She shrugs and stretches in her sheets. It doesn't matter anyway.

The proclamation ticker says: 'This shift's efficiency rewards include two lemons imported from the upside!' She realises with a certain shock that she can go and pick a basketful of lemons from the tree outside, right now.

She gets up to shower and she can't help comparing her body to those of the browns she's seen. They're so bizarre, but there's something about them… Their shape is much more uniform than normal people's so they can all wear the same specification of apparel. She once watched a couple of brown Shoppers at the Mall and they looked more like some sort of arthropod, but the apparel does work well on them. Is that proof that apparel was invented upside first?

Penter shakes her head. A stupid idea.

When she compares her body with those exotic brown bodies, why is it that she feels inferior? They're the freaks, not her. But there's something about the relationship between the world and the upside that idealises them and makes normal people second best. The various Ministries' cravings for upside resources and supplies, whether Scrupulist or Player, the sheer amount of time and energy they spend on courting browns, somehow gives the whole world a great inferiority complex.

She soaps herself and stands for several moments under the water. This is a luxurious by-product of the missed penetration. Normally she would automatically shut the taps after three moments, but she's standing here wasting water, and more importantly, the energy to warm it. Kark it, it's upside energy anyway; it probably comes straight from that burning sun.

She puts on the apparel designed by the project researchers – it's the outfit that the Mother in some television document wears – and goes downstairs to make breakfast for the family and the tame brown. That is what Mothers do. She turns on the television and watches the upside documents while she prepares the meal. The television is a primo tool for language acquisition.

'Pastel tones can inject an aura of summer into every living space,' she repeats. 'Reaching the final four is my whole life,' she repeats. 'A cook-off doesn't get tenser than this,' she repeats.

Chapter 4

RYAN

The dying afternoon sun sprawls over Julie's bed. It's not yet soft enough to flatter her, so Ryan looks away, out through the wood-framed French windows into the manicured garden. It's peaceful here and Ryan almost doesn't want to leave. It reminds him of those dirty weekends in luxurious bed-and-breakfasts he used to take with Karin before Alice was born. So long ago. They were so young.

Everything got fucked up and there's no way to reverse it.

Julie strokes his thigh with her little hand. She offers him a cigarette but he declines, watching instead as she wraps herself in a sheet, trails out of the French windows and lights up on the patio. He knows she feels his eyes on her back while she smokes. He knows she wants him to come out there, but he doesn't move. He thinks instead about the new girl, how those grey eyes locked into him. Julie exhales her last lungful, grinds out the butt, comes back inside, dropping the sheet as she walks, and curls into his side.

He's been in this house, in her bed, three times now; that's probably enough.

'I'd better go, ma'am,' he says, using a fragment of the banter they employed to get here. Bored housewife and maintenance man. It works for her, he figures, so it works for him. She's a nice enough woman, small enough, and certainly enjoys her afternoon excursions.

'There's no rush. Artie will be back around eight and Dino's away, as always. Dubai this time. I could… we could…' she says tentatively, knowing that she's crossing a line. This isn't their arrangement and she doesn't want to show him that she wants more.

Ryan is painfully sensitive to need – it's another of his big problems. He can't help reaching out to people who need love, who need to be held; he never wants to hurt anyone, but he's powerless when the urge to fulfil that need strikes. It's his downfall. Others might think it's cruel, but all he's ever wanted is to be kind. But not this middle-aged woman. Not now.

He leaves her lying on the bed instead, and goes to take a long shower. Why not here, a room-sized shower, multiple heads, a toilet that flushes properly, rather than the sporous, stenchy shared bathroom at his hovel? He changes, slings on his backpack and blows Julie a kiss as he heads out to the front hallway.

As he reaches for the handle, the door thumps into his hand and knee. Ryan winces before he sees someone standing on the threshold.

'Who are you?' A fat kid, up to Ryan's chest, squeaky voice all over the place.

'Uh, plumber.'

Then from behind him, a sound in the passage. 'Befo—'

The kid looks past him, goes purple, then looks away. Ryan turns and there's Julie, with nothing on but a G-string. She clasps her arms over her chest. 'Artie, honey, it's…' She scurries back to the bedroom.

'Plumber, my fucking arse!' the boy shouts.

'Hey, wait a minute. Show some…' Ryan stops before he makes himself sound stupid. But, seriously, an eleven-year-old kid?

Speaking to him like that? Despite the fact that he's the father of a thirteen-year-old himself, he has no idea how to handle kids, especially not boys. He's not sure whether to admire this kid's balls or give him a smack.

The boy seems set on making his decision for him. 'I'm going to tell my dad and he's going to fucking kill you, you arsehole.' The kid's taking out his cellphone and is aiming it at him.

'Hey! Give me that!' Ryan grapples the phone out of the boy's hand, but not before a couple of faux shutter clicks have fired off.

'Hey! Fuck you. Give me my fucking phone!'

Ryan holds the struggling boy off with one arm, gripping and twisting the sleeve of his T-shirt, and thumbs through the images with the other hand. Nothing but hand-shadow. Good.

'Mom!' The boy's about to cry.

'Come on, come on,' says Julie behind them, now dressed in jeans and a sweatshirt. She comes to the doorway where Ryan and the boy are still standing, awaiting orders. She holds out her hand to Ryan, who deposits the phone into her palm.

'You'd better go now,' she says.

'Yeah, I know,' he says. In the calm now, he can feel a thump start up at his temples. He winks at Julie – now she's having none of it – then heads out the door. As he saunters down the driveway, the gate starts to slide open. He's not sure whether Julie's watching him leave or knows how long it takes someone to walk down the drive. The driveway curves towards the road, so there's no direct view of the gate from the house. Ryan scans for cameras: there don't seem to be any up over the gate, and they're not likely to be hidden, not in a normal suburban house. Big cameras are a deterrent to would-be thieves.

Ryan walks out onto the pavement and buzzes the intercom. He hears the cluck and static of the line opening. She doesn't say anything. He's really pissed her off. It's not surprising, really, that she would defend her child. Isn't that what mothers are supposed to do? 'Thanks, I'm out,' he says. 'Sorry.' The gate trundles shut in answer and he ducks back inside just before it closes. He stashes his backpack under a bush near the entrance and skirts around the side of the house to the main garden. It's dark now, and the security lights studded along the inside of the perimeter wall are on. There aren't any motion-activated lights that Ryan can see, and it's unlikely that Julie arms the external beams or interior passives before she and Artie go to bed.

The French windows to Julie's bedroom are still unlocked and he slips in, stands quietly. There's plenty in this room that he might consider taking as a memento: Julie's gold lighter, perhaps; an item of jewellery she'd never miss? Or he could take something that belongs to the absent husband, he thinks, going into the bathroom, opening the cabinets. A shaving brush, a razor. He's tempted to pocket something of Julie's anyway, but there's no reason, it won't satisfy the urge. Ryan's not a sentimental man.

He pads soundlessly across to the bedroom door. The modern house's mix of thick carpeting and travertine tiles make sneaking much easier than the creaky wooden floors of older houses. He puts his ear to the gap. There's the sound of shooting, explosions, hard music: the kid's in the lounge, playing games. He can't tell where Julie is until she speaks.

'Artie?' No answer. 'Artie?' She's calling from the kitchen. Still he doesn't answer. *Show some respect to your fucking mother*, Ryan seethes inside. The passage from the bedroom leads to a T-junction in the front end of the house. Ryan sees Julie cross from the kitchen to the lounge. 'Artemis?' he hears her say in a conciliatory tone before she goes to where he's sitting and her voice is lost behind the noise of the game. Neither of them is likely to come back to the bedrooms for a while. He hurries out of Julie's room and into Artie's, the next door down on the left.

The kid's room is unnaturally neat, obviously tidied by a house-keeper every day. Again, Ryan is reminded of a bed-and-breakfast or boutique hotel, as if the child's a short-term guest in this lavish room. Instead of rock stars or models, idealised scenes of forests and seascapes decorate the walls. The only hint of the boy's person-ality is a row of comic-hero figurines lining a clean, white shelf above a desk. On the desk is a small pile of school textbooks and a wafer-thin Mac.

No way can he take that. But he needs to punish the boy just the same. Take something. The compulsion isn't as strong as it was in Duvenhage's office, but it's there all right, manifesting itself as a low throb behind his eyes this time. He opens the built-in ward-robe and a funk of pubescent boy wafts out. He scans the shelves of precisely folded clothing, and then, down there at the bottom of the closet, a neat, white, woven-cane toy box. Ryan opens it. It's stuffed full of plush toys and plastic cars that the kid probably doesn't play with any more, but there's something else down there. Ryan shoves his arm in, scratching around towards the bottom, transported back immediately to when he was a boy. There was always something shameful and illicit you had to hide far away from judging eyes, but at the same time it was always within reach. Eleven years old, precisely when shameful compulsions and the taste for risk emerge from their cocoon.

Right at the bottom he feels something soft, a tightly folded silky something.

Shit. He hears a door click open, too close by. Ryan freezes, afraid to look around. But the door closes again and he realises it's the bathroom, hears the boy pissing, scrambles to the side of the bed where he can't be seen from the doorway. If the kid comes into the room, he's fucked. He scans for escape routes, but the window is security-barred and the only way out is the door.

There's a flush from next door; the basin tap runs and the door clicks open again. *Go back to the lounge, go back to the lounge, you little fucker.* Ryan can't hear which way the kid's going. Fuck those tiled and carpeted floors.

Ryan waits for a minute, lets his breathing calm down, tunes his ears again. The kid's probably gone back to his game. If he were going to come into the bedroom, he would have done it by now. Ryan shifts back across to the toy box and digs in again. He's not going to take the boy's stolen underwear; it's probably not very clean. Probably his mom's.

He's beginning to lose the taste for this, rifling around in some boy's secrets. But as he's drawing his arm out of the box, his fingers scrape past something hard and velvety and sharp. He brings it out: a yellowed, time-logged paperback, *The Dominion of Slaves*. Not a history text: three rouged and chained and half-naked women sigh at him wantonly from the cover. Ryan smiles. This will do.

Something about the smell of the book, the specific funk of sweat and semen and mildew and guilt, takes him back to his boyhood again and he's hit by a wave of nausea. Christ, kids are *supposed* to keep soft porn and sticky underwear in their rooms; they're supposed to be allowed to. Ryan's own father, curse his rotten fucking degenerate soul, would have beat the shit out of him if he found something even as silly as this book in his room; it wasn't even that Ryan had to learn better methods of evasion, they were just *in* him, hardwired from the time he was a baby, when, presumably, his father would hit him for shitting in his nappy.

He imagines Artie's reaction when he finds his book missing. He'll know someone found it, but he'll never know who. He'll look at his mother differently after that. Fuck him; kid has to learn, doesn't he? That's the difference between boys and girls. Girls deserve love and tenderness; boys need to learn to toughen up. Ryan pockets the book, closes the wardrobe and exits the room.

Slipping back through Julie's room, he lifts the gold Zippo anyway, but it's an empty gesture; the impulse to take something has already been sated. He drops the lighter on the carpet and closes the French window behind him. In the shadow of the curve of trees at the front gate, he puts the book in his backpack and scales the wall.

It's eight thirty when he gets back to his boarding house. He makes toast from stale bread and spreads peanut butter on it. He feels like a beer but he's out, so he has a glass of water to complement his dinner.

Ma Beccah bustles in and clatters a cup and saucer into the sink. 'There was a man here looking for you, Ryan.'

'For me?'

'He said he was a friend of yours and you borrowed something from him and he came to get it back. That's what he said.'

Shit. He doesn't have friends, only enemies, a list as long as a toilet roll of people he's stolen from or pissed off in some way. But borrowing, that's something he doesn't do. He owes nothing to anyone – not money or favours, that is – and that's one thing he can be proud of. Karin's brother, maybe? Karin and Alice have been staying with Ziggy and he always takes care of Alice whenever Karin loses it. Maybe it's something to do with Alice, but why wouldn't he just phone? But then again, Ryan can't remember the last time he used his phone or charged it. He thinks it's in his bag. Fuck, he should be a more responsible parent, keep it with him for situations just like this.

'Did he say his name?'

'No.'

'What did he look like? Was he tall? Well-built guy?'

'No, he was short. Sort of round face. He looked... I don't know... like he wasn't telling the truth. He asked me to let him into your room, he'd find the thing and just go. I said no ways, he must speak to you.'

'Thanks, Ma.' Whoever the fuck it was, it's definitely—

Oh, fuck. Duvenhage. Of course. Ryan had completely forgotten about the flash drive. He feels in his pocket. The little dove is still there where he stuffed it earlier today. 'Was he wearing a grey suit, maybe?'

'Yes, that's right.'

Fuck, how could Ryan have been so stupid? He slumps down at the kitchen table and stares at his toast. He should have known Duvenhage would miss something like that. The first thing Ryan used to do when he started up his computer was stick in a back-up drive. And why had he filled in his real address on the job application in the first place? Who does that? This is getting out of hand. The things he's taken before have always been completely anonymous. Now this compulsion is directing him to do dangerous things. Steal from his boss, for Christ's sake. And then the kid. Going back into Julie's house for no reason at all. He's never done anything that risky before; he could have been arrested, for fuck's sake. Julie knows exactly who he is and where he works. There was no reason, he knows, except he was angry with the kid.

He was angry with Duvenhage too, speaking to him like that, and Ryan just had to nod and smile and suck it up. He can't let it get out of control. Two items in a single day. It's as if he's trying to sabotage his life; as if his own fucking mind is trying to destroy him.

'Are you all right?' Ma Beccah asks.

Ryan realises he's sitting there, his hand clasped over his mouth. 'Yes, sorry,' he tells her. He tries to shake himself out of it. If there's any chance of him keeping his job, he's got to replace the drive back in Duvenhage's office without him noticing. And he needs his job to keep any hope of living with Alice again. It's school assembly first thing, so he can do it then.

But if Duvenhage's so keen to get that drive back, there might be something of value on it. There are different ways of looking at this problem. How badly does Duvenhage want it back?

'Hey, Ma Beccah. Do you have a computer I can use?'

'No, but Fransie next door lets me use his when I need to send an email or go online. I'm sure he won't mind if you ask him.'

'Okay, thanks.'

Fransie next door is not the first person Ryan would like to visit. The situation there is weird. Fransie and his alcoholic dad living there together in that filthy, dilapidated house with Fransie's little girl, Tess. No mom, no auntie, no nothing. He's seen Tess playing in the front yard a couple of times when he gets back from work. She told him that she's ten, that she goes to Ridgefield Primary, central Malvern's run-down government school. She's sweet and polite, almost too polite. There's just a bad feeling about it. But Ryan's in a rush and he has little other option at this time of night. He goes to his room and scratches through a desk drawer until he finds the back-up drive he used to use at work, takes a deep pull from the Three Ships in his backpack, then heads over to Fransie's house.

The rusted metal gate squeals as he pushes through it redundantly. He could just as easily step over it. Fransie's father is sitting in a wicker chair on the paint-peeling veranda in his usual stained wife-beater. His eyes follow Ryan as he climbs the six steps and crosses the veranda to the front door.

'Evening,' says Ryan, and the old man grunts.

Ryan knocks at the door, and after a minute Fransie comes out, scanning ahead of him before smiling and opening the door wider. 'Hey, brother. What can I do for you?'

'Hi, Fransie. I'm Ryan from next door.' He holds out his hand and Fransie gives it a limp, distracted shake; his small hand is rough and dry.

He narrows his eyes at Ryan. 'Ja, bru, I know.'

'I'm sorry to bug you so late, but... I have a thing.' Ryan's about to launch into a lie about needing a document for work but feels less comfortable lying to a man like Fransie than to the middle-class suckers over the hill. His tribe, who he understands much better. 'I wonder if you can copy this drive onto this one.' He displays the little flash drive. 'Ma Beccah says you have a computer.'

Fransie snorts back a laugh. 'Sure thing, brother. You don't mind waiting out here? Keep my pa company, hey?'

'Of course. Thanks.'

Ryan's relieved not to be invited in. He's unsettled enough as it is, and he wouldn't want to see what it's like inside. He sits down on the top step of the veranda, thinking about Tess, what it must be like to stay here, wondering about where her mother is, when the girl appears out of an overgrown thicket at the side of the house like a spirit summoned. She's still wearing her school uniform, which is as grubby as her face. Her hair is tangled with leaves and twigs.

'Hello, Mr Ryan,' she says.

'Been exploring?' he says.

She laughs.

The old man grunts behind Ryan. She looks up at him and shrugs. She doesn't appear to be scared of him, that's something at least. But then the door opens and her face freezes and she looks down at her shoes.

'Here you go, brother.' Ryan stands and Fransie passes the drives back to him.

Without a word or a glance, Tess slips up the stairs past Ryan and into the house. Something dark starts uncoiling inside him. He needs a drink.

Chapter 5
TARA

Tara sits slumped at the kitchen counter, absently toying with the mug of coffee she made over an hour ago. It's going on for seven thirty – usually the most chaotic time of her day – but she hasn't yet showered or even brushed her teeth.

The stench of burnt oil still lingers in the kitchen. Fortunately, Stephen managed to turn off the heat and throw a tea towel over the pan before any real damage was done to the stove or surrounding units, but he left the ruined pot on top of the dishwasher, where it still sits in silent accusation.

Not that she's worrying about that right now. She's got other things on her mind.

She spent most of the night obsessively clicking on that photograph – zooming in and out, freeze-framing on the baby's face, the sewn-shut eyes, the little pursed mouth looped with thread. Could it be some kind of perverse joke, some bastard screwing with her mind? But who? It can't be Martin – if the infant in the pic isn't real (and she's still not sure it isn't), it's been photoshopped – and while Martin may be a mendacious little shit, he doesn't have the skill to pull that off. There's Martin's mother, of course, a woman who can hold a grudge for Africa, but Tara can't see Olivia doing something like this. It's too passive-aggressive. There's too much attention to detail.

She's aware, of course, that there are others who have an even stronger motive to cause her distress. The story is still up there on the internet, including a detailed transcript of the court case, but as far as she knows, no one from the old days, with the exception of her mother, knows that she's holed up in a Joburg suburb, thousands of miles away from New Jersey. She's glad she ignored her feminist principles and took Stephen's surname; it makes her harder to trace.

But what if it *isn't* some kind of sick joke? What if the baby in the photograph *is* real? After all, this Batiss is undoubtedly foreign, and if he or she is a bereaved parent longing to own a replica of a possibly deceased child, could the mutilation be some kind of North African or Middle Eastern burial practice she's never heard about before? Or perhaps it's even worse than that – some sick fetish. A while ago, her sister sent her a link to a site showcasing pictures of a novelty Voldemort Reborn, complete with snake-like eyes and red-veined skin. That turned her stomach, but it doesn't hold a candle to Batiss's photograph.

So the response she'd written, 'Is this a joke? If so, I'm not laughing,' remains unsent in her drafts folder.

She should really get moving, make sure Martin is up and dressed, but instead she continues to swirl her spoon around the mug, trying to ignore the sick throb of what she hopes isn't the beginning of a migraine.

She hears a door slam, the flush of a toilet. The thump of feet in the hallway.

Martin slinks into the kitchen, scowls when he sees her. 'Where's Dad?'

'Left early.' Tara can't actually remember Stephen leaving for work this morning, although she has a vague recollection of him muttering something about an early meeting.

'Aw *what*? But I need him to sign something for me.'

'Why didn't you ask him to do it last night?' She knows she's picking a fight, but after the night she's had she can't be bothered to tiptoe around a twelve-year-old, however big the chip on his shoulder.

'I forgot.'

'Well, I can sign it, can't I? What is it?'

He pulls a crumpled piece of paper out of his bag, hands it over reluctantly. Tara smoothes it out on the counter. The text is slotted around an anthropomorphic soda-pop can that appears to be leaping for joy, a speech bubble leaking out of its mouth with the words 'Quizzes! Prizes! Body Art!' She scans the rest of the flyer:

Hey, Learners! Do you want to experience something Exceptional? Something that will help you Change Your World and those Around YOU? Something that will help you be more:

Exciting!
New-found!
Creative!
Original!
Unbelievably cool!
Nifty!
Terrific!
Entertaining!
Right!
Suitable!

Then come to ENCOUNTERS! Connect with us every school afternoon from March 12 to March 18 from 4 till 6 for sharing, caring and loads of FREE FUN with a capital F!

'You seriously want to go to this?' Tara asks. It doesn't seem like the kind of thing Martin would be into. Ever since Tara's known him, his world has revolved around rugby, gangsta rap and violent computer games – perfect ingredients for a thug in the making. This 'Encounters' flyer smacks of the kind of thing the hokey religious groups used to post on the notice board at Raymond Scheider Primary, luring the kids into abstinence programmes and the like with the same dubious promise of FREE FUN with a capital F.

But then again, she thinks, maybe if the little shit found Jesus he'd get off her back.

'Are you going to sign it or not?' he says.

'Who gave this to you?'

'What do you care?'

'And you want to go today?'

'It's every day. That's what it says. You can read, can't you?'

She scrawls her signature, hands it over. He snatches it out of her hand.

'Aren't you going to say thank you?'

'Whatever, bee-atch,' he mumbles.

Something inside her snaps. 'You know what, Martin,' she says, unable to stop herself. 'Why don't you go fuck yourself.' The savage glee she feels at the sight of his stunned expression only lasts momentarily, but it's almost worth it.

It doesn't take long for him to recover. 'You can't talk to me like that!'

'Looks like I just did.' Tara realises that part of her really is enjoying this.

'I'm telling on you!'

'Get your stuff together. We're going to be late.'

His eyes narrow. 'Mom says you're a freak. She says you're sick.'

'Does she?' Tara tries to feign disinterest, but she can feel a familiar knot of tension starting at the base of her skull, suspects that it will claw its way up to join the headache simmering at her temples.

'She says that you only make those stupid ugly babies because you can't have your own.' His voice is rising, getting shriller. 'She says you lost your baby because you deserved to, that you stole Dad because you're a bitch. A slut. A stupid, ugly, fat, American cu—'

Her hand flashes out before she can stop it. He staggers back, ugly red splotches appearing on the pale skin of his left cheek.

Oh shit, she thinks. Oh God. What now? 'Martin, I...'

Tears bubble in his eyes. 'I hate you!'

'I didn't mean to—'

'I'll get you for child abuse! I can do that! I can call Childline. I can call—'

'You can do all of these things,' she says, trying to inject calm into her voice. 'But it will make you late for school.' As if that's going to make any difference, she thinks. Except, oddly enough, this does seem to quieten him.

'Whatever,' he mumbles. He turns away, kicks at his bag.

'You ready to get going?' she asks brightly. The mark on his cheek is fading, thank God. She can't have hit him that hard after all.

'Where's my lunch?'

Goddammit. She's forgotten to make him his packed lunch – a chore she usually completes the night before. She digs in her handbag, finds herself handing him a fifty-rand note for the tuck shop, five times too much. Awesome. First child abuse, now bribery.

She waves him towards the front door.

Martin turns around and shoots her a hate-filled look. 'You're going to be sorry,' he says.

I'm already sorry, Tara thinks. But all she says is, 'Let's go.'

She sits in the car in a shady corner of the staff parking lot. Although her headache hasn't actually morphed into a migraine, she's feeling that same sense of detachment and nausea that comes over her just before the black spots start dancing in the corners of her eyes. Probably just stress. The drive to school wasn't pleasant. She tried to make conciliatory, over-cheery conversation, but Martin spent the journey in a fug of resentment, not even kicking at the back of her seat. She rests her forehead against the steering wheel.

Did she actually hit him?

In all the years she was teaching, she never once struck a child; never even came close. Even in the early days, when she was forced to take a series of positions as a teaching assistant in the rougher districts, in schools equipped with metal detectors and their own security guard squads. Schools where six-year-olds used the word 'motherfucker' more frequently than they said 'please', where the older kids mouthed 'bitch' at her when she passed them in the corridors.

How could she have sailed through that and allowed a little snot like Martin to push her over the edge?

She knows she should really phone Stephen, tell him what's happened before Martin gives his own version of events. But she can't face hearing the sigh in his voice. The unspoken 'I thought you said you were *good* with children, Tara.'

Maybe she's overreacting. It was a just a slap. Big deal.

But it is a big deal. At least to her.

She doesn't have to be in the library until ten today, for the first batch of readers; she usually uses the time to head to Woolworths and stock up on groceries, dropping them off at home before she heads back to the school. But today she doesn't have the energy. She can't bear the idea of going home, knows she'll just end up brooding, obsessing about Martin. She could always go and sit in the library, help Clara catalogue the books. Or maybe hole up in the staff room while the teachers are at assembly. Volunteers are allowed to use the facilities, although Tara never has. In her opinion, the teachers are as cliquey as the Mother Tribe. No, the library will do.

The security guard hasn't yet locked the front gate so she's able to slip in without ringing the bell. She can hear the muffled boom of a man's voice echoing from behind the double doors that lead into the hall – a blank-walled area with pointless arched steel roof struts that make the space look more like a pretentious modern-art gallery than a school.

Curious, she tiptoes over to the doors, pushes one of them open slightly and peers in.

Mr Duvenhage looms over the lectern on the stage at the far end of the hall, staring down at the orderly rows of children sitting cross-legged on the floor below him. The teachers are perched on chairs along the sides of the hall, and Tara spots Clara sitting stiff-backed at the piano a few feet from the front.

'I'm afraid I have a rather serious issue to air,' Duvenhage is saying. 'I have heard disturbing reports from Mr Duma that several pieces of chewing gum have been found stuck under the desks. I don't think I need remind you that desecration of school property is...' – he pauses – '*sickening*. Does anyone want to admit to this crime? Or perhaps one of you *saw* someone doing it?'

Holy crap, Tara thinks. Is he encouraging the kids to rat on each other? She's amazed to see several hands shooting up into the air. She recognises Martin's chunky frame in the third row from the front; realises that he's one of the kids squirming with enthusiasm to be picked.

'Very well,' Mr Duvenhage says, pointing down at him. 'You. Martin Marais. Please stand up.' Martin gets to his feet, turning around to grin at one of his friends.

'It was Kyle de Villiers, Mr Duvenhage,' Martin says. 'He did it. I *saw* him.'

'I see. Thank you, Martin. You will be rewarded for your honesty.'

Mr Duvenhage clears his throat. 'Kyle de Villiers, please stand up.'

A skinny child with a shock of black hair stands up, his hands twisting behind his back.

A chill creeps up Tara's spine. She's reminded of that Shirley Jackson short story she used to teach – 'The Lottery'. She doubts the kids are going to start lobbing stones at Kyle, but even from her post at the back of the room, she can sense the atmosphere in the hall, a pregnant mix of excitement, schadenfreude and fear.

Mr Duvenhage peers down at him like a vulture assessing a carcass. 'Is Martin's assertion true, Kyle?'

Kyle nods miserably.

'What do we say to Kyle, children?'

'Bad eggs will be thrown out, good eggs will be served,' the children drone in unison.

'Correct. Kyle, I will see you in my office after assembly for castigation.'

Kyle nods, murmurs, 'Thank you, sir,' and sits down.

Poor kid, Tara thinks. She is uncomfortable with Mr Duvenhage's disciplinary methods but has to admit they probably work. She's fairly sure it's the last time Kyle will be tempted to 'desecrate' school property, and come to think of it, since Duvenhage was appointed, Stephen hasn't once been called in to discuss Martin's behavioural issues. Not that his behaviour at home has improved, but she supposes it's a start.

Mr Duvenhage claps his hands. 'Today's theme is belonging. Please stand for this morning's meditations.'

Tara's phone beeps and she steps back, shutting the door softly behind her. She fumbles it out of her bag, clicks onto her inbox. Sees she has one text message from a private number.

Varder Batiss. It has to be. But her cell number's not listed on her website. She taps in a reply. <how did you get my number?>

<methods>

Methods? What methods? <are you serious?>

<we are humourless about this. Are you?>

What in God's name does that mean? Tara paces back and forth in front of the door, trying to phrase a reply. <that photograph u sent. Is it real? A real baby?>

<it is the baby we require>

< I'm concerned about this commission> Should she be more specific? She doesn't want to offend this Batiss person if he or she is, in fact, a grieving parent.

<no need to agonise. the deposit you claim is made into your account. we hope you find this tolerable>

Before she can craft a response to this, another message pops up. It's from ABSA customer services, alerting her to the fact that her account has just been credited with R75021.67.

She stares down at it, unbelieving.

She quickly does the maths. That's nearly ten thousand dollars! Way too much.

<it's too much>

<you accept?>

Jesus, she thinks. Is this Batiss person serious? Could this be some kind of scam? But for the life of her she can't figure out what kind of internet scam-artist deposits seventy-five grand into their target's account up front. No, Batiss must be deranged in some way; highly eccentric, perhaps. What should she do? Should she take advantage and just run with it? After all, this could set her free. Keep her going until her permanent residency comes in. Hell, if what she's heard about the South African Home Affairs Department is true, seventy-five grand could *buy* her permanent residency.

Her phone beeps again. <repeat: you accept?>

She types in **<yes>** but something stops her from sending it straight away. She needs to consider this. There must be some kind of catch.

The sound of singing floats through the door. She recognises the tune, realises that it's one of the songs the beardy religious group used to sing to the kids back in New Jersey, a simple, catchy number that she would catch herself humming for days afterwards. Still, as much as she dislikes it, the sound of it sparks a wave of homesickness and regret.

She pushes the door open again as carefully as she can, peers through it, sees Clara banging away at the piano, Duvenhage leading the children in song, his voice deep and strident.

Tara remembers that the irritating tune wasn't the only reason she disliked it; its message is dodgy as hell: *don't be an individual, kids, it's safer to follow the herd*. She's about to close the door when Duvenhage suddenly stops singing. He's too far away from her to be sure, but she has the distinct impression he's staring straight at her.

She jumps back as if she's been caught doing something illegal, fingers slipping on the door; it shuts with a thunk. She hurries down the corridor, knowing that she's overreacting (so what if she looked in on the school assembly?), but she only relaxes when she hears the sound of singing starting up again.

She stalks past the school secretary's office, turns the corner to the library. She tries the door – it doesn't give. Locked. *Goddammit.* She'll have to get the key from the rack next to Sybil Fontein's desk. And while she's there, she can root around, see if there's a couple of Disprin to take the edge off her headache.

She retraces her steps, is about to enter the office when a man slips out. Tara steps back to give him room, then realises that it's that new maintenance man – the pirate. She finds herself blushing, running a hand through her dirty hair. She's uncomfortably aware that she's not wearing any deodorant; that she's dressed in a pair of baggy leggings and a faded Obama-For-President T-shirt – the first clothes that came to hand when she flumped out of bed. God, she must look awful.

'What are you doing here?' she blurts.

'I work here,' he says.

His eyes skate over her face, her hair, down her body, linger, for some reason, on her sneakers. It's a shameless, almost brazen, assessment, as if he doesn't care if he's making her uncomfortable.

'You're American,' he says.

'That obvious, huh?' She crosses her arms over the slight bulge of her stomach. 'Um… how long have you been working here?'

'Why?'

'Just making conversation.'

'Why? I don't know you, you don't know me.'

What to say to that? Tara can't tell if he's being plain rude or trying to be witty. She's saved from having to answer him as a door slams, followed by the scuffle of feet approaching down the corridor. The assembly must be over.

He ducks his head, brushes past her. There's plenty of room for him to pass, but she feels the bare skin of his arm sliding against hers.

A mass of children streams towards her, en route to the classrooms on the first floor, and Tara's struck again by how subdued they are; there's barely a whisper or a giggle, just the shush-clump of their shoes as they shamble along. She presses herself against the wall to give them room.

She feels a tug on her hand, sees the new girl staring up at her. She looks grubbier than she did yesterday, streaks of grease in her weird dyed hair, her makeshift uniform leaking threads. If she's not an outreach kid, could she be a neglected child? In this sort of privileged school? Why not? After all, it happens everywhere, however prosperous the area. She should know.

Tara smiles down at the girl. 'Hello. I remember you from the library. What's your name again?'

'Jane, miss,' the girl whispers.

'Sorry?' Tara's sure she heard something else yesterday.

'Jane. My name. It goes like this: Jay Ay En Ee.'

'That's a pretty name,' Tara says, hoping she sounds convincing.

The kids streaming past them don't give the girl a second glance, although a couple of the reading-difficulties kids wave shyly at Tara.

'You're new here, aren't you?'

The girl nods.

'And... do you like the school?'

Jane bares her teeth in that strange approximation of a smile Tara remembers from yesterday. One of the girl's incisors looks like it might be rotten, the grey enamel pitted with white flecks, as if she's tried to cover it with Tippex. Poor kid.

She sees Martin shuffling past. He scowls at her, whispers something to the boy next to him – a kid Tara recognises as Jonah Hallock, another thug in the making – and smirks.

'Freak,' Jonah hisses as he passes the girl, slipping away before Tara can remonstrate with him.

'Mrs Marais!' she hears Clara calling over the heads of the kids. The girl skitters into the throng, her limp less pronounced than it was yesterday. The other children part to make room for her, as if they don't want to brush up against her.

Tara tries to smile as Clara approaches. It isn't reciprocated. 'That's the child I was talking about yesterday,' Tara says, gesturing at the girl's back. 'The one who came into the library.'

'Oh yes. You mean the new intake.'

'Is she...' Tara searches for the right word, but in the fog caused by her increasingly throbbing headache all she can come up with is 'normal', which won't go down well in this environment where students are 'learners' and remedial kids are 'learning-challenged'. 'Is she... okay?' is what she finally settles on.

'Of course. Why wouldn't she be?'

'She's limping. And the other children don't seem to—'

'It can take a while for new learners to feel at home in Crossley College,' Clara interrupts. 'I'm sure the other children will make her belong soon enough.' Strange choice of words, Tara thinks. 'What are you doing here at this hour, Mrs Marais? You are far too early for library duty. Is everything in order?'

Tara imagines spilling her guts to this woman. *Oh, it's nothing really, Clara. I hit the crap out of my stepson and a creepy stranger wants me to make them a replica of a possibly dead, but certainly mutilated, baby.* Yeah, that would go down well. 'Everything's fine. I... um, thought I'd pop in early and help you with the new books.'

'I see.'

'Um... I caught a few seconds of the assembly. Is that normal? Asking kids to rat on each other?'

Clara stiffens as if Tara has personally insulted her. 'I'm sure you understand the need for strict discipline, Mrs Marais. Now that we are no longer able to use physical methods, Mr Duvenhage likes to emphasise teamwork and sharing and caring – collective responsibility, if you will. You are, after all, not from this country, are you? Some of our practices must seem strange to an outsider.'

'I guess.'

'But who knows, perhaps you won't *always* be an outsider.'

'What do you mean by that?'

Clara leans in closer, as if she's about to impart something confidential, and Tara's hit with a whiff of her lavender scent. 'You have a teaching degree, do you not?'

'Yes.'

'And I believe you're just waiting for the wheels of bureaucracy to turn before you find yourself a position?'

Now how in the hell does she know that? Tara wonders. She's never discussed this with Clara before, and she's only mentioned her past and her ongoing war with Home Affairs in the vaguest terms to the members of the Mother Tribe. 'What are you getting at, Cl— Mrs van der Spuy?'

'Just that if a vacancy comes up, perhaps you might consider being part of our family.'

'You serious?'

'Always, Mrs Marais. Now. I hope you don't mind me saying, but you're looking peaky. Why don't you go home, have a hot bath. We can do without you for one day.'

Actually, Tara thinks, maybe that isn't a bad idea. After all, she's got a hell of a lot of issues to process, including Clara's left-field offer. The school may have a strange method of naming and shaming, but so what? Most of the schools she's taught at over the years have had some kind of hokey philosophy underpinning them. It's the kids that matter, and surely they need someone like her – level-headed, concerned for their welfare – to balance out the other, more... disturbing elements? And if she went back to teaching she could make her Reborns on the side. Hell, maybe she wouldn't have to sell them at all. If she gets her work permit and permanent residency, that is. Which isn't entirely out of her grasp now, is it?

She pulls out her phone, opens the drafts folder and flicks through to her unsent <yes> message.

Before she loses her nerve she presses the send button.

There's a response almost immediately: <primo J>

It's only when she's climbing into her car that she realises her headache has gone.

She dumps her bag on the kitchen counter, switches on the oven – she'll need it at the right temperature to set the paint – then flies up the stairs.

Giving Baby Paul's drawer only a cursory glance, she clicks on the computer and prints out the photograph. Now that it's in hard copy, it looks much clearer – she should have done this last night. She pins it above her work table, traces the lines of the baby's lips and eyes with her finger. If it is photoshopped, it's a brilliant job. Apart from the thread sealing its eyes and mouth, the baby's features are regular and even, he or she looks perfect – almost alive. She'll have to decide on a sex; she can't tell from the pic if it's male or female. It's so generic, in fact, that Tara realises that she could, quite easily, get away with using the Baby Gabby head she's currently working on, with only a few minor adjustments. Batiss's baby's skin is a delicate pinky-white, soft blue veins showing through the skin of the forehead, and she finds herself automatically working out which pigments she'll need to mix to overlay that shade on Baby Gabby's darker skin tone. Its skull is only slightly dusted with hair, so she won't have to spend weeks rooting its scalp, and she can use her new nasal drill to widen Baby Gabby's nostrils to make them match Batiss's baby. She tries not to think about how she'll feel when it comes to adding those all-important finishing touches; for now she has enough to get on with.

Her phone beeps again. She snatches it out of her bag. It isn't Batiss this time, but Stephen. <we need to talk> is all the message says.

Yeah right, she thinks. Talk about what? Why he lets his son treat her like shit? Why he won't even broach the subject of her getting pregnant again? Or perhaps why it is he no longer races home after work, but seems to slink in later and later each day? Then it hits her. Could Martin have told him about the slap? Is that what he wants to discuss? And if Martin's told Stephen, isn't it likely he would have also told Olivia?

She deletes the message without replying, and feverishly unwraps her new batch of Genesis paints. She doesn't want to think about Martin, about Stephen, about anything except the baby in front of her.

She screams through the school gates, tyres squealing. She's been so lost in her work that the afternoon slid away from her – she's over twenty minutes late to pick Martin up from his Encounters group.

She races into the parking area, sees him waiting alone in the gloom next to the 'Differently Abled' sign, steels herself for the usual barrage of snide comments and a marathon sulk session.

She pulls up next to him, winds down her window. 'Sorry I'm late.'

Martin shrugs.

That's odd. It's not like him to pass up an opportunity to give her a hard time. 'You okay, Martin? How was your meeting?'

Martin mumbles something under his breath that could be anything from 'go fuck yourself' to 'great, thanks for asking'.

'Listen, Martin,' Tara says, before he climbs into the back seat. 'About what happened this morning. I just want you to know, it was all my fault. I shouldn't have raised a hand to you.'

She's expecting him to say, 'No you shouldn't, you stupid bitch,' or words to that effect, but he just shrugs again.

'We'll talk about it when your father gets home this evening. We'll sort it out.'

'I don't need to talk about it,' Martin says.

'Your father should know what happened, Martin. Unless... unless you've already told him. Have you?'

He yawns. 'No. Why would I?'

Tara experiences a twinge of guilt at the relief she feels. Is it possible that this could be buried? It's not as if she's been abusing the kid, is it? It was just a moment of madness. Could've happened to anyone. And no one could say she wasn't provoked.

He straps himself in without having to be asked, yawns again and starts humming something under his breath (Tara hopes it isn't 'I Just Wanna be a Sheep'). She's so used to seeing him continually fiddling with his iPhone that it's disconcerting to see him without it. And does he look paler than usual? He rests his head against the window, a faraway look in his eyes.

'Martin?' she asks, twisting round in her seat. 'Are you feeling okay?'

He stops humming, looks straight into her eyes and says, 'Yes, thank you, Tara. I'm just primo.'

Chapter 6

PENTER

Penter pokes her head around the gate and looks at the road outside the precinct. There's a constant stream of the machines going by and from the documents she's seen, there are even more on other roads. She's amazed that the browns don't all just smash into each other and terminate themselves. Despite herself, she feels another prickle of admiration for their organisational skills. To live at such speed and not cannon into one another is a feat in itself.

She shuts the gate and retreats into the quiet precinct. If she were here longer, or if her role were different, she'd need to venture out, but as it is, she has work to do in the precinct and there's no reason to brave the rushing machines.

On her way back to the house, she looks up into the bewildering sky and stops to feel the sun's warmth. It's like when she was a half-pint and would move too close to the heat vents. She knew it was hazardous, was parching her skin, but at the same time the warmth in her muscles and bones was irresistible. She'd heard about the sky and the sun, of course – everyone has; everyone dreams of them secretly when they're due for a renewal, she's sure – and the Ministry warned her just how uncanny they were, but nothing could have prepared her. The thin air out here makes her feel like she's floating and about to evaporate away. The sun is like a prophetic floodlight, like all the faulty wiring in the world coiled into a single, massive point of danger. The sky is like all the garment dye ever produced and she doesn't know how it could have been manufactured, how they could have made it so big, how they could have used so much material, and how it still stays floating above them.

She detours through the garden and marvels at the opulence of green, the acrid breath of the trees' leaves. She plucks a sappy leaf off a berry tree, consciously suppressing her guilt at the desecration. Up here, there's an abundance of plant life, leaves are left to coat the ground and rot into the soil. Fruit is left to fall and is given over to the insects and the birds – those creatures that swirl in the ether like solid breath. She looks at the living green tissue in her hand and a drop of white sap leaks out of the end of the stem and spills onto her palm.

Some of the trees are higher than the central victual court at the Mall, higher than the prefab palms in the piazza at the Apartments. And all around her, the birds are singing songs that make her chest ache. Animals that fly! With their colours, they swoop in the open air and they soar off into the nothingness above. Everything lives exposed out here, stretching and growing and moving and moulting.

The tame brown has been tending a patch where vegetables grow on living wood. Even the soil, something she knows well, smells different here. No matter how well they prepared her, it's overwhelming.

She walks upstairs to the television room, finds Father on the couch, scanning through a sheaf of mimeographs from the evening session. She watches him for a moment without him noticing. She'd never met him before she was assigned, doesn't even know his real name, just as he is unaware of hers – up here, he is simply Father, and she is simply Mother. He finally looks up, nods distractedly at her.

'Was it a good session?' she asks from the doorway.

'Yes,' he says. 'Plenty of viable. The Ministry's prognosis was sound.'

Realising that he is busy, Penter turns to leave.

'Mother?' he says.

'Yes, Father?'

'The meal you prepared. "Breakfast". It was… interesting. In the sense of unpleasant. I think you could make some more effort to prepare a meal that allows the family to remember the comforts of home.'

The bubble of good feeling she was nurturing is rudely burst and she's stung. 'May I remind you that I am a Deputy Node Liaison for the Ministry of Upside Relations, and not a victual servant?' A terrified thrill runs through her. Her disregard is a direct result of the thought-seep. Despite her status, Father is the team leader on this project and she knows she would never address a team leader in these terms back home.

'May I remind you,' Father says, still smiling coolly from the couch, 'that here you are Mother?'

Penter walks further into the room. 'My name is Penter Ulliel,' she enunciates. When she embarked on her path, she was assigned the name by the senior Node Ministry Commissioner himself. He told her that she was named after an auto-loading haematology analysis device which he had admired on a visit to the Wards, but after he was depreciated, she realised that he had mispronounced the word, so now she has a unique name. Despite its idiosyncrasy – or perhaps even because of it – she's proud of her name.

But, she realises, this is another extraneous conceit that won't worry her when the assignment is finished and she goes back home and has her penetration renewed. She won't be arguing with her superiors either. By the look on Father's face, he's enjoying the unusual exchange as much as she is.

'That notwithstanding, Mother,' he says, 'your organisational role in this project team is to behave as the female head of an upside nucleated family does, which the research has clearly shown' – he indicates the television set in the corner – 'definitively includes victual preparation. Nourishing, comforting victual preparation.'

She shakes her head but she knows he's right. Still tingling with the thrill of disregard, she goes downstairs to find the tame brown and send him out for some proper ingredients.

Chapter 7

RYAN

'You wanted to see me, Mr Duvenhage?' Ryan says. As expected, he managed to sneak in while everyone was religiously at assembly and drop Duvenhage's flash drive on the floor under the desk, as if he'd just mislaid it himself. He looks forward to seeing the man backtrack. 'My landlady said you came to visit last night, but I was out. She said you didn't leave your name but described you, and, well... you're the only person I know who—'

'Yes, yes, okay, Mr Devlin.' Duvenhage's standing in the doorway, clutching the doorknob. His skin is as pallid as ever, but even more sweaty. 'I, uh, I have a meeting.'

'I just wanted to check, sir. Was it you? How can I help, sir?'

'Uh, yes, it was...' Duvenhage straightens, draws the door shut behind him and steps towards Ryan in the corridor. 'Yes, Mr Devlin, it was me. I thought I had lost something and I wanted to ask you about it. It was something very important.'

'What was it? I can tell you if I've seen it. It must have been very important if you—'

'Thing is, I found it. So there's no problem. But frankly, yes, I suspected you. Locking my office door like you did yesterday.

Really, that's suspicious behaviour. An important part of being seen as honest is behaving, at every moment, in an honest fashion.'

'I'm not sure what—'

'It's fine. I need to go now. My associate is expecting me.'

'Yes, sir,' Ryan says to Duvenhage's back. 'I'm glad it's all sorted out, sir.' He sighs with relief as Duvenhage goes and notices Sybil Fontein staring at him. He smiles at her and heads out of the administration wing and towards the staff room, where he should be helping Thulani clean.

It's just after one, the last teaching session of the day, and most of the teachers are in class. Even though this room is a hundred years newer than the one in his high school, Ryan still gets the same feeling from it. When he went to school, kids were not allowed near the staff room unless they were handing in punishment work or doing a chore for a teacher; neither was desirable. And despite the fact that this staff room is only eight years old, it still somehow has the same outdated green coffee mugs on a tray and scale-encrusted stainless-steel urn bubbling away for nobody, the same bland dove-grey vertical blinds that always get snagged up and droop from their cheap and broken plastic catches, the same square, butt-indented chairs covered in sticky green polyvinyl that haven't been properly washed in all their days. Ryan's fucked if he's going to scrub between those seams.

'Hey, Ryan,' Thulani says, smiling. Ryan doesn't know how the man can be so cheerful. He's been here since the school was established, and before that he was a night janitor at a shopping mall. Cleaning up after other people all his life. But he's always smiling from his grey-peppercorn-dusted cheeks and has a different loud shirt for every day of the week which he makes sure shows from between the buttons of his overall. Is that all happiness takes? Just a small, quiet assertion of individuality?

'Hey, Thulani. What do you need me to do?'

'Bins and vacuum?'

'Sure thing.'

Ryan starts by picking up the larger bits of paper and detritus strewn on the staff room's floor. The same teachers who'd administer a beating to a kid for littering... But then again, they don't beat kids at school any more. How do they control them?

Since this morning, he's been feeling twitchy, unsettled and he can't think what's caused it. He managed to damp the symptoms each time they appeared yesterday. It's seemed like weeks since he last had the compulsion, and suddenly yesterday it was like a flood... But he calmed the ache each time it appeared – first the drive in Duvenhage's office, then Artie's book. What could be causing it now?

Oh, shit. His mind's got to be fucking with him again.

Tess. He hasn't felt that for a long time; he wished he never would again, but here it is. There was nothing he could do about it last night, so he just went to bed, drank the rest of the Three Ships and forgot about it. Until now. When he woke up this morning, the memory had gone like a dream; blurred by the hangover throb in his head.

He shovels the rubbish into a big black plastic bag, slivers of newspaper, misprinted test papers used for scrap pads, and flyers printed on yellow, pink and baby-blue paper. As he's emptying the bin near the coffee counter, he notices a yellow page that has been scrunched up into a tiny ball, not just casually, but with some force. He's interested to see what could have provoked such a strong reaction. He unballs the paper with long fingers, avoiding the gum and wet spots and smoothes it out on the carpet.

It's an invitation for a meeting of some group called ENCOUNTERS, and it's got a jumping Coke can with a smiling face on the picture. 'Quizzes! Prizes! Body Art!' it yells. One of the corners is missing, torn off. Ryan looks up at the notice board above the counter and there it is. The little yellow corner, still pinned against the navy felt. Somebody ripped the flyer down and crumpled it up angrily. One of the teachers objecting to a marketing roadshow being allowed in the school?

Ryan stands and takes the paper to where Thulani is standing on a short ladder reattaching the drooping blinds. 'Do you know anything about this?'

'What is it?' Thulani unplugs his earphones and takes the paper.

'Do you know anything about this group?'

'Looks like some church group, youth group, something. I don't know.'

'Do you ever get the feeling that this place is... weird in some way?'

Thulani laughs and raises his eyebrows. 'Like how?'

'I don't know. They're always banging on about their "ethos".'

Thulani shrugs.

'And the headmaster, Mr Duvenhage. He's new, isn't he?'

'Yes. Started this year.'

'What happened to the old head?'

'He retired.'

'What does Duvenhage actually do?'

Thulani's eyes dart around the room. 'It's a different system here since he started. Mr Duvenhage is like the business head. Fundraising, partnerships and things like that. I don't know.'

'Is he even a teacher?'

'It's a different system here since he came in,' Thulani repeats. 'It's very different from the schools I went to.'

'Yeah. Mine too.'

'But a lot of things were different back then.'

'Of course.'

'Listen, Ryan. I've learnt in my life, and at this school, that it's better just to do your job and not to ask questions. Keeps you happy.

The answers don't matter really, do they?'

'I suppose not.'

Ryan's changing out of his overalls when he sees the new girl drifting towards the maintenance sheds across the middle-school playing field. The bright green grass and the dusty blue sky behind her, and just the lone girl in her tan uniform remind him of something. A scene from a movie or a music video or something. He can't remember. But with her bleached hair and her dead-pale skin, her disconnected attitude, she looks like an inverse goth, like a different subspecies of those girls who wear black layers and paint their lips and their eyes and their hair black. Not that there are girls like that at this school. If they go out on weekends dressed like that, they make sure to hide it at Crossley College. He's never got close to girls like them; they'd simply never open up to a man like him. He appeals to a different sort of girl, girls like Tess next door.

But this girl's too young to be a full-blown goth, or whatever she is, surely? She looks like she's about ten, but at the same time she seems older, more experienced. It's something in her eyes, and as she comes closer he realises he's staring at her through the window of the shed, the overalls half off, his hands frozen at the button at his waist. And she's staring back at his bare chest. Now she's just a few metres away, coming up the slope off the playing field, her eyes still trained on him. Is she coming towards him? His heart jerks.

Ryan pulls his T-shirt on and straightens his hair and now she's passing the window. Is she coming around to the door? He goes across and opens it, but she's not outside. He goes back to the window, but she's not there. He jogs out of the door and scans the path, looks around the side of the shed, but she's disappeared. There's a knot of kids waiting over at the car park for their lifts. She was probably heading that way after all and just blended in. Ryan blushes, even though nobody saw his embarrassing little performance.

But she was looking at him, that much he's certain of. And that girl does not blend in.

He finishes dressing and walks through the parking lot, disturbed by how irrational the girl makes him. Another picture of Tess and how lost she looked last night jumps, unbidden into his head. He passes an olive-green Land Rover. Julie.

He ducks away, but it's too late.

'Hello, Ryan,' Julie says.

'Hi,' he says. 'How are you?'

She ignores the question. 'You scared me last night. You scared Artie.'

Ryan shrugs. 'I didn't hurt him, did I? I just wanted him not to take my picture. It's very rude to take someone's picture without asking.'

'You don't think... what he saw... that would be a bit upsetting for a boy?' He can see her eyes hardening. She's not going to cry. 'I'm sorrier than I can ever say that we were doing that.'

'Are you serious? I don't understand. Why should it matter to him? Your husband is obviously a—'

'You know, there's something wrong with you. Something missing.'

'What do you want, Julie?'

'I just want to be sure that you're not going to... tell anyone about our...' She retracts into the car. She looks afraid.

'Listen. It's over. It was over before you even fucking knew it. Out of my mind. Don't worry. I won't tell anyone about our little mistake. It's nothing I'm proud of.'

She stares forward. 'Good. Then that's fine.' The window starts going up.

'*I dumped you*, bitch. I fucking dumped *you*,' he thinks.

Another embarrassing scene, and Ryan simply can't understand what Julie's problem is. She's the one who seduced him. And he didn't hurt the boy. He'll get over it. Today's turning into a bad one. He needs a drink.

He walks the short way along Smith Street to Bedford Centre knowing as he does so with his faded jeans and his grubby backpack that he's starting to look more and more like someone who belongs outside, no longer a complacent suburbanite. Now he's forced to scuff through the city's grime with the rest of the poor people, get painted brown by its filthy air. When last *was* he a clean and complacent suburbanite, a shiny-smiled middle-class dad? Now the dirt has become ingrained in his skin, the sun's had its way. And the booze, he supposes. Soon, he'll look like someone the security guards might turn away at the entrance to the mall. But not yet. They'll take his money while he still has it.

He heads straight to the bottle store and buys another couple of litres of Three Ships. He stashes one in his backpack and keeps the other in the blackish plastic bag and twists open the top. That crack of a bottle top; as satisfying as a good, spine-crackling stretch. He used to get wasted at cafes and bars, but now this is all he can afford. The alcohol's the same chemical however and wherever you drink it.

He sits on a bench in the mall's middle level, where he can get a good view of the franchise restaurants and the escalators and glass-sided lifts. He watches the late-afternoon shoppers going past and takes a furtive slug from the packet. Just one more for courage. He remembers pushing Alice in the grocery trolley right here. It would be their special time – Karin would get a morning off mothering and Ryan and Alice would do the weekly groceries. She must have been – what? – two or three when she sat in the front kiddie seat of the trolley, and she'd help him choose what they were looking for. As they went, he'd select her some fruit cuts and a juice to keep her happy.

If tonight were any other night of the week, he'd head straight back to his room, but not on a Wednesday. On Wednesdays Alice and Karin get take-aways, and sometimes it's at this mall, and

Ryan's always waiting. It means that he gets to see his girl every couple of weeks, and if the circumstances are right, he might even get to speak to her. She never tells her mother; she's good that way.

A few slugs later he sees Karin's stick-thin frame clipping up the escalator, with Alice in resentful tow. His heart lifts, despite the fact that it looks like they've been fighting. Alice is wearing black again. Each time he sees her, she's a bit moodier, a bit fatter. What the fuck is Karin doing to her?

Ryan follows at a distance, knowing from past experience that they're heading either for the Pizza Supreme or the Island Health Foods, depending on their collective mood. He follows them past Island Health Foods. Pizza is the mood tonight. He watches them place their order. Karin sits on the couch in the waiting area and grabs a magazine. She smiles up at Alice but Alice stays standing, arms folded. Then she says something and Karin starts up, slams the magazine on the couch and stalks off. Alice sits, and pages through the magazine, her body slumping.

'Hey, girl.'

'Daddy!' The smile that lights up Alice's face seems to slough off all that extra baggage. She straightens up. 'She's gone to Pick n Pay.'

'Sweetie, is she treating you well?'

'She drives me mad. I miss you.'

Ryan's heart fills up. 'How're you doing?'

'Fine.'

'And how's school?'

'Okay.'

'I got you something.' He rummages in his backpack, painfully aware of the sound of bottles clinking as he does. He shuffles past the boy's soft porn that's still in his bag and pulls out the Harry Potter book.

'Oh, thanks, Dad.' She's trying hard to keep her smile on.

'What's wrong?'

'I already read it. Long time ago.'

'Oh, I thought... We used to read the first one together, bfore... when...'

'That's a long time ago, Dad.'

'I suppose it is. I'm sorry.'

He reaches out to take the book back, but she pulls it herself. 'Oh, but I want it, of course, Daddy.' She puts on a smile knows, to please him. He loves her more for the effort. 'I'm keng it! You know, I can swap it for something else. Say it was a

'Okay. I'm glad you like it then.'

She looks at him. Her face is still the same. 'Dad

'Yes, sweetie?'

'When do you th—'

'What the *fuck* are you doing here?'

'Listen, Karin. I was just... here. I saw Alice. she is. J say hello?'

'*No,* you can't! Now fuck off.'

'Jesus, Karin. Is that any way to speak it of Alg looks to Alice for support, but she's already She's across the restaurant entrance, looking at no foldin. 'So so hard she could twist herself in two. He ack to how's it going? Fucked any dealers lately?

'Fuck *you,* Ryan. Get the *fuck* away fr She ts at him with her hand and he grabs her wrist an s backor sleeve. There's nothing — no track marks, no b no nohing. She's clean. *Dammit!*

'Get your hands off me!' she scream not you... I've got over you and your little hobbies.'

'What do you mean by that?' he asks ough he nows.

'You know what I mean, you sick fu

'Excuse me. Excuse me!' The restau manager's grappling at him now. Ryan pushes him off.

71

'I've got a job now. I'm going to get visitation rights back. I'm going o tell them that you're not fit to be a mother.'

'Loc at me, Ryan.' She puffs herself up, extends her scrawny neck li a chicken. 'I'm better. I'm over you. You'll never see Alice again. I you think the court's going to grant visitation to a strung-out dru After what you did to A—'

He gr her mouth, mashing her lips, grinding her jaw, making it hurt. ' shut the fuck up,' he snarls. 'I never hurt her!'

The re rant manager is still grabbing at him and he sees two security ds jogging along the corridor.

He lets picks up his backpack and crosses to Alice. 'I'm sorry. You know at she's like...' Alice is crying but she doesn't move to wipe he . He reaches out to hold her arm but she jerks away.

'I'm sor ay.'

Nothing

'See you

He walks He hears the slap and the shear of the book being wn behi n. It skids all the way to his feet. He bends to pick and loo or Alice, for one last moment of connection, but treate the shadows of the restaurant.

Rya

and wat g, he's tried reading, he sat with Ma Beccah the gashe p on television. None of it is helping to patch link Tes d on this godawful day. He wishes he didn't seeing Al ation last night; he doesn't want that. And been think g: s evening has only made it worse. So he's and the compulsio he faces the temptation and then says no, He's stronge now, s away. He can try that with Tess, can't he? He goes down the e? He can control himself. He'd be free. sprays on deodorant. idor and showers, puts on clean clothes, backpack over his sho checks his watch. 11.47. He slings his r. The girl's going to be fast asleep now, but maybe just being outside her house will resolve something. Besides, he's not going to get any sleep in this state, so he may as well get some air.

Coming out the front door of Ma Beccah's house, it's the sort of crisp night he wishes he was a smoker. Smokers have a built-in reason to stand around outside and watch. You see someone standing on a pavement in the middle of the night, not smoking, and you know he's up to no good.

But here he is, not smoking, standing outside Tess and Fransie's house. It's dead quiet, not a car or a pedestrian, not a cat. The streetlights through the dying leaves paint unwavering stencils on the pavement. The city thrums in the distance and he can hear the faraway rush of the highway, the bleat of a train down in Cleveland. The rocker on the veranda is vacant, but Ryan can almost imagine the shadow of Fransie's malignant father shunting it back and forth in the cool air. The single fluorescent bulb at the front door flickers.

Is it his imagination, or is he feeling calmer? Or is it just the fresh air after all? 'Hello, Mr Ryan.' She's come out of the overgrown side of the garden again and is standing alongside him, on the other side of the low precast wall. She's wearing cheap tracksuit pants and a loose T-shirt, thin flip-flops on her feet.

'Jesus, Tess. Christ, what are you doing here?'

'Uh, it's my house?'

'I mean, what are you doing out? Why are you up?'

'I couldn't sleep.'

'Where's your father?'

'Out.'

'Is anyone looking after you?'

'Grampa's there, but...'

They don't love this girl like they should. She's all alone in the world.

'Hey, Tess,' he says, 'I got you something.' He drops his backpack to the pavement and squats over it. He brings out the book and hands it to her.

She looks like a child on Christmas morning. The way children are supposed to react. 'Oh, Mr Ryan! That's awesome. I saw the movies. I always wanted to read Harry Potter. Thank you! Thank you!'

'It's a pleasure, love. I got it specially for you. Because I know how nice it is to escape into stories. I'm sure you've got a great imagination.'

She blushes, looks down. She strokes the cover of the book and then decides something for herself. 'Come, Mr Ryan. I want to show you something.' She takes his hand and he remembers when Alice used to do that. It feels so warm, to be needed. He steps over the wall and she leads him down the side of the house, into the over-grown bushes. They push through a narrow opening in a thick, rough hedge.

Tess clicks a camping light hanging on a lopped branch and the space is illuminated. Instead of more tangled branches there's a clear space surrounded by growth; it's a little room.

'This is my castle,' Tess says.

'Like in a fairy tale?'

She doesn't answer but she watches him proudly as he looks around. There are three cracked plastic kids' chairs, a muddy quilt rolled up in a corner, a couple of cushions. A half-empty bottle of Coke, a purple plastic box, some comic books.

'Do you sleep here, Tess?'

'No. No. Only sometimes. When's Dad's out, and...'

'They don't take care of you, honey. They should take better care of you.'

'I'm okay. I'm fine. I wanted to show you because... because you're kind to me.'

'You know you deserve to be loved, don't you, Tess?'

He realises she's still holding his hand. It's sweating. She's looking at him with an open expression, as if waiting for something.

Beep-beep. Beep-beep.

Her cheap digital watch sounds a new hour. She lets go of his hand and looks at the display. 'Twelve o'clock,' she says.

'Midnight,' he says. 'You know what happens in fairy tales at midnight, don't you?'

'What, Mr Ryan?'

'Poor girls turn into princesses.'

Chapter 8

TARA

Tara's been working steadily, and Batiss's baby's face is already taking on that newborn rosy glow. She's christened him Baby Tommy, deciding that he is a boy, after all. She's always loved the name – secretly planned to use it for her own firstborn son in fact – but it just seems right that he should have it. It suits him.

She gently places his head on its stand, decides that before she starts the finicky vein work on his forehead, she'll sort out the colours she needs to re-mottle the Baby Gabby limbs. She digs out her sponges, readies the paper towels she'll use to blot up the excess paint.

'Tara!' Stephen yells up the stairs. She listens to his footsteps flumping down the corridor towards her sanctuary, reluctantly unlocks the door, blocking his view into the room with her body.

Stephen's face is pink and puffy. His blue work shirt is crumpled and sweat-stained. 'What the hell are you doing, Tara?'

'Working.'

'But Martin hasn't had his supper yet – *I* haven't had my supper yet.'

'Martin knows where the fridge is, so do you.' Although she hasn't eaten all day, Tara isn't even slightly hungry. There's a tube of Pringles stashed in her bottom drawer if she needs them. She goes to shut the door in his face, but he shoulders his way in.

'What the bloody hell are you—' He stops dead as he takes in the printed photographs tacked up on the wall above her desk. To help her with those all-important details, she's created a collage of blown-up images of Baby Tommy's anatomy: close-ups of his features, his little bunched fists, his darling chubby legs and, of course, his eyes and mouth. Seeing it through Stephen's eyes, she realises it probably resembles a murder board – the kind of prop that's always hovering in the background in crime shows.

'What the hell is this?'

'My commission.'

He moves closer to the enlarged print-out of Baby Tommy's mouth, the black thread puckering the delicate skin around his lips. 'Jesus, Tara. That's sick.'

She swallows a snappish response. Baby Tommy isn't sick. Can't he see how beautiful he is?

'Who would want something like this?' Stephen asks, voice thick with disgust.

'A client.'

'Who is this client?'

'What do you care? They're paying me.'

This makes him pause. 'How much?'

'Five thousand,' she says, without a twinge of guilt at the lie. He knows that most Reborns go for between two and three thousand; the lawyer in him will approve that she's upped her rates.

He turns away from the photographs with a shrug of revulsion. 'What's wrong with Martin? Is he ill? He's shut himself in his room.'

'He's your son, why don't you ask him?'

'I *have* asked him, I'm asking you. Christ, first you almost burn the house down, now you hole up in here for a measly five grand. What's got into you?'

'I could ask you the same question.'

'What do you mean by that?'

She can feel the electric charge of a major row crackling in the atmosphere between them. A showdown is way overdue – they need to clear the air – but if she gets into it now, it will use up valuable Baby Tommy time. She'll have to backtrack, try and nip it in the bud. 'Nothing, Stephen. I didn't mean anything. Look, I'm sorry about supper, I guess I just got carried away in here, forgot the time.'

His body language loosens instantly and Tara feels a jab of triumph – it's so easy to play him, almost *too* easy.

'It's fine. I know Martin can be difficult.' He reaches out and takes her hand. 'And I know I've been... distant, preoccupied lately. There's big shit going down at work again.'

She slaps a practised expression of concern on her face. 'What sort of shit?'

'Trouble with the trust account.'

'Again? You want to talk about it?'

He runs his hands through the sweaty clumps of hair at his temples, starts to ramble on about the audit that has the senior and silent partners squirming. Her ability to listen calmly while he unpacks his day is one of the fundaments of their relationship, although he usually prefers to spill his guts to her just after they've made love. But that hasn't happened for a while, has it? In fact, she can't actually remember the last time they had sex. Was it a week ago? Two weeks? A month? Hard to believe that just over a year ago he used to sneak out of the office, drive across town to the Melrose apartment she shared with a bunch of students, and all so they could have twenty hurried minutes together. She watches his lips moving, a bubble of spittle popping at the corner of his mouth. The thought of his hands on her now makes her skin crawl.

She finds herself wondering – as she does more and more these days – what would have happened if instead of staying in Joburg, letting herself slide deeper into their affair, she'd carried on with her round-the-world adventure, caught a flight to Buenos Aires as she had planned to. She allows herself to dwell on the forbidden issue of whether he would have even consented to the hurried divorce, the hasty marriage, if she hadn't fallen pregnant. More and more these days, she doubts it. She has to face it. If it wasn't for that ill-fated pregnancy, she wouldn't be trapped here. She'd be back in New Jersey, or possibly teaching in another state, praying that the school administrators didn't dig too deeply into her background (she is, after all, just one Google click away from being found out). Still, she can't afford regrets, and in any case there's something about this place that's got to her, squirmed its way under her skin. It's not the city itself; she's still struggling to get a handle on its aura of suppressed violence, clogged highways, paranoid security estates and sprawling townships. She's not sure what it is, suspects it's because there's so much *need* here. If what she's read on IOL is true, there are thousands of South African children locked in an epidemic of foetal alcohol syndrome and abuse; casualties of a country ripped apart and slapped back together, the seams still showing. Kids like Jane, for instance. Staying here and helping needy kids like her, well, it would be a way of doing penance for what's gone before, wouldn't it?

'So what do you think?' Stephen says.

'You poor thing,' she says, hoping that he won't ask any specific questions. 'No wonder you're so stressed. Sounds like a nightmare.'

It's the right thing to say – all he needs. 'How about we go out for supper at the weekend? Just the two of us.'

'That'll be nice.'

'I'll order take-away tonight, shall I? What do you want? Pizza? Simply Asia?'

'Whatever you want, Stephen,' she says, willing him to leave, fingers itching to pick up her mottling sponge.

'That's my girl.'

He wraps his arms around her, buries his face in her hair. She pulls back, catches the fleeting look of distaste on his face as he gets a whiff of her unwashed body and stale breath.

She doesn't care.

She's only had three hours' sleep, but this morning she feels more alive than she has for weeks. Freshly showered and dressed in a newly ironed shirt and pair of Levi's, she smothers the temptation to check on Baby Tommy – the lure of him is so strong she can feel it in her gut – and pads down to the kitchen.

She makes herself a cup of instant, pulls open the fridge and sees they're out of milk. Goddammit. Now she'll be forced to go shopping after library duty instead of heading straight home to Tommy.

She should really go and check on Martin. Make sure the little bastard is up and ready for school. She drains her coffee, makes her way up to Martin's room and taps on the door. No response. She knocks again. 'Martin? You up?'

'Go away!' There's a panicky edge to his voice she's not heard before.

'You okay?'

'Don't come in!'

She presses her ear to the door – hears what she thinks is a muffled sob.

Should she go in? There are no locks on Martin's door; Stephen confiscated the key months ago after he'd locked himself in to avoid being punished for smearing the word 'Bitch' on her car window with mud. She turns the handle, steps inside, sees him frantically trying to push his bed linen into the wash basket. The pungent odour of urine fills the room.

He rounds on her, cheeks wet with tears. 'I told you not to come in! Get out!'

'Hey,' she says, 'it's cool.'

'It's not!' He drops the sheets on the floor and screws his fists into his eyes like a much younger child. It's the first time she's ever seen him cry.

'Here,' she says, 'let me do that.' Careful not to show any disgust, she rolls the sodden sheets together, wraps them inside the duvet cover.

He wipes his snotty nose on his sleeve. 'Don't tell Dad.'

'Of course I won't. Besides, it's no big deal. It happens to every-one.' Does it? Isn't late-stage bedwetting one of the signs of a psychopathic personality? She chides herself for being so unsym-pathetic. Poor kid is in a state.

'I had a bad dream,' Martin says.

'You remember it?'

He shakes his head. She can tell by the way his eyes shift that he's lying. 'You want to stay home today?'

'No!'

'You sure?' That way, she thinks, with only a hint of shame, she'll have an excuse to carry on with Baby Tommy instead of doing library duty.

'I'm sure. You swear you won't tell?'

'I swear. It'll be our secret. Really, you can trust me, Martin.'

He sniffs.

'Hey, what went on in that meeting last night? That Encounters thing?'

'Just stuff.'

'Is it a... Christian-type thing?'

'No!'

'What then?' She's heard that the Scientologists have spread their tentacles throughout South Africa. But even Mr Duvenhage wouldn't allow that kind of hokey shit at the school, would he? She remembers the soda can on the flyer – perhaps it's some kind of marketing drive.

Martin sighs. 'It's just stuff. Primo stuff.'

'And that word – primo. Where did you hear it from?'

He shrugs. 'Dunno.'

'Is it like a new slang word? Like rad or lekker or whatever they say here?'

'S'pose.'

'Have you told your father about Encounters?'

'Why should I? He won't care. He's always busy.'

Fair enough, Tara thinks. 'Well, if you are going to go to school, you'd better hustle. I'll pop these into the washing machine, it'll be as if it never happened.'

'Tara?' he says as she turns to exit his room.

'Yeah?'

'Thanks.'

'You're welcome.' In all the time she's known him, she's longed for him to show her the tiniest sign of gratitude or respect, but now that he has, why does she feel so uneasy?

The morning's class streams into the library, and Tara's surprised – and oddly pleased – to see Jane trailing in after the others. Her uniform looks even grubbier today; her hair greasier. Dark circles ring her eyes as if she hasn't slept. Tara tries to catch her attention, but Jane heads straight over to the starter-reader shelf and drops to her knees.

'Who *is* that?' Malika says, nodding in Jane's direction and wrinkling her nose.

Tara feels a stab of irritation. It's not Jane's fault that her uniform is tatty. If she is one of the outreach kids, her parents probably can't afford to wash it every day. 'She's new. She was here yesterday. Didn't you see her?'

'God. That hair. What was her mother thinking? I'd never let Sienna and Ruby out looking like that.'

'Maybe she doesn't *have* a mother, Malika.'

Her harsh tone goes right over Malika's head. 'Maybe. You okay to deal with her?'

'Sure.'

Tara makes her way over to where Jane's rummaging through the shelves. 'Hey, Jane. You want to read with me today?'

Jane looks up at her and grins. She's getting better at it; hillbilly teeth aside, it looks less like a snarl.

'Which book would you like to start with, sweetie?' Tara remembers how Jane was holding that book upside down. What if she can't read? Is that likely? At age ten?

Jane immediately hands Tara one of Duvenhage's vile self-published picture books. The front cover shows a group of smugly grinning children, their arms around each other. Off to one side, a small boy with angry slashes for eyes appears to be aiming a vicious glare in their direction. It's an appalling cover – the children's heads are way too large for their bodies; they look like pumpkin heads – and the garbled title, *There's No Team In Individual*, looks like it's written in blood.

'You sure you want this one, sweetie?'

'Yes, miss,' Jane says.

Tara scans the first page. It's all in rhyme, and terrible rhyme at that.

'Will you read it to me, miss?'

Tara smiles. 'You're supposed to read it to *me*, sweetie.'

Jane stares at her expressionlessly.

If Jane can't read, the last thing Tara wants to do is embarrass her in front of the other kids. 'How about I start and you can join in?'

Jane nods solemnly.

Buzzy bees are all the same, they like to work not play.

They buzz around in flower stalks, making honey all the day.

They like to follow, keep the faith, they like to keep in line.
They know that if they act real nice their lives will turn out fine.
Children too, like me and you, we like to have our chums.
As long as they are GOODLY ones, not deadbeat scummy bums.

Jesus, Tara thinks. What the hell was Duvenhage or Clara thinking ordering a dodgy book like this for the library?

'What are chums, miss?'

'It's an old-fashioned word. It means friends, buddies, you know.'

'Oh.'

She's about to suggest to Jane that she fetch another book, when the fire siren whoops.

Clara's office door slams open and she scurries towards Tara. 'It's probably just a drill,' she says, 'but I should really check what's going on. Can you escort the library children outside, Mrs Marais?' She peers down at Jane, frowns slightly.

'No problem.'

'Good,' Clara says. With a last confused glance at Jane, she heads out into the corridor.

Tara claps her hands. 'Okay, everyone. Line up by the door.'

The children silently pack their books away and line up. She does a swift head count, then instructs them to hold hands and keep together. Jane is standing apart from the others, that awful book still clutched tightly in her arms.

Tara beckons her over. 'Hey, Jane. Why don't you hold Skye's hand?'

Jane drops the book onto the floor and limps forward, but Skye steps back, shoves his arms behind his back. 'I don't want to, miss,' he whines.

'That's not very nice, is it?'

'Please don't make me,' he whispers, and Tara sees the wobble of tears in his eyes. She understands why he isn't keen, of course.

Jane isn't exactly the most approachable of children, but this is an extreme reaction, surely? There's always one outsider kid in every class – he or she usually ends up being a bully-magnet – but she gets the impression that Skye's reluctance runs deeper than being caught being nice to the weird kid.

Malika is already leading the line through the door.

Tara sighs. 'Go on, then, Skye. But you are being very rude.'

'Thank you, miss,' he whispers, fleeing after the others.

'Well, it looks like you've got me,' Tara says over-brightly to Jane. She takes the child's hand in hers. 'Don't worry about what Skye said.'

'Oh, I'm not worried, miss,' Jane says. 'He's just a brown.'

Tara blinks. A brown? Is that some sort of racist statement? Unlikely, as Skye is as white as she is. 'You shouldn't use words like that, Jane.'

'Like what, miss?'

'Brown. If you... um... use it in the wrong way, people might think you're being racist.'

'What's racist?'

'Where people discriminate – I mean judge or treat badly – other people because of the colour of their skin.'

Jane looks up at her through those grey, unreadable eyes. 'And not because they're depreciating? Mother says that the problem with browns is that they depreciate too quickly.'

'Depreciate? What do you mean by that, Jane?' The child shrugs. What kind of parents has this child got? It sounds like she's being fed a steady diet of ignorance and casual racism. 'Are you finding it okay in the school, Jane? The other children... Has anyone been mean to you or anything like that?'

'Mean, miss?'

'Cruel. You know...' God, she thinks, she's really making a pig's ear of this. She must be getting rusty. 'Teasing? Bullying? You can always speak to me about anything that's worrying you, you know that, right?'

'Are you my chum, miss? Like in the book?'

'Yes. I suppose I am.'

'Do you have a baby in your tum?'

'What? What made you ask that?'

'One of the halfpints told me. Is it factual, miss? He said they come out of here.' Jane pulls up her shirt, and points to her belly button. Tara gasps. The girl's stomach is sliced with scar-tissue.

Jesus, Tara thinks. A car accident? 'What happened to you, Jane?'

'Happened, miss?'

'Your stomach. The scars.' Come to think of it, aren't they more like burn scars? Tara's not really sure. And there's that limp. Tara can't see any sign of a leg-brace, but perhaps that's also an injury from some sort of accident.

'Oh. Mother says I shouldn't talk about my carcass. She says that browns won't embrace that. Do you like television, miss?'

Tara's struggling to follow Jane's train of thought. 'Yes. I suppose I do. Don't get to see much of it, though.'

'I love television, miss. You sound like television.' She drops her voice, puts on an American accent. 'Motherfucka, I'm a gonna shoot a cap in ya ass.' And then she laughs – it's a shrill sound, but it makes Tara smile all the same.

'That's another word you shouldn't really use, Jane.'

'Which word, miss?'

'That cuss word.'

'Cuss?'

'That... um... word beginning with "m".' She isn't getting anywhere. 'Come on. We'd better get going.'

By the time she and Jane make it outside into the playground, the other children are already lined up in perfect, silent rows, Duvenhage pacing up and down in front of them like a sergeant major. She ushers Jane over to Ms du Preez's line at the far side of the yard.

Tara feels the weight of eyes on her back. She turns, sees the swarthy maintenance man next to the grounds staff and cleaners a few metres away, looking in their direction. She lifts her hand in acknowledgment, but he doesn't respond. She's about to dismiss this as more of that rude behaviour she encountered outside Sybil Fontein's office, when it hits her that it's not *her* he's staring at, after all, it's Jane. While Clara briskly does the head count, an exercise that takes several minutes, he doesn't once lift his eyes from her; he doesn't seem to notice Tara's increasingly pointed glare. His intense expression is making her feel uneasy. It's almost... hungry.

She's relieved when the children are dismissed and Jane follows her classmates safely back into the school. Tara thinks about confronting the maintenance man, asking him what the hell he thought he was doing staring at a child like that, but he's already making his way to the groundskeepers' shed and she's not in the mood to make a scene. Besides, it's almost break time, and Baby Tommy is waiting.

She isn't late to collect Martin this afternoon from Encounters, but it's a close-run thing. It had been a real effort to drag herself away from Baby Tommy. She's finding the work so... fulfilling somehow. And it's not just the money. The feeling of bringing him to life is far more intense than when she Reborned her first baby, Baby Pooki; even stronger than when she created Baby Paul.

She waves at Malika, who's lounging against her black BMW convertible, waiting for her older daughter, Sienna, to slouch her way to the car. Tara isn't a fan of Sienna, a twelve-year-old mini-Malika with highlighted hair and painted acrylic nails. Tara remembers meeting her at Martin's birthday party last year. She seemed older than her years, spent most of the party huddled in a corner with a couple of mini-skirted pre-teens, and Tara had overheard them making bitchy comments about their classmates. She has a vague recollection that Sienna and her sidekicks were accused of picking on one of the outreach kids – something about creating a Facebook hate group.

Martin picks up his bag and slinks into the car.

'How are you feeling, Martin?'

'Fine, thanks,' he says, his polite tone surprising her.

But he doesn't look fine, Tara thinks. He looks exhausted, his face muscles slack, his shoulders drooping. 'How was Encounters?'

'Excuse me?'

'The meeting?'

'Fine, thanks.'

'Have fun?'

'Yes.'

She follows Malika's car up the driveway, is about to accelerate into the main road, when she spots a small, familiar figure standing among a cluster of commuters waiting for their taxi home. She'd recognise Jane's odd-coloured hair anywhere. What is she doing here? She should have been home ages ago. Has she also been to Encounters?

'You know that kid, Martin?'

'Huh?'

Tara gestures in Jane's direction. 'That girl. She in your Encounters group?'

'No.'

She makes a decision, shoots out into the traffic, switches on her hazard lights, brakes sharply and pulls over next to her.

'What are you doing here, Jane?' she calls out of the window, ignoring the furious blare of horns from the cars forced to stream around her.

'I'm waiting, miss.'

'You shouldn't be out on the road, sweetie. It's dangerous.' It's worse than dangerous, Tara thinks, remembering the predatory way that maintenance man stared at her. 'How do you normally get home?' She can't walk, surely. That would be asking for trouble.

'Danish.'

'*Danish?*'

'Danish takes me home.'

'Who's that? Your brother?'

'No.'

Maybe it's her mother's deadbeat boyfriend. Tara pictures a tattooed thug, breath stinking of booze, screeching up to the school gates in a muscle car with blacked-out windows. Her imagination is really running away with itself. 'Isn't he coming to fetch you today?'

'No. I told him not to.'

'Why not?'

'I wanted to exit with you. You're my chum, miss.'

'Oh, sweetheart,' Tara says. Is the poor kid so lonely that she's waited all this time on the off chance that she'll turn up? Thinking about it, how *did* Jane know Tara would be back to fetch Martin? And if she didn't go to Encounters, what has she been doing in the hours since school let out? 'It's not safe for you to be out here by yourself.'

There's another flurry of beeping horns, followed by, '*Move, bitch!*' She'd better get going.

'Get in, Jane. I'll give you a lift.'

Tara waits for Martin to protest, is surprised when all she hears is a muttered 'Aw what?'

The girl smiles and jumps into the front seat. Martin always sits in the back as if Tara's his taxi driver; it's pleasant to have a passenger next to her for once.

'Put your seat belt on, sweetie.'

'Belt?'

Hasn't the poor kid ever been in a car before? Maybe she only travels by minibus taxis – coffins on wheels, as Stephen calls them. Come to think of it, maybe those horrendous scars are the result of a car accident after all. Tara leans over her, pulls the belt across the child's skinny body.

'Can I have a hug?' Jane asks, in the same gruff American accent she used before.

Before Tara can answer, Jane throws her arms around her neck and Tara finds herself hugging her back. Jane's frame is fragile, feels almost like it could snap under her embrace. She smells of dried leaves and strawberry essence.

Tara feels her chest tighten. Shame, poor kid must be starved for affection. She gently disentangles the girl's arms from around her neck, indicates and pulls the car up onto the pavement so that she isn't blocking the traffic.

'Martin, say hello to Jane.'

'Whatever,' he says, but so drowsily, it sounds like he's about to fall asleep.

'Hello,' Jane says, turning round in her seat to wave at him. 'How are you today I'm fine thanks kay bye.' She pauses, stares at Martin for several intense seconds. 'You're a forespecial.'

Martin shakes his head and curls up against the window.

'Where do you live, sweetie?' Tara asks.

Jane digs in her backpack, pulls out a laminated pink card and hands it to Tara. The childish script on it reads: 'If lost please restore to 67a Excelsior Avenue, Bedfordview.' Jesus, Tara thinks, it's like something you'd tie around a dog's neck. The address doesn't sound like a slum area, but as far as she can tell, in this country, names mean nothing. Tara taps it into her GPS, waits for the gadget to boot up. That's odd, she thinks, the house is only a couple of kilometres from Crossley College. Tara's used to Joburg's messy and often contradictory layout – shanty towns sitting cheek-by-jowl with Tuscan-style mansions – but as far as she's aware, the school's surrounding area is resolutely upper class, peppered with Virgin Actives and delicatessens.

Tara pulls out into the traffic, follows the GPS's directions. Jane leans over and fiddles with the radio dials, filling the car with static interspersed with gabbling radio chatter. If Martin had done this, Tara would have stopped him immediately, but she doesn't have the heart to spoil Jane's fun. Poor little mite clearly has a hard enough life as it is.

The GPS woman guides her through a complex warren of side streets, and within minutes Tara turns into Excelsior Avenue, an upmarket street lined with McMansions and gated complexes. She hadn't expected this. Perhaps Jane isn't one of the outreach kids after all.

'You have reached your destination,' the GPS voice says as Tara cruises past a property she's noticed before – well, she could hardly forget it. Scores of statues, most of which look like they've been bought wholesale from a garden centre, are cemented into its towering stucco walls. A triple row of dryads, half-naked nymphs balancing water urns and cherubs with smiles so poorly rendered that they look like grimaces of pain, jostle for space either side of a rusting gold gate. Stephen had driven her down here a couple of months ago, slowing down so that they could gawp at the house. 'Probably some Greek drug lord's half-completed vanity mansion,' he'd sneered. 'More money than taste.'

Assuming that the GPS must have made a mistake, she prepares to accelerate, then spots the gold curls of the number '67a' mosa-icked onto the bare breasts of a concrete nymph.

Ensuring there are no cars behind her, she reverses, and swings the Pajero around onto the grass verge.

'*This* is your house, Jane?'

Jane nods.

What now? She can't just drop the kid off and run. What if no one's home? Besides, she should probably have a word with Jane's parents, tell them that their daughter was hanging around in the main road – a job she's not relishing in the slightest. What if Stephen's right and they are gangsters or drug dealers? But she doesn't have much of a choice.

She turns to Martin. 'I won't be long. Keep your door locked.'

Martin shrugs and mumbles something she hopes is a 'yes'.

She helps Jane unclick her belt, and together they approach the gates. Tara searches for an intercom, but Jane steps forward and nudges the vast plate-metal slabs open. So much for security. The house itself is fronted by packed dirt peppered with weeds and pools of dried concrete – more like an abandoned building site than a front garden. Its partially completed facade, which appears to have been designed with the Parthenon (or a cheesy casino) in mind, is similarly adorned with statues. In among the generic cherubs and Michelangelo's Davids, Tara makes out several like-nesses of the Hindu goddess Kali, as well as mythological figures she doesn't recognise. She recoils at a male figure with the head of what looks to be a squid, a woman with three breasts and a stump for a hand. Jesus. She's almost sure that a couple of the cherubs' heads are fused together like conjoined twins, but before she can look closer, Jane grabs her hand and tugs her towards the plain wooden front door, which, in comparison to the rest of the place, looks reassuringly benign. Used to entering South African houses by running the gauntlet of security guards, intercoms and Trelli-dors, Tara's shocked when Jane pushes it open – she doesn't even need to turn the handle.

She's expecting to walk into some kind of over-the-top recep-tion area – after the house's insane exterior, she's imagining a pink marbled floor, maybe a statue of Venus – so she's taken aback when they step straight into an unfurnished, double-height entrance hall that stinks of damp concrete. Work must have been halted mid-renovation, Tara assumes as she checks out the plastered walls and bare, screeded floor. To her right, a partially tiled staircase sweeps upwards, the top steps disappearing into darkness.

Jane skips towards an arched doorway to the left and leads Tara into a vast kitchen, which, in stunning contrast to the neglected entrance hall, looks like it's been cut straight out of a model-home catalogue. It's bright in here – too bright. Rows of strip lights range the ceiling, and it doesn't take her long to realise they're the only source of light in the room. The windows have been sealed shut with wood panels. Why would they do that? The room reeks of burnt coffee beans, and it's not difficult to discover why. There's an extensive collection of appliances arrayed on the kitchen counters, including three coffee machines burbling with black liquid.

'Is your mother in, Jane?'

'Mother's always in, miss,' Jane says, for once sounding animated, almost cheerful.

'Could you fetch her for me?'

'Yes, miss.' Jane disappears through a green door at the far side of the kitchen, slamming it behind her.

The minutes tick by, and Tara begins to get antsy. She can't leave Martin alone in the car for much longer but she's reluctant to follow Jane through that door. She paces up and down the room, pausing when she notices a cardboard box, the word 'Research' scrawled on its lid in amongst the jumble of appliances. She knows she shouldn't pry, but she can't resist peeking inside it. It's full of DVD box sets: *Jersey Shore*, *The Real Housewives of Orange County*, *Desperate Housewives Series 3*, *Rock of Love*, *50 Classic Survivor Moments*, *The Wire*, as well as several films – *Independence Day*, *Pretty Woman*, *Lars and the Real Girl*, *Saw 7*, *Love Actually* and *Bringing Out the Dead*. Eclectic taste, Tara muses. Shoved to the side of the box there's a battered cookery book. Checking to make sure she's not about to be disturbed, Tara hauls it out. It clearly dates from the sixties or seventies; there's a grainy photograph of a shiny chicken on the cover beneath the words 'Family Meals for Four'. She flicks through it, almost drops it as several photographs flutter out from its pages onto the floor.

'Shit,' she mutters, bending down to retrieve them. Most seem to be close-ups of plants and vegetables, then she comes across several snaps of a man and a woman posing next to a station wagon. Jane's parents? Tara hopes not. The woman is skeletally thin, with brick-red hair and lips that are so puffed with silicone they look ready to split; the man's skin is too smooth to be natural, and his nose looks far too small for his face – clearly the result of too much plastic surgery.

'Good afternoon!' a woman's voice calls from behind her. Tara whirls around, sees the woman from the photograph slipping through the arched doorway. Tara tries not to gawp at her outlandish appearance, which is accentuated in the flesh. Her ballooning lips are smeared in orange lipstick, white scalp patches show through the red curls of her hair and she's dressed in the same skin-tight lacy bodysuit she's wearing in the photograph.

'Hi,' Tara manages. 'Sorry to barge in like this, but—'

The woman takes Tara's hand in both of hers, flutters a series of air kisses around her head. 'Welcome to home,' she says, trying to smile, although those swollen lips make it near impossible. 'It's so pleasant of you to drop here like this.'

Is she foreign? Tara can't place her accent. It doesn't have that clipped South Africanness about it, but nor does it sound Russian or European. 'Um, I volunteer at the library – you know, at Crossley College. I drove Jane home. She let me in and I—'

'You *drove* Jane home? That's pleasant of you. Can I offer you a refreshment? Coffee? We have lots of coffee.'

'I'm fine, thanks.' Tara can't keep her eyes off the woman's neck, which is several shades darker than the smooth plastic of her face. The remnants of a disastrous fake tan, perhaps? 'Look, Ms... I'm sorry, I don't know your name.'

The woman attempts to smile again. 'That's because I haven't told you what it is.'

Tara waits for her to give it, but the woman simply stares at her as if she's waiting for her to continue the conversation. After several awkward seconds, Tara says, 'I'm afraid Jane got it into her head that I would take her home.' The woman still doesn't respond. Is she drunk? Could this be the source of the neglect? 'She was waiting outside on the main road. She said that someone called Danish usually fetches her.'

'Oh that karking *Danish*!' The woman laughs as if Tara's just said something hilarious. She looks at the photographs Tara's left littered on the counter top.

'I'm so sorry. I shouldn't have been prying. Really, there's no excuse—'

'Do you like this?' the woman asks, gesturing to a close-up of the man.

'Um... very nice.'

'Isn't he scenic? He could be a mascot, couldn't he?'

What the hell does that mean? A mascot like in a baseball game? Like the Mets' Mr Met or something? God, Tara thinks. Poor Jane. With a mother like this, no wonder she has trouble fitting in. She reaches for something to say. 'Um. Your house, it's very... interesting.'

'Is it?'

'Unusual.'

'Tara?'

She looks over her shoulder, sees Martin hovering nervously at the doorway that leads into the entrance hall. 'I'm coming,' she says to him. 'Go back to the car.'

Martin stares at the woman for several seconds, then does as he's told.

She's reluctant to leave Jane in the hands of this woman, but what else can she do? Looking like a freak isn't a crime, is it? And to be honest, she's desperate to get out of here. She turns back to the woman. 'I really should go now, but—'

She jumps as the muffled sound of a scream penetrates the room.

'*Tara!*'

It's Martin.

Chapter 9

PENTER

Penter finds Jane sitting in front of the television, watching one of her favourite upside movies, *Revenge of the Driller Killer III*. The violence isn't to Penter's taste. She's not delicate – she was a recycling apprentice before her redeployment to Upside Relations – but she prefers the movies that end with weddings and parties and laughter, even though she knows this partiality for upside fancy verges on disregard. In the normal world, movies are only for the eyes of Shoppers, but up here she's allowed to indulge in these non-factual story-documents as part of her research.

The more she watches, the more non-facts she finds in upside documents. They seem so concerned with vague abstractions like worshipfulness, symbolic currency, concepts like *values* and *national pride*. How can browns spend so much time and energy on perpetuating this nonsense when there are beans to grow? When they could just go out and look at the sky?

Father says that the most accurate reflection of brown life is found in the product advertisements, and he keeps encouraging her to spend more time watching these. But he must be mistaken. If the advertisements are a true reflection of society in the node, female browns always eat *yogurt* together. She tried the glutinous substance once; it made her projectile. The women also talk about detergents and cook while singing. If this is true, then she understands them less every day.

Before she makes dinner she needs to file a report about the brown educator's unexpected arrival in the kitchen, but she's unsure what to say. She's sure she interacted with the educator according to protocol, but its offspring behaved in a grossly disregardful fashion. She doesn't know whether she caused offence in some way, or whether she should take offence. Despite this, she imagines wearing lightweight apparel, talking about yogurt and detergent with the educator, or maybe discoursing about *love*.

This 'love' is the most interesting upside abstraction, and it is the subject of several movies. In the name of research, she used the computer in the television room to investigate the concept. She has memorised the definition she found: 'Love is both an action and a feeling. The action of love generates a blissful feeling called by the same name. When the action stops, the blissful feeling is replaced with pain. Every person is capable of great love (and its opposite, fear, which generates all painful emotions such as hate, greed and jealousy).'

Penter wonders if she is capable of blissful love, or even fear. She supposes that it is possible now that she has gone several days without a penetration renewal. But how will she know if she *does* feel it? She doesn't think it can be like regard – which she has felt many times, of course. Regard is what makes the world function. According to her research, the greatest love is supposed to be between a Mother and an offspring, although Penter cannot understand how this could be. In many documents, like the ones entitled *Love Actually* and *Pretty Woman* (a disconcerting title as the female protagonist in it is unsightly even by brown standards), love is nothing to do with offspring and everything to do with violent debate, naked parasitism, speeding around in upside machines and festivities that make Shoppers' cocktail sales look like halfpints' vat-leaving parties.

She looks away from the television as a man strapped in a chair starts screaming. 'Jane,' she says, 'can I talk to you?'

Jane does not lift her eyes from the screen. 'Yes.'

'Why did you bring that brown to the house?'

'Father asked me to interact with it.'

'Why?' She knows that questioning Father's instructions could be seen as disregard, but she is curious.

'I don't know. The educator says it is my chum.'

'Chum?'

'A friend and a buddy, you know? And I thought it would be interesting to converse with it.'

'Was it interesting?'

'No.'

'How is the scouting going?' When she asks Father anything about the project, he tells her she doesn't need to know.

'Fine.' Jane watches as the screaming brown's eyeball is popped by the tip of a whirring drill.

Penter smiles brightly like she's seen the Mothers do on the television. 'And how was your day?'

'Motherfucking typical,' Jane says. The halfpint absorbs language from the television like a root-fibre rag. Penter's envious of Jane's young, flexible mind. 'Mother, can I have a pet?'

'A pet?'

'A creature who will be my constant companion, like a My Little Pony only not so much scum. Can I ask Danish to scout me one?'

'I'll ask Father for you.'

Without taking her eyes off the screen, Jane intones, 'Thank you, Mother. I love you, you are the bestest awesomest raddest person in the whole world.'

Penter knows that Jane is just replaying the upside cant she's seen in the movies, but shouldn't those words still make her feel blissful?

'I love you too, Jane,' Penter tries. She feels nothing. Perhaps she has a subviable heart.

She goes out into the precinct to look at the beans. Yes, when she touches the little green shoots she feels a shift in her chest. She taps the bony nodule just below her neck, listening to the hollow rap. She touches the beans again, but the feeling is gone.

Aware of the luxury of the act, she pulls a bean off its stem and places it in her mouth. The victual documents always show the servant rinsing the produce under running water, as if their stomachs cannot process soil. This must be an affectation of the browns, and such a waste of fresh water. If there's one thing a real downsider is used to, it's soil. The Ministry research report confirmed that downsiders' constitutions are more robust than the frail systems of upsiders, although whichever Ministry drone typed this report has clearly never tried youngberry-flavoured yogurt.

She plucks another bean, rubs it against her face. She likes how it feels; a whole, viable living thing that has sprouted out of nothing. The documents talk of *miracles*, which seems to be a catch-all term for everything their intellect cannot encompass. If she were retarded she might, today, standing in the produce patch, rubbing a bean on her skin, believe in the meat tree.

'Mother,' she hears Father say behind her. 'I thought I'd find you lurking in the garden.' She turns to face him. Danish is shuffling behind him, carrying a basketful of coloured packages. 'We have selected two primary viables, faster than I anticipated. All is slick.'

'Primo news, Father.'

'Yes.' His smile falters. Penter knows what this means. If the primaries have been selected, it cannot be long before they return home.

'I have brought you a gift,' Father says as Danish places the basket at her feet. It's full of plastic packets of soup like the kind on the advertisements, and icy boxes labelled 'Chicken Nuggets', 'Hash Browns', 'Cheesy Corn Dogs', and 'American Fries'.

'Tasty and convenient victuals to make your Mother work less odious,' Father says. 'Father knows best!'

'Thank you.' The food in the basket doesn't look appealing. It reminds her of the scum traded at McColon's and Bleed back home. In fact, she would far rather eat a bowl of unwashed beans than a cheesy corn dog, but as the Mother, she must prioritise the needs of the family. And, she reminds herself, this gift is a sign of Father's regard.

'I must report to the Ministry,' Father says. 'And you must go chain yourself to the kitchen sink.'

'Father... Jane brought a brown to the house today.' She watches his face – by anyone's standards he's scenic, although, like her, he has had only limited modification – and tries to interpret his expression. He looks unfazed. 'Why did you ask Jane to interact with her?'

'That information is on a need-to-know basis, Mother. And you don't need to know.' Penter has wondered what Father does while he locks himself away in his office for all those hours. Evidently watching upside movies is among his duties.

'Is it a new regulation from the Ministry? I am... not sure what to say in my report.'

'I'll handle the report. It is not in your purview to do so.'

'But it is part of my protocol to—'

'Do not concern yourself, Mother.' He smiles at her gently and turns away.

Confused, she watches him return to the house. She wonders what it would be like to feel love for him. For Jane. To be part of an upside family. Then she shakes her head and reminds herself who and what she is.

She's the Deputy Node Liaison for the Ministry of Upside Relations, Penter Ulliel, not a yogurt-eating, love-prattling brown.

Chapter 10

RYAN

Ryan can't sleep. He gets his phone and dials Ziggy. He needs to know if Alice is okay; he needs to know if he blew it with her last night.

'Hello?'

'Ziggy. Hi, it's Ryan.'

'Jesus... It's... six o'clock in the morning.' Ryan hears the distorted rustle and creak of Ziggy getting out of bed, creeping out to the hallway. He's always suspected that Ziggy has a crush on him. Ziggy doesn't want to lie in bed next to his boyfriend and talk to Ryan, but at the same time, he's not going to hang up. 'What do you want, Ryan?' he says now, in a quiet voice.

'When Alice came in last night, how was she?'

'What do you... Do you mean you don't know?'

'Know what?'

'They don't stay here any more. They moved out.'

'When?'

'About three, four months ago. Yes, New Year's Day.'

'Where did they go? How could Karin—'

'She's doing well, Ryan. She's got a permanent job. At a bank.

Perks and everything. You mean you seriously don't know?'

'No. So where are they staying now?'

'I'm not telling you that. You weren't even supposed to know that they had come to stay with us. After what you did, I shouldn't even be talking to you.'

'Jesus, Ziggy. Don't start that. You know I never hurt Alice.'

'I think I do. That's why I'm talking to you. But you need to give up. She's moved on, she's doing well. Don't drag her back.'

'I'm not the one who's fucking dragging her back. Karin's the fucking—'

'Stop, Ryan. She's my sister, and I'm on her side. You may not have hurt Alice – that I believe – but there are reasons Karin doesn't want to be with you, doesn't want Alice near you. They're compelling reasons and there's no chance you're getting them back. You must give up and forget about them.'

'But—'

'I don't know what else to say. I've been quite clear.' The phone muffles again and Ryan can hear Ziggy talking to someone. 'I'm going now. Thanks for waking me up, by the way. This is the problem with you, Ryan. There's a missing piece somewhere in the empathy department. Just give it up.'

Ziggy cuts the call before Ryan can say anything. There's nothing to say, though, is there? 'Something missing'? Didn't Julie say something like that yesterday? All of a sudden he's surrounded by shrinks, by holier-than-thou saints who know what his fucking *problem* is? *They're* his fucking problem, that's what. He slams his phone onto the bedside table, knocking over a half-empty coffee cup. Fuck!

He grinds the heels of his hands into his eyes. It's only then that he remembers going outside to get some fresh air, and… What in hell possessed him? Tess lives next door, for Christ's sake. It's only a matter of time before her father finds out, and Ryan doesn't rate his chances against Fransie.

Ryan's panic doesn't flitter and zing, it curls up and stiffens like an animal playing dead, waiting for the moment to run. Because that's what he's going to have to do. He's going to have to cut and run. Again.

What in hell possessed him?

While he was with Tess in her little hideaway, he kept thinking of the new girl down at Crossley College, the strange one, that pale one who looks like she has so much hidden deep inside; pain, fear and, yes, a sort of uncanny confidence. He wants to get beneath her skin, but somehow he can't even come close. And now he's fucked it up again, because of her. He's going to have to leave, take what he can grab, and go. All because of her.

He showers and gets dressed quickly and heads straight for the school, darting a look at Tess's house as he passes. Even this early, Fransie's father's sitting there on his rocker, watching him as he passes. He watches everyone, Ryan tells himself. He watches everyone. Would Tess have told her father already? He hopes that the normal rules will apply, just for a couple of days. Even though they did nothing wrong, she'll believe it's wrong, that somehow she was to blame – she approached him after all – and she won't want to get him into trouble. But sooner or later Fransie will find out, and he can't be here when that happens.

What the fuck is he going to do? Where is he going to go? He's got nothing left.

'Hello, Mr Ryan.'

Oh, Christ, not now. She's ambushed him from behind the wall, just like she did last night. 'Oh, Tess. Hi. How are you?'

'Okay. I'm just... I was just...' She's already in her school uniform.

'You're up early.'

'Uh, yes.'

'Well, have a good day, okay?'

'Uh. Um… Mr Ryan… You want to come visit again later?'

'I…' Ryan's about to refuse. He wants this girl to be under no illusions, there's no fucking way he's going to 'visit' her again. But if he can keep her onside – keep her from talking – for today at least, it will work in his favour. 'Uh, sure, okay. But not so late, all right? You should get more sleep.'

Her face lights up in a big smile and the clump inside Ryan lightens a little with it. The girl's happy. That's all he ever wanted.

'And Tess…?' He lowers his voice.

She moves closer to him, replies softly, taking his lead. 'Yes, Mr Ryan?'

'You can't tell your father, okay? He won't understand. You'd get in big trouble.'

Her face becomes serious for a moment, and then she smiles again. 'Of course, Mr Ryan. See you later,' she says as she skips back into the garden.

Ryan darts a look back up at the veranda; the old man shows no sign of having heard anything. And then he remembers something: Cinderella turned back into a kitchen girl at midnight; it wasn't the other way around. She didn't turn into a princess like he said. Alice would have challenged him, she would have told him he was talking rubbish, but Tess just smiled and accepted it. Christ, she's ten years old. Of course she'd know her fairy tales better than he does. Did Tess believe him, or does she just think he's stupid? Is she secretly laughing at him?

Whatever, he's got more important things to worry about. He had thought getting himself straight would give him the chance to get Alice back into his life. But if what Ziggy says is true, that chance evaporated months ago. Besides, there's no way he can keep the job now. Fransie will easily find out where he works; Ma Beccah would tell Fransie in a minute if she heard what he did. Seeing Karin last night was a shock: how clean she looked, how… responsible. Maybe deep down he knew it was over when he saw her. Maybe this thing with Tess was just his mind running ahead of him, forcing him to move on.

So today's the big break. He's got to take what he can and disappear. He runs through his inventory. It's a quick exercise; he's got nothing to his name. He can't steal from Ma Beccah — she's got nothing either — so he's going to have to take something from the school and burn that final bridge too. When life gets beyond you like this, it's sometimes comforting just to go with the flow, cede all control.

So what should he take from the school? They don't hold much cash, as far as he knows. He hasn't noticed a safe in Duvenhage's office, and there wasn't anything of instant value in his desk when he looked through it the other day… Hang on. He's got the copy of Duvenhage's flash drive. It was Duvenhage's urgency that gave him the idea to copy it; there might be some valuable information on it. Ryan's not especially practised at blackmail, but these are extraordinary circumstances.

'Morning, Mrs Fontein,' he says with his best smile. 'I wonder if you could help me.' He holds up his flash drive. 'My daughter typed out this essay at her mother's house and she forgot that I didn't… well, I don't have my own computer to print it out for her.'

Sybil Fontein glances across the hall at Duvenhage's closed office door. 'It's not long, is it?'

'No, no. Just a few pages.' He smiles again and Sybil brushes the front of her blouse. 'She put so much effort into it, and I really hate to let her down.'

'Of course, of course, Ryan. You can use Cheryl's work station. She's not in till later.' Sybil Fontein leads Ryan behind a partition and logs into the computer at the admin assistant's desk.

Ryan sits and slides the drive into the port. Sybil hovers behind him. He looks up over his shoulder at her. 'It might take me a while to find the essay. All this other stuff on here. You know how teenagers are.'

'Oh, all right. Just let me know when you're done.'

'Thank you, Mrs Fontein.'

In truth, the flash drive only contains two files and a subfolder. Ryan clicks open the first file, which is in a generic text format. A row of blaring capitals spells out: '***THIS DOCUMENT IS THE SOLE, PRIVATE AND STRICTLY TRUSTWORTHY PROPERTY OF THE MINISTRY OF UPSIDE RELATIONS THE MOST STRINGENT CORRECTION WILL BE APPLIED TO DISREGARD OF THIS NOTICE***'

The Ministry of what? Jesus, Ryan thinks. Must be some kind of religious thing Duvenhage is into. And it's so private and confidential that Duvenhage doesn't even password-protect it. Ryan scans the text below it – an email or letter, dated six months ago.

```
Sir,
     As discussed, we would be most gratified if you
would peruse our prospectus on upside life for
accuracy and take note of the halfpint assessment
exemplars appended.

Regards,

First Minister Cardineal Phelgm
Ministry of Upside Relations
```

The letter is just as garbled and incomprehensible as the memos he had to read when he worked at the office. He moves on to the next file to see if it will clarify anything.

The second text file is some sort of essay or speech in mangled English:

At present, take appropriate measures to stop
the future. Teach children to respect everyone,
regardless of all obstacles, man-made and our
peers to establish their own separate. Next time,
colleagues or friends, talking humour, humour and
laughter just be a part of the crowd. Do not even
say "I do not like this joke," because in addition
to negative energy. Of course you do not keep
silent when you see someone abusing others. But
remember the violence can take many forms. Create
a standing friends, and abuse of mental capacity
of a joke. Whether the person is in word space to
create negative energy. Mental health agencies
and practitioners almost unanimously agree that
the other people who like to abuse others and
bullying, teasing, harassment of other people,
whether victims of such treatment or those with
low own opinions, so much attention, feel better
than others. Say not a word that does not mean
you have to prove such an act. Could prove to be
convinced by the way, if they do not do anything.
In supremacy march and those who witnessed the
assault case and did not stop, they have been
identified that tolerates such behaviour. A young
woman who still believe that faith save supremacy,
the man who beat other people screaming hate those
who, instead of holding. Simply standing between
the audience and protect human rights it does
not add any negative energy. In today's society

through a commitment to all hate crime, it is
almost impossible to deny the existence of

Shit. Why did Duvenhage want his drive back so badly? Pages and pages like this. Could it be something Duvenhage has been drafting to deliver at school assembly or a board meeting? At any rate, Ryan hasn't got the time to waste. Nothing here is going to make him any quick money, and that's what he's here for.

'How are you getting along, Ryan?' Sybil Fontein asks, her bust popping over the partition wall in front of him. She glances nervously across at Duvenhage's office again. 'If you just want to leave a copy of the file, I can print it later. It's just that...'

'That's just the thing, Mrs Fontein. I haven't found the file yet. The girl needs some organisational training. I realise you're going out on a limb for me, and I appreciate it. I won't be long, I promise.'

The well-spoken and polite-worker routine works on her and she retreats back to her desk. This is his last chance. Ryan clicks on the folder named 'Edification Hub 1:307:561/h Exemplar Viability Assessment Mark-Up'.

Holy. Shit.

This is it. The mother lode. No wonder the sick fuck wanted his flash drive back so badly. Ryan clamps his hand over his mouth. Swallowing the bile down, he manages to get his finger to scan through the directory. This is too much in one place.

There are pictures of naked children here. Boys and girls, laid out like a gallery of... of corpses. He can't bring himself to look at the details but the gallery scrolls before his eyes like some evil film. Snuff, that's what it's called, or some sort of sick horror porn. My God. So that's it: 'the Ministry' must be some sort of underage brothel.

The bodies are laid out on plain white-sheeted gurneys, each of them drawn on with a dark marker like an anatomical diagram, almost like those pictures you see in butcher's shops showing the different cuts of meat.

He can't bring his mind to believe that the children could be dead. They can't be, surely? But their eyes are closed and they lie straight and docile on their backs, their arms loosely at their sides.

They have to be sleeping. They have to be acting. This has to be some sort of joke.

And now Ryan does vomit. He grabs the waste bin from beneath the table just in time and empties out his stomach. As he's retching he remembers to reach up and switch off the computer screen just as Sybil Fontein rounds behind his desk.

'Ryan!' She scans the cubicle angrily before eventually asking if he's all right.

'I'm so sorry, Mrs Fontein. I'll clean this up.'

But she stands there. He has a mesh drum of vomit oozing onto his lap but he can't move until she's gone. He needs to eject the drive properly, clear the cache. 'Uh, do you mind bringing me a towel?'

She huffs and stares at him as if this is the sort of thing she knew would happen when she let a worker into the administration area. This is why there are rules, Sybil. But at length, she turns and walks across to a supply cupboard. By the time she's back, Ryan is standing with the drive in his pocket and the computer shows a pacific field of tulips. Sybil Fontein stands as far away from him as possible as she dangles the towel towards him. Another ally lost, another bridge burnt.

He wraps the towel around the bottom of the seeping pail and hauls it down the corridor to the boys' toilets. The faces of those children on the computer, their bodies – so quiet, so limp – are burnt into his eyes.

No, he says to his mind, before it even phrases the question. No. There's the entire world of difference between Duvenhage and him.

Ryan's mowing the fields on autopilot, planning when and how to confront Duvenhage. He's obviously more of a freak than he imagined, and Ryan's going to have to be careful. There's too much evidence here for a quick shakedown; he's going to have to keep it to himself and come up with a long-term strategy. If he plays it right, this could pay off decently.

At the same time, though, Ryan knows he should take this right to the police, go straight to the Child Protection Unit and rescue those children. But why would they believe him? Respected school head versus washed-out labourer? Besides, even though he's never been convicted of anything, he wants to stay far away from the police and not invite their attention. With all the hints Ziggy was dropping, who knows, maybe Karin's building a case against him already. Maybe he's on some sort of watch list. So the police are out of the question. That's not to say he can't still blackmail Duvenhage. The sick fuck just has to believe that Ryan might out him, whether or not he would.

But he's still concerned for those children. Assuming they're alive – and he has to assume that, otherwise the darkness is too deep to contemplate – where could they even be? Are they in some institution, are they lost kids being held somewhere? They can't all have been treated like that and then just gone home to their parents – something would have happened, it would be in the news, people would be after the culprits, surely? He would have heard about it. Those kids were probably living on the streets or in some orphanage or home. There are plenty of vulnerable kids in this city.

The children in the pictures could be suffering right now. Ryan really should do something or tell someone.

But he needs money. He's got to leave his job and his room tonight and disappear, or else he's dead tomorrow. He's got to play Duvenhage carefully from a distance, get as much as he can in the shortest possible time. Then he'll send the pictures to the police anonymously. It's the best he can do.

'You okay, brother?' Thulani says as he comes up the line with the marking machine. 'You're not looking so well today.'

'No. I'm a bit sick.'

'You want to knock off? See you tomorrow?'

'Sure, uh, okay. Thanks.'

Ryan goes back to the maintenance shed and moves everything from his locker into his backpack. Two spare T-shirts, an old pair of jeans, a pair of socks, a can of deodorant and a hairbrush. Is this all he'll be carrying with him? Will it be safe to go back to Ma Beccah's tonight?

He looks in Thulani's locker, feels through his pants pockets. There's R70 and change crumpled up there. He briefly considers taking it, but doesn't. Instead, he searches in the equipment lockers for anything he can easily sell, but the only things he can fit in his backpack are trowels and forks and rolls of weed-eater cord; light bulbs, multimeters: no fucking value at all. The lawnmowers and ladders are top of the range, the tools are quality, but he'd get nothing for those in a hurry. He could pawn a R3000 toolkit for fifty bucks up on Jules Street, but it wouldn't half look suspicious if he hauled one of those through the security booms.

He stashes a handful of screwdrivers and a multimeter in his bag, but he'll have to go back to the administration block if he's going to get anything of value. He remembers no cash or jewellery or special equipment in Duvenhage's office when he was there on Tuesday, but he wasn't looking very carefully. He's going to have to get back into Duvenhage's office somehow, and get past Sybil Fontein in the process. Fuck knows how.

But when he gets into the administration lobby, the red fire-alarm button stares at him from the wall. Of course.

He elbows the glass and punches the button, then dashes into the staff toilets as the alarm screeches and the unnaturally orderly evacuation begins. Desks shuffle politely and the kids file quietly down the stairs and out of the building, the only noise coming from the megaphones quacking out from the front quadrangle.

After a couple of long minutes, he goes back into the admin lobby and peers around. All clear: Sybil and her assistants are gone. The office doors are still closed. He knows Duvenhage will be down in the quad and sergeant-majoring the evacuation. But whichever teachers are on marshal duty will find the source of the alarm soon.

Just to make sure, he knocks on Duvenhage's door and listens for a moment, knocks again. No answer. The door's unlocked. Ryan slips inside and locks it behind him.

He moves to the desk and opens the top desk drawer. He hasn't got much time. Neatly stacked cardboard folders with thin sheaves of paper. He hurriedly flips through them, not even lifting them out of the drawer – there's no time – there's nothing of interest; he needs to find cash. It's become that simple.

He changes tack and pulls at the drawers of the filing cabinets: each is filled with suspension files, neatly arrayed, each one with a name printed on it and a photo clipped against the cover. Student dossiers.

Those folders would have the home addresses of the students in them, wouldn't they? He hauls open the drawer containing the Grade Five files. Think, Ryan. When he saw the new girl the first time the other day, it wasn't break time. She was walking with her class. The teacher was leading them to the biology lab. What was her name again? He flips through the files. Here it is: 5C, Mrs du Preez. That's her class. He walks his fingers through the folders until he sees the girl's photo. The sight of her face gives him a jolt. Those grey eyes, that same frank stare with a worldful of need behind them. 'Jane Smith' – that's her name. The address is 67a Excelsior Avenue. That's surprising; it's a rich area, and he's thought of her as another poor and neglected child, something like Tess. Maybe she's the daughter of their domestic worker? Stranger things happen these days. He memorises the house number and closes the cabinet.

He heads back to the desk, trying all the drawers again. More neatly stacked documents in the middle drawer, but the bottom one is locked. This is it. He picks the lock easily with a pen clutch and a paperclip and slides open the drawer. He's blocked out the fire alarm but now listens to it for a second. It confirms that they still haven't found the trigger.

There's a locked top-hinged box inside the drawer, but it's made of flimsy sheet metal, a nod to security that might keep idle toddlers out. Ryan soon has it open.

He hears voices on the other side of the door. He slams the lid shut and tiptoes up to the door and listens.

'Here. Here it is, Keith.' A heavy click and the alarm dies. The silence whooshes into Ryan's head.

'Is there any problem here? Any fire?'

'No, not that I can tell. We'd be able to smell it, right?'

'Ja, I think so.'

'But then who…?'

'I dunno. Vandals?'

'You mean a student? Little fuckers wouldn't dare, surely.'

'Yes. But… there's no fire.'

'Yes. What are we going to tell Mr Duvenhage?'

Keith doesn't answer, but Ryan hears the men's footsteps retreating back down the corridor. Ryan's running out of time. He hurries back to the desk drawer and flips it open again. It's not quite the jackpot he was hoping for. Just a thin scattering of fifties and twenties – a petty-cash box. He pockets the notes; it's probably only a grand in total, but it's better than nothing. He shuts the box and closes the drawer. Nobody will know it's been tampered with until they open it.

He carefully unlocks the office door and peers through the crack. All clear. He walks out of the admin building, skirting the rows of students on the piazza. The kids line up, silent and subdued.

He's on his way to the main gate when he sees a group of middle-grade children in their gymkhana row, but this one's got a kink in it. The children stand curved around an invisible obstacle, like there's a force field. In the middle of it is the new girl.

His eyes are drawn to her and he stops walking. She draws him in like a magnet. She's compelling – it's as if she's looking right into him, begging him to help her. *I know where you live*, he telepaths back to her, *I will come and help you*. Ryan forgets about the stolen money in his pocket, and the fact that he should be running; for a minute he even forgets that he may never see his daughter again. For now, the girl's eyes invite him in, and he wants nothing more than to go there with her. He feels a profound connection...

which is broken by someone's hand waving. That library volunteer who he saw the other day. Christ, is she waving at him? He ignores her and tries to re-establish the connection with the new girl, but now she's looking away, at nothing in particular. Ryan feels a flash of rage towards the library woman, but then remembers what he needs to do. He needs to go. Now. Before Duvenhage looks in his drawer and finds it unlocked.

He doesn't know where he's going to go. Despite the fact that in the last twenty-four hours he's lost everything that's important to him, burnt every bridge, he still feels anchored here. Just knowing that Alice is nearby – they must be near if they still come to Bedford Centre for take-aways – makes him loath to leave. But he must, and when he's on his feet again, he'll find her.

So he'll head back to Ma Beccah's. He's going to take some clothes and whatever else he can carry and start off before Fransie gets back from work.

By four in the afternoon he's out in Bedfordview walking along Excelsior Avenue, past the hideous electrified mini-mansions and being glared at by bored security guards and rich wives in their X3s. Ma Beccah was out so he just left her a note and a week's rent.

Julie's house was somewhere around here. Just two days ago he was lying in her bed, her little hand rubbing his thigh, and he had felt almost happy, like life was in balance. But it never is, is it? There's always something – someone – who comes along and fucks things up for him.

He has no particular plan for what he'll do once he's there. He crests a rise in the road and sees the most grotesque mansion on the street. He's driven by it several times but this is the first time he's ever walked past it. He gets the full effect of its hideous kitsch now. Its wall is studded with concrete statues of naked gods of one sort or another, but not tastefully placed twenty metres apart. These are crammed along the wall, another recess with a mismatched sculpture every two metres. The wall is at least four metres tall, crenellated with ramparts and topped by a clicking electric fence. It's a massive stand, three or four times bigger than most of the properties on the road, and the wall goes on for perhaps a hundred metres, studded by those kitsch concrete statues.

As he walks downhill alongside the wall, a little Pajero turns into the drive and stops by the front gate, which glares gold light back at the car. A woman steps out and goes around the back of the car to its far side. He's no more than twenty metres away from the car when the woman comes to the gate with her passenger.

Ryan stops short. It's the girl. It's the new girl and that library teacher. She's giving the girl a lift home. He thought he was still in the 50s, but here it is. Number 67a.

He stands still, willing himself invisible as the woman and the girl push through the gates. All this security and they're not even automated? They must be broken. There's a boy in the Crossley uniform in the back of the car but he's lost in his phone or game-pod or whatever, and he wouldn't look at a guy walking along the pavement anyway. Ryan ducks in front of the car and through the gates, keeping his distance behind the woman and the girl.

Inside the walls, the house is like some failed fantasy castle theme park, cluttered with more concrete statuary and balconies and balustrades overlapping each other at insane angles, like an Escher drawing. The walls are all plaster, only painted in patches, and the ground is packed red soil, as if they stopped building in the middle of the process.

The girl and the woman move on towards a white facade, perhaps an older house that's now the core of this bewildering new structure. The woman looks back nervously and Ryan ducks under a deep portico. He peers out at their backs disappearing into the house and decides to wait. Once the library woman's gone, he can decide on his next move.

He looks around the space he's in. Rather than a portico, it might have been designed as a garage for multiple cars. He counts eight columns, each spaced a good car-width apart and each adorned with more statues. There's one of a voluptuous woman and a muscular man kissing, naked but for a drape of cloth obscuring some of their private parts. But as he paces between the columns, out of sight of the windows in the white house, he begins to notice that some of the statues are strange – not just standard Grecian stuff you'd get in a garden centre. Some might be Egyptian or Indian or something, men with animal heads and women with many arms, some with knives, some with nasty leers and drooling teeth. These must have been hand-moulded and custom designed, and a chill runs through him. What sort of person would want these images in their house?

But there are even stranger ones. The columns in the middle of the garage area are supported by sculptures of much more modern-looking people – or creatures, because these people are lopsided, some have amputated legs or massive, misshapen heads; something about them makes Ryan think of Duvenhage's photos, and the recall sends a bilious rush up his oesophagus. Despite himself, despite the fact that he's nauseated, he can't look away. He paces between the columns. These statues have arms that look like they've been... sharpened. They come to a hook-like point. Almost like tentacles, and the figures probe at each other in foul ways. What sort of sick imagination could conjure such a—

There's a slam outside and the gate squeaks open again on its massive hinges. The boy from the car comes stomping up the sandy pathway towards the door, cursing under his breath as he goes.

Ryan steps back into the shadows and watches him pass. He tells himself to stop looking at the decor of this place, shut his eyes and calm down, make a plan. What is he doing here? He should be finding a place to sleep, not hiding out in the front yard of a weird schoolgirl's house. He has to start again and get himself together this time. If he carries on behaving like this, he's never going to get Alice back.

He's right. He should just go. He slings his backpack over his shoulder, ignoring the pull of the captivating girl inside – if he can't see her, she can't pull him in like she did earlier – and heads back towards the gate.

His muscles are frozen by a shrill scream.

What are they doing to his girl?

Chapter 11

TARA

Stephen paces in front of the bathroom door, gripping his cell-phone and sucking his teeth. 'Martin! Come out of there now!' He bangs his fist on the door, glares at Tara. 'What the hell is he doing in there?'

Tara doesn't reply. Asshole. How would she know? Martin seemed fine when she knocked on his bedroom door early this morning. Sure, he was a tad subdued, but nothing like the state he'd been in yesterday evening when she found him shaking in the driveway of that strange house, refusing to say why he'd screamed. She'd been seriously worried about him then, but by the time they'd arrived home he'd appeared calmer, almost back to normal, making her regret the panicked phone call she'd made to Stephen en route. Stephen had been all for storming over to Jane's house; he insisted that Tara was hiding something from him, that something *must* have happened there to spark off his son's screaming fit. Refused to listen when she said that she hadn't seen anything out of the ordinary (a massive understatement considering the freakishness of that woman and the house's extraordinary decor). He also refused to accept Tara's argument that Martin's odd behaviour had started after he'd been to that first Encounters session, that if Stephen had bothered to take an interest in his *own fucking son* he would have noticed this. Back and forth they'd raged, the argument reaching a head when Stephen insisted on phoning Olivia. Tara's now dreading the mammoth 'We Need to Talk About Martin' session that's planned for tomorrow evening, with Olivia valiantly flying back from her business trip to rescue her son from the clutches of his evil stepmother.

Her phone beeps. Without even looking at the screen she knows it has to be Batiss. She's right. <please confirm time as to baby deliverance date>

Goddammit, Tara thinks. She didn't have a chance to do any work on Baby Tommy last night, preferred to keep him locked in her sanctuary, untainted by the toxic atmosphere. Still, if she's able to work on him solidly this weekend – Martin and Olivia permitting – a week should be enough. She taps in <Next Friday okay?>

<we need sooner. please accelerate to this monday your calendar>

Monday? Batiss has to be joking. <sorry but this is impossible>

<nothing is impossible when you have sunbeams as your friends. bonus for timeous conveyance will be forthcoming>

Bonus? <what bonus?>

<we repeat: baby needed aye-sap. double-time moola bonus if delivered timeously chop chop>

Does this mean Batiss will double the money? Jesus. Who *is* this person? She's now sure it can't be a scam – the seventy-five grand is in her account, she's double-checked. No, Batiss must be very rich or very deranged. Or possibly both. Double pay would mean almost R150,000. That could really set her free. And, thanks to the fact she decided to use Baby Gabby as a base, she has to admit that most of the work has been done already. If she pushes, she could just about make it.

<will do my best>

<we do not have the liberty of understanding you. Confirm: YES/NO>

Jesus. <YES>

She knows what the response will be. She's not disappointed. <primo J> Another message immediately follows: <note penalty clause additional for late deliverance. contract dispatched to your electronic address>

Penalty? Probably just another one of her client's idiosyncrasies. She'll get it done by Monday.

'Who's that?' Stephen snaps.

'My client,' she says.

Stephen rolls his eyes. His own phone has been beeping and buzzing all morning, but apparently *that's* okay.

The bathroom door finally clicks open, and Martin emerges. Tara's relieved to see that he looks none the worse for wear, although his wrists are red as if he's been scrubbing at them.

'You doing okay, my boy?' Stephen says to him, ruffling his hair. 'What were you doing in there?'

'Nothing.'

'You want to have the day off school today?' Stephen asks.

'No! I have to go to school.'

'You sure, bud?' Stephen says, compromising his concerned-parent act by glancing at his frantically beeping phone. 'Hold that thought, I've got to take this.' He stalks into the bedroom, slams the door behind him.

Martin glances at Tara. 'I have to go to school. It's Encounters this afternoon. I can't go if I'm off sick. It's the rules.'

'It's not up to me, Martin. Your dad doesn't think you should go. He thinks it's what's caused all this.' She's not going to mention that she was the one who put that idea in Stephen's head.

'It didn't, Tara. Really, it didn't.'

'What's so cool about it anyway?'

Martin scratches at the back of his neck. The skin is raw there, looks like he's getting a nasty pimple. 'I like it. It makes me feel... special.'

Again, Tara has to concede that, last night's disturbing behaviour aside, he's certainly been more pleasant to be around since he started to attend those meetings.

'I know you don't want to talk about this, Martin, but back at that house, why did you scream?' His eyes flick away from hers. She smiles down at him. 'I don't mind telling you, that place made me feel a little bit like screaming, too. What did you see?'

'I didn't see anything.'

'You can trust me, Martin. You know that now, right?'

He nods miserably.

'So what was it?'

'I'm... I'm not sure,' he whispers. 'It was a... a... thing.'

'What kind of a thing?'

'Ja, Martin,' Stephen says, appearing behind them and making Tara jump. 'What kind of thing?'

Martin shrugs. 'It was a just a snake, Dad.'

'A snake? All this for a fu— for a bloody snake? What are you, a moffie?' Stephen chuckles. But Tara can tell he's relieved. For all his bluster, she knows that the last thing he wants is more complications.

'So I can go to school, then?'

Stephen shrugs. 'Don't see why not, sport.'

'And I can go to Encounters?'

'Long as we're not going to have any more of these episodes.'

'I'm fine, Dad, I promise.'

Stephen ruffles Martin's hair again. 'That's my boy.'

Martin flinches away from his father's touch, gives Tara a curious half smile that looks, she thinks, almost conspiratorial.

'You sure you're feeling well enough to go to school?' Tara asks, pulling into the teachers' parking lot and turning off the engine.

'I'm fine.' He unclicks his belt and slides out of the car. 'Laters.'

She watches him drift towards a small gang of kids who are hanging around in the basketball quad, dragging his bag behind him. The group shifts, and Tara makes out Jane's shock of artificial-straw hair. She's crouching down, appears to be staring intently at her cupped hands.

Goddammit, Tara thinks. Is she being bullied? It certainly looks like it. She hurries out of the car, jogs towards the group. 'Hey! What's going on here?'

Several of the kids start guiltily, duck their heads and scurry towards the entrance hall. Martin shrugs at her, shoulders his rucksack and slouches after them. 'Hey!' she calls after them. 'I'm talking to you!' She tries to remember faces and names, in case she needs to report them. She recognises Jonah, Martin's vile buddy, but that's all.

Jane hasn't moved. Tara drops to her haunches and gently touches the girl's back. 'Hey, Jane. Are you okay?'

Jane looks up and Tara gasps. Jesus. She's wearing thick, dark foundation, false eyelashes and a smear of orange lipstick. 'What have you done to your face, Jane?'

'I'm cosmetically prettified, like the browns on television, miss.'

Tara digs a tissue out of her bag. 'We should wipe some of that off your face before your teacher sees you. We don't want you getting into trouble, do we?'

'Okay, miss.' Jane keeps absolutely still as Tara does her best to remove the lipstick and ghastly foundation. 'There. Much better. You're far too pretty to need make-up, sweetie.' Tara taps Jane's cupped hands. 'And what have you got there?'

'A present, miss. Danish scouted it for me. It's awesome-fuckentastic.'

'Can you show me?'

'Yes, miss.'

Jane opens her hands and Tara can't hold back the scream. 'Jesus!'

'It's okay, miss. It's depreciated.'

Tara recognises the (thankfully) dead creature sitting in Jane's palm as a Parktown prawn, a giant cricket that resembles the unholy marriage between a spider and a crawfish. 'What are you doing with that?'

'It's my chum, miss,' Jane says brightly. 'Like you.'

Tara hears the morning siren whoop. They should really get inside. 'I wouldn't show it to any of the other children if I were you, Jane.'

'Okay, miss.' She slides it into her pocket.

'Shall we go inside?'

'Yes, miss.'

Jane takes Tara's hand, looks up at her. 'You know what, miss?' Jane says, putting on her American accent. 'You're my number one ho on the whole freakin' strip.' She smiles her strange smile. 'I love yous, miss.'

Jane wasn't in today's starter-reader class. Really, Tara's getting seriously worried about that kid. Well-adjusted children don't tell virtual strangers that they love them, even if they are quoting from some sort of gangsta flick. And what kind of mother allows their daughter to go to school made up like a child prostitute? Although reluctant to get involved – it's impossible to forget that the last time she interfered, her life went into freefall – she decides that she has to let someone know about her concerns. But who? She's never met the school counsellor – who she's heard from Stephen was worse than useless anyway when she dealt with Martin – and she certainly doesn't feel like approaching Duvenhage.

She waits until the last of the reading class leaves, then knocks on Clara's office door.

Clara glances up from her computer. 'Is everything all right, Mrs Marais?'

'Could I ask your advice, Mrs van der Spuy?'

'Of course. Please, sit.'

'It's about Jane. You know, the new girl. I'm worried that maybe there's something... *off* about her home situation.'

'Off?'

'Well, I'm worried that there might be some... neglect.' Tara tries to hide her shock as Clara leans back in her chair and yawns. 'I realise I might be meddling, but yesterday she was hanging around outside the school on the main road. I offered to give her a lift and...' And what exactly? Her mother has appalling taste in architecture and clothes? So what?

'Mrs Marais, I appreciate you bringing this to my consideration, but let me assure you we keep a very close eye on our learners here.'

'Sure. I appreciate that. But it's not just that, this morning—'

'How is Martin doing, Mrs Marais?' Clara interrupts.

Tara blinks. 'What does Martin have to do with Jane's situation?'

'Everything fine at home?'

'Yes. Why—'

'But he *has* had trouble in the past, hasn't he?' Tara knows exactly what Clara is driving at. She may as well come out and accuse Tara of calling the kettle black. She swallows the twinge of anger she feels, decides not to rise to Clara's bait. Clara attempts her version of a sympathetic smile. 'It can't be easy being a stepmother. Really, you have my sympathy.'

Shit, Tara thinks. Time to change the subject. 'Um... There's something else. This Encounters group. Have you heard of it?'

'Of course I've heard of it, Mrs Marais.'

'And... well, what goes on there?'

'It's one of Mr Duvenhage's projects, I believe. Designed for our learners who need a more... directed approach. If you're at all concerned, then perhaps you should sit in on a meeting. I'm sure that wouldn't be an issue.'

'Thanks. I just might.'

'Is that all?'

'Yes.'

Clara turns to her computer, rattles her fingers over the keyboard.

Tara slinks out, feeling as if she's just been disciplined. She heads down the corridor, listening to the soft hum emanating from the classrooms, hurries past Duvenhage's office. All she can think about is heading home to Baby Tommy. Just the thought of him waiting for her in her sanctuary makes her feel calmer.

'Mrs Marais?' a voice says behind her. She turns to see Mr Duvenhage approaching, his pink, prissy face sheened with perspiration. 'I wonder, could I have a word?'

Oh God. What's Martin done now? 'Sure. What's it about?'

'Oh, this and that,' Duvenhage says. 'Would you mind joining me in my office?'

Unlike Clara's saccharine-postered nightmare, Duvenhage's office is as impersonal as a bank manager's, although Tara detects the whiff of rot from the stained ceiling boards.

'Please, sit.' Duvenhage waves her towards the hard-backed chair in front of his desk. It's way lower than his own, and Tara is forced to look up at him.

'What's this about, Mr Duvenhage?'

Duvenhage digs in his desk drawer, hands her a sheet of paper. She takes it from him, almost drops it when she reads the heading at the top of the page: 'Raymond Scheider Primary School Child Sex Abuse Scandal (US)'. Judging by the typeface and the '[citations needed]' peppered throughout the text, it's a print-out from a Wikipedia page. She's never read this particular account before; it's been months since she's dared to Google her name. She scans it quickly.

In 2008, seven children, all of whom attended Raymond Scheider Primary School in Mayton County, New Jersey, were removed from the custody of their parents amid accusations of sexual abuse and involvement in an alleged satanic cult. The children's welfare came under scrutiny after several teachers at the school approached the school's consulting child psychologist, Dr Raphael Blake, to investigate what they believed was abnormal behaviour and rumors of ritualistic abuse. Using a controversial technique called reflex anal dilation[1] as well as conducting several in-depth interviews with the children in question, Dr Blake concluded that in all seven cases, sexual abuse had occurred. Dr Blake subsequently reported his findings to the region's child welfare office, and the children were immediately placed in foster care.

Consistently denying the charges, the parents approached the media. In 2009, after an extensive enquiry, it was ruled that the evidence was seriously flawed and the children were returned home. The teachers' accusations, Dr Blake's conclusions and the welfare officers' findings were all found to be wholly unwarranted. No foundation to the many claims of satanic abuse was ever proven.

Two of the teachers involved, lay minister Carlos Androna, and Lana Ivey, were thought to have been influenced by their staunch religious beliefs, fuelled by rumors of a cult operating in the area [citation needed]. The third teacher, Tara Elizabeth Himmelman, stated that she was motivated purely by concerns for the children, who she thought were acting 'in a peculiar fashion consistent with the behaviour of sexually abused children'.[2]

The parents of the children involved have filed a class action suit against Dr Blake and the three teachers involved, citing psychological trauma, stigma and job loss. So far the case has not come to court.[3]

Duvenhage rests his chin on steepled hands, looks straight into her eyes. 'You are Tara Elizabeth Himmelman, are you not, Mrs Marais?'

'How did you find out that was my name?'

Duvenhage wafts a manicured hand. 'Methods.'

Now where, Tara thinks, have I heard that before? 'And you're showing me this, why?'

'I believe you've been talking to Clara van der Spuy about concerns you may have about one of our learners.'

That was fast. Clara must have been on the phone the second Tara left her office. 'How long have you known about this?'

'Oh, Mrs Marais, you must understand that we thoroughly research the backgrounds of all of our volunteers.' He eyes the Wikipedia article.

'I was sure that the parents in question were guilty of abuse, Mr Duvenhage. I still am.'

'Yes, yes. That's not my concern. You do understand that the school takes the welfare of its students very seriously.'

'I see.' Tara does see – she sees very clearly. The last thing that Duvenhage and the board of trustees wants is a re-run of the Raymond Scheider Primary scandal. 'You're blackmailing me.'

'Blackmailing you?' Duvenhage laughs. 'Certainly not! I am simply pointing out that accusations like these... Well, as you know, they can be blown out of proportion. I know Jane's... family personally. They may be a bit...' – he chuckles – 'eccentric, but that's as far as it goes, I assure you. Morality is important to us here at Crossley College. It's the basis of our very ethos. We maintain a high standard of responsibility to our learners – both within the walls of the school and within the broader community.'

He stands up, holds out a hand. She's being dismissed again. Clara and Duvenhage make a hell of a tag team. Tara tries not to wince as her hand is gripped by moist, pudgy fingers. 'We do appreciate all the primo work you do for us here, Mrs Marais.'

Primo. That word again. It's just a coincidence. A new South African buzzword that's doing the rounds. Has to be.

'In fact,' Duvenhage continues, 'Mrs van der Spuy says that you might be interested in joining us at the school on a more... permanent basis.'

Tara draws back. 'Even now? Now that... you know?'

Duvenhage chuckles again. 'Oh, Mrs Marais. Everyone can make *one* mistake, can't they?'

Chapter 12

PENTER

'Mother! Mother. It is time for you to kindle.'

She opens her eyes, looks up into Father's face, his skin bathed in blue light from the television screen. She must have fallen asleep on the couch in the television room. After last night's victuals, a projectile-inducing mess of soggy corn dogs and noodles that only Danish seemed to enjoy, Penter had retired here. She meant to research more of the advertisements to please Father, but as she clicked through the channels she paused on a channel called SKY. Thinking it would be a document about the ether above her, she was shocked to see violent, sometimes blurry images that were more disquieting than those in Jane's documents: crying and naked halfpints, broken and burning houses, enraged browns, modified browns in sale apparel talking about war, economic crises, bloodshed and 'terrorists'. She watched for hours, hypnotised. She eventually realised that this SKY, unlike *Pretty Woman* or *Love Actually* was a factual document, not a story. Why had the Ministry guidelines not warned her about this?

She touches her cheeks. Her face is wet. 'What is wrong with me?'

'You had a nightmare.'

She looks at the clear moisture on her fingers. 'What is this?'

'An extrusion of thought-seep. It won't bother you when we return and your penetration is renewed.'

Penter knows that the question is disregardful, that if Father wants to volunteer non-essential information he will, but she can't help herself. 'Do you suffer thought-seep?'

A pause. 'Yes.'

'And Jane?'

Father smiles. 'She does not seem to be so affected. She's a primo scout.'

Once again, Penter marvels at the halfpint's adaptability. She suppresses a pang of what she understands to be jealousy. 'Is it time for me to prepare breakfast for the family?'

'Almost. But first, do you want to see the viables?'

She's not sure how to answer. Is he testing her? The selection of viables is not in her purview; she is the unit's Mother. Father wouldn't try to trick her into committing disregard, would he? Only Players would do that, and playing is not tolerated in the Ministry of Upside Relations. Why does he want her involved?

She is curious, though, so she nods, hoping that he will invite her to explore his study, the only room in the house she has never entered.

He doesn't. Instead, he plugs his gelphone into the slow tech at the base of the television. The screen flickers, and then she sees a recording of twelve small browns, six males and six females, sitting on chairs in a large white-walled room with wooden floors, their heads drooping like the beans in the garden. She is full of admiration for Father's methods. Not one of the halfpints moves as he uses the device and the mark-up pens.

'Are you sure that they will not recall their experiences here?' Penter is confident to ask questions because Father seems so relaxed.

'Entirely,' Father replies. 'The Ministry's brain-sweep technology is perfectly efficient. The halfpints you see on screen are the viables Jane scouted,' Father says. 'Halfpint browns with top-percentile destructive capacity which could be rechannelled. The viability formula for this programme is adapted from the Walters-King scale used in the Wards,' he continues, as if excited to be sharing the information with a willing audience. 'The calculation is dependent on the mean actuarial concordance between poundage and depreciation rate.' He smiles at her confusion. 'The halfpints whose flesh is most likely to withstand ongoing penetration renewal and conditioning.' Penter nods. Most of the full-grown browns scouted by Mall Management and Ward Administration have a far faster depreciation rate than normals. The theory underpinning this project suggests that halfpints will assimilate faster than full-grown browns and last longer in the environment. She hopes so, otherwise their mission here will have been nothing but a waste of energy.

'When will the selected viable be assimilated?' she asks.

He shrugs. 'A matter of shifts.'

Penter remembers an image she saw on SKY last night. A crying Mother, pleading for her offspring to be returned. They did not say where it had gone, only that it was lost. 'If browns... disappear... won't this cause their families distress?' She is not sure why this concerns her, but it does. She glances at Father to see if he finds this question disregardful.

'Browns disappear all the time, Mother. They are not like us. They wander, they scope. As a default, they hold their family units and other browns in disregard. You have seen this?'

She has. Not only on SKY, but in the movies that Jane likes. 'Which one is the primary viable?'

'We have two options.'

He zooms in on a corpulent halfpint with a mess of yellow hair. 'Ugh,' she says. Then she realises that she has seen it before. It's the brown that came to the precinct with the educator. The disregardful one. She is not surprised it has been chosen. The other one is female, not as odious, but also in need of urgent modification to make it less unsightly.

'This is good work, Father,' she says.

Father looks down at his gelphone and frowns. 'Thanks you.'

'Why did you show this to me?'

He doesn't answer, only stands up and says, 'I must conclude some business.'

Without another word, he leaves the room. She gets up quietly and follows, not sure what she's looking for. As always, he's locked his study door behind him, but she squats down and peers through the keyhole, aware of the risk she's taking.

Father's drafting a message on his gelphone. He can't be conversing with the Ministry – they require only daily reports. She looks at his naturally primo features in the glancing sunlight and feels a cramping in her stomach. Remembers the words from the computer. Is this fear? She isn't sure. Could it be love? No. It doesn't feel blissful, more as if she is about to projectile. She watches him place his gelphone in his pocket, then hurries down the stairs and into the hallway, hearing Father's footsteps behind her.

Unwilling to let Father see her face, she opens the front door, stares out into the grounds. Danish is approaching, moving faster than usual. She can't decipher his expression – he may have been modified, but he is still a brown. He hobbles up to the door and hands a piece of paper to Father. Sometimes she wonders what the Ministry was thinking providing them with a tame brown who cannot speak, however admirable his oral modification work may be.

Father reads it, then turns to look at her. 'There is an unauthorised brown in the precinct.'

Penter blinks. Tries to remember the correct protocol. 'Shall I report?'

'No. I have... an idea,' Father says. 'Perhaps it could be of service.'

Penter is shocked. 'But that is not in our purview.' She's heard rumours that treasonous Players have been scouting browns unlawfully for the Modification Ward and that the Ministry is displeased. Unlawful scouting is a terminal offence. Is Father a Player after all? Is this what he was doing with his gelphone? As a Node Liaison it would be her duty to report him.

Jane shuffles past her and enters the kitchen, distracting her from these confusing thoughts. Which is the greater disregard: treasonous thoughts against Father, or a wariness about doing her duty to the Ministry? At this moment, confronted by the mute tame brown, an intruder, Father's secret messages and Jane's peculiar needs, Penter longs for nothing more than a renewal. All the questions trouble her and she longs for the quietness of clear direction. How do the browns exist without order?

She follows Jane into the kitchen, hands her a bowl and pours the colourful nuggets of dry sugar that have become the halfpint's favourite breakfast. She distributes a similar bowlful to Danish and he limps into the corner of the room to enjoy them.

She joins Father at the door. 'If we attempt to recruit the intruder without authorisation,' she whispers, 'will we not be in disregard?'

'We have an open-ended brief when we are in the field, Mother. It does take time to acclimatise to the freedom. In this case, I am secure that the Ministry will be felicitous if we scout a rogue brown beyond the specified purview of the project. How does the advertisement say it? *We go the extra mile.*' He waves a hand in Danish's direction. 'It will not be long before that will depreciate. We may need a replacement. This project has been a success and there will be others, I'm sure.' Father smiles at her, places a hand on her shoulder; it's the first time he has ever touched her. She feels a sharp tug in her chest, something that hurts more, is more blissful, than regard. When he removes his hand, she thinks she can still sense the weight of it pressing down on her.

He cannot be a Player. It would be impossible for her to have such regard for him if he were.

'You are correct about Danish, Father,' she says, returning his smile. She notices that Jane is watching them both carefully as she spoons sugar from the bowl into her mouth. And, she thinks, Jane did say she wanted a pet.

Chapter 13

RYAN

There's a grinding sound in his right ear. The cold smell of wet clay and concrete. A monster is looming over him, a spider-woman, all arms and breasts, knives and malicious smiling. Something else is cutting over him, like a laser, burning into his skin.

It's a sliver of early sunlight. Ryan props himself up on an elbow and tries to rub life into his face. There's fine sand all over his cheek, on his brow. He brings his hand into range in front of his eyes and sees the earth-red of clay, not blood. His body is so stiff he can only haul it over and up like a carcass. His knees crackle and burn, the nerve bundles down his spine object.

The spider-woman with the knives leers and he remembers that she's made of concrete. He's been sleeping in the back corner of this half-built McPalace's eight-car garage. He sits up cross-legged and chases the cobwebs away. The grinding is still vibrating through the ground, as if there are major earthworks happening deep below him. He listens intently in the dead still of dawn and fancies he can hear a high-pitched whining beneath that grinding, a keening sound.

There's a swirl of faces listing through his head: Karin, Julie, Tess, Alice, but most of all the new girl, her polar face superimposed over all the rest. She's somewhere near, he remembers, and the lurch that this causes in his system is a different sort of lurch to the knots of fear and regret the faces of Tess and Alice cause. As for Julie and Karin, those pathetic old hags, they leave him cold.

After hearing the kid screaming yesterday, Ryan had ducked under the portico out of sight and waited. A minute later, the library volunteer woman came out, dragging her snot-faced son down the driveway. The kid was pale, tear-streaked, but oddly passive, quiet – shocked. Ryan realised that it was that boy who'd been screaming, not the girl, and he felt a wash of relief. Dusk was falling by then and Ryan knew that this was as good a shelter as any, better than many. He'd be able to hide out in the back of this half-constructed shell and make more plans tomorrow. He'd have to go hungry tonight, but he'd been hungry often enough before. An almost-full bottle of whisky would give him all the fuel he needed.

At some stage in the evening he called Ziggy, begged him for Alice's phone number, but of course Ziggy laughed him off. He also tried Karin, but she didn't answer. He can't leave things like that, Alice hating him. Is his only option to stake out Bedford Centre again on the next take-away Wednesday? He can't allow her disappointment in him to fester and crystallise into loathing. He's got to get in touch with her and make things right. He did nothing wrong, it was all her bitch mother's fault. He never hurt her.

The sunlight's slanting in more powerfully now, but Ryan still doesn't feel elastic enough to move. He imagines the sun's rays warming his muscles and joints and cleansing him. The grinding below has stopped, he notices, and he hears birdsong in the trees of the garden. He should be hearing cars on the road – it's not that far away, but the gate and the wall are high and thick enough, he supposes, to block out the sound. Ryan's never been rich, even when he was a salaried and productive member of society, and he's always had to live with other people's sounds and smells, but this silence and seclusion, this is why people rate being wealthy. You can buy your own private world.

Who lives here? he wonders. Can that pale girl really belong to a rich family, the type that would have eight cars to park? Or is she the daughter of a servant who lives on the property? When she's looked at him he's been branded by her wordless appeal – for help? For rescue? For attention, care, love? Something in that girl's gaze cries out with need.

The slice of light falling on his body flickers off and then on again. Someone has passed the mouth of the garage. It flickers again as the figure returns and stands staring at him. It's just a silhouette. The broad shoulders and round middle make Ryan suspect it's a man. The head seems too big for the rest of the body and he appears to be leaning on a cane. Ryan thinks of a drawing Alice once made, which he hung on his office partition all those years ago; this shadow is like that child's drawing come to life.

Ryan draws himself up straighter but doesn't stand. Let the man come to him. Ryan concentrates on exuding confidence, like he belongs here. If the man's tacitly asking what the hell Ryan's doing in his garage, Ryan counters it with a wave of what the hell are you looking at.

The shadow man stands there looking for a minute more, then passes by again in the direction of the main house.

The spell is broken and Ryan packs his bag, readying to leave.

He's slung his satchel over his shoulder and is on his way towards the gate when he's confronted by a woman. She's a peculiar woman, with curves in all the wrong places – sort of… knobbly. But that doesn't stop her from wearing a form-fitting lacy body suit, almost as if she's a member of one of those I'm-a-freak-and-proud-of-it brigades. The first thing that goes through his mind is that he can probably beat her in a fight. She's tall, but probably quite light.

He hopes that it doesn't come to that; the fact is he doesn't want to touch her.

When she speaks, he's surprised by her friendly tone. 'Good morning, mister,' she says in an unplaceable accent, but given her odd get-up, he assumes she's a recent import from Eastern Europe. It all suddenly fits into place: the semi-constructed house, the nouveau-riche tastelessness. She must be the wife of one of those gangsters on the run from the former Yugoslavia who've set up shop in South Africa. People like that don't get house bonds or building loans: all their transactions are strictly cash. That explains the bizarre decor, and the fact that work seems to have halted.

Ryan doesn't want to be caught squatting in a Serbian gangster's house-in-progress.

'Oh, hi. I've just been admiring your... art.' He waves a hand at the freakish statues. 'I didn't mean to trespass, I'll be on my way now.' He offers her his smile, which bounces off her unnoticed – her gaze remains one of open curiosity.

It's as if she hasn't heard him or understood him. She reaches out her hand. 'My name is Mother,' she says. 'Danish reported you were here. You are one of those browns – uh, upside citizens – who has no home? It is charming to meet you.'

Ryan can do nothing other than take her hand and shake. She has an unsettling handshake, crimping her fingers and holding them straight and rigid, and it's cold and clammy at the same time, almost like one of those hook-tentacled statues. Perhaps she's palsied or something. He had better stop being so judgemental, Ryan thinks, if he's going to survive on the road. From this woman's perspective he's the freak here – homeless and dirty-brown, it's true. He'd better start being nice.

'Hello, um, ma'am,' he says. 'Yes, you're right. I actually don't have a home at the moment. But I'm used to living on the road. I'll be fine. Thank you.' He turns to go.

'But we have an ample home. We have extent for twenty... upsiders, maybe thirty if they are small and we load them correctly.'

Ryan laughs. 'I don't think your... family... would be so happy if you started taking in homeless people. I don't know where you come from, but that's not the way things work here.' But the thought of family brings back the image of the girl. Is she this woman's daughter? That would explain a lot – a recent immigrant with no friends and out of touch with local customs.

'My family' – the word clunks out of her mouth like a stone – 'would be felicitous. You see, as we are organised according to documented periurban kinship configurations to this node cluster, I am the executive manager of the domestic precinct, while Father is the family's financial procurement manager. We have Jane, whose organisational role is to acquire project-specific knowledge and liaise with local halfpints, and of course, Danish, our tame brown. He guides us through the node.'

Ryan just nods. This woman is evidently insane.

Mother – if that's what she wants to be called, like she comes from an Appalachian farm, so be it – rests a hand on one of the lumpy bits on her side and continues. 'There is a tradition of accommodating operatives within a precinct, is there not?'

'Excuse me?'

'There is a tradition of accommodating operatives within a precinct, is there not?'

'I'm sorry, I don't understand.'

'Oh, please. My apology. I'm learning to speak more clearly for upside citizens,' she says, more to herself than to Ryan, and when her voice drops that false public cheer, Ryan can see how this woman might be taken very seriously. She clears her throat. 'You. Work. You. Stay. Here?'

'Work here?' he answers.

'You clean? You lift?' she says, as if addressing a child. Or, in Ryan's experience, the way employers address their manual labourers.

'Yes. Yes, I do.'

'You will be remunerated and stay on the precinct. That's "the way things work here", yes?'

'Yes. Yes, it is. But how much… remuneration… are we talking?'

Mother's long hand dips into the neckline of her bodysuit and emerges with a fold of blue notes. She flicks off a wodge as if at random. 'This? Per one week?'

Ryan takes the money and stuffs it in his back pocket. 'You've got a deal.' He extends his hand.

'"You've got a deal",' she repeats, smiles a lopsided grin and returns a stiff, point-fingered shake. As Mother leads him into the house, Ryan can't believe how suddenly his luck has turned. He's got what must be a couple of grand in his back pocket, a place to hide, and – what pleases him most of all – he's living on the same property as the girl. He's going to be able to get to know her, find out what she needs. This time, he's not going to be stupid like he was with Tess. This time he can let things take their course.

The room Mother opens for him is in the new wing, a blocky modern construction that seems to have been built up against the large old house at a jaunty angle. It's still vacant and dank and all unpainted plaster. The dust-coated alabaster floor tiles make the room feel like a hallway or stripped bathroom more than a bedroom, but the weather is still warm and the sense of closeted safety – nobody from his past life will find him here – makes him feel more relaxed, he realises, than he has felt for ages. The knowledge that he will never have to go back to that school and work for those petty tyrants, have to be nice all the time, comes to him as an overwhelming relief. He hadn't appreciated just how much working in that environment stressed and prickled him. A quiet domestic job for this odd but genial woman is just what he needs.

Behind these grotesque walls, he might as well be in a different country, a different world.

But he has one more engagement with the outside world to wrap up before he can slink away and gather himself. Duvenhage. Ryan will make him pay whatever he thinks his silence is worth; it will be interesting to know just how badly Duvenhage wants to hide his perversity from the public gaze.

Mother watches him put down his bag and test the mattress on the basic cot. It's new and comfortable – it still smells of the polythene wrapping in which it was delivered.

'Mister?'

'Yes? My name's Ryan, by the way. Do you mind if I start work this afternoon? I have an errand I must run this morning.'

'Please find me when you have completed your errand.'

Although it's above ground, this room, he notices, has no windows. The walls and the ceiling seem to push in on him. It's like a bunker in here. But where better than a bunker to hide?

'Please regard the notices,' the woman continues. 'Feel free to ramble throughout the house and grounds, but do not transgress on the first floor. There are clearly demarcated notices. Those quarters are for the family only.'

'Okay,' Ryan says, not quite understanding what she means, but if the notices are clear he's not likely to run into any trouble. 'I'll do that. No problem.'

'Primo!' She smiles. 'We will converse when your errand is complete.'

When Mother has left, he washes up and puts on a clean T-shirt. The bathroom next door has a sink and a shower and a pile of painters' drop cloths in one corner. There's no toilet. He lifts the cloths but there are just more tiles. In the end, he pisses into the basin. He'll have to explore the house more later, but for now he's in a hurry.

He shrugs on his backpack, aware of the lightness now that he has only one bottle left in it. But now with the cash he's just been paid, he'll be able to stock up on supplies. He mustn't forget food – there's no guarantee he'll be fed here.

He heads straight down the corridor the way he came in, into the recesses of the parking garage and across the sandy driveway, and pushes through the gold gate, scalding his hand in the process – it's already been super-heated by the morning sun and is obviously not designed for manual use. He turns west on Excelsior Avenue, back towards the tiny suburban shopping centre halfway towards the Key West strip mall: it's just a corner shop, a cheap draper's, a print shop cum internet cafe and a bottle store.

When he gets there, the little shopping centre feels like part of the compound, an extension of the foreign enclave of his own city. He feels anonymous, like he's travelling some far corner of the world where nobody knows him. By avoiding the busy thorough-fares of Bedford Centre or Eastgate, he can keep the illusion alive that he's far away and untouchable.

He orders a coffee and a danish at the internet cafe and sits at the old computer, registers a new webmail address: 'payback666@webmail.com', a dramatic little touch. Then he inserts his flash drive and scans through the copied thumbnails, careful that nobody's able to look over his shoulder, before selecting a moder-ately disturbing one, a naked girl laid out, with blue skin, and marked up like meat at a butcher's. He sends it to Duvenhage with-out a message, reads a news site and waits. It's Friday morning – Ryan checks his watch, nine-thirty, after assembly – and Duven-hage is quite likely to be idling complacently behind his desk.

Two minutes later, a reply.

'Who are you? What do you want?'

Ryan replies with a picture of a naked pubescent boy, similarly cold and scrawled on. 'I have them all.'

A sip of coffee. 'What do you want?'

'I have uploaded the pictures to a secure server.' That sounds right, doesn't it? 'You will receive ftp credentials in exchange for R100,000 in cash.'

This time Ryan has time to finish his coffee, scan two articles without reading them. Damn, has he overplayed it? Is he sure that nobody can trace this address? No, he's not sure. He doesn't know about any of this spy-tech shit. This is his only play.

Then, from a new address, kennethd@snazzymail.com: 'You're being absurd. I don't have that money.'

Ryan has to take a flyer. He scans through the drive for the letter, for some detail to make his threat sound authentic. 'Do you want me to ask the Ministry?' It's a long shot, but Ryan's gut tells him it's the right move.

It is. 'Where? How? EFT?'

EFT? He's going to get blackmail money transferred into a registered bank account? He's not that stupid.

'Leave it in the dustbin next to Post Office Box 2190 at Gardenview post office. Noon. One minute late, the files go to the Child Protection Unit. If I get the money, I send you the login and I'm gone.'

'How can I trust you? You won't just take the money?'

'You'll have to take my word, won't you?'

'I know this is you, Ryan Devlin.'

Oh, fuck. How do blackmailers do it? They always seem to get away with it in the movies, but there are a thousand fucking pitfalls in this process. He should just cut and run. But Duvenhage doesn't know where he is, and even if he's got some way of tracing the email to this print shop, he'll be long gone. He's got to try. This could make his life a lot easier.

'Noon,' he types. If he were Duvenhage, he'd have the place crawling with friends who'd come and kill him the moment he picked up the money. What the hell is he going to do? Can he get someone to pick it up instead of him? No, they'll just as easily take that person. This shit doesn't work. 'You don't know who I am. If the money does not get back to me safely, the address goes to the Child Protection Unit. Don't fuck with me.' Backspace backspace. 'Don't play with us.' That sounds better.

Another too-long delay. 'Noon,' Duvenhage responds. Ryan checks his watch. He's got two hours. He doesn't even have someone he can call to do the pickup. Nobody would help him. He's got to do it himself. He knows Duvenhage will be watching, and will see that it's him, but he'll have to bluff his way out of it somehow. Duvenhage knows he's got the pictures, so he's still got some high cards in his hand. How about if he holds his phone up, finger on the button, as if he'll press send if anyone comes near? That'd work. Duvenhage wouldn't know his phone's so kak that it doesn't have internet access.

Yes, that should work.

Chapter 14

TARA

The house is quiet. *Too* quiet. She's not used to it being so peaceful at the weekend. Martin usually spends most of Saturday and
Sunday attached to his Xbox, killing zombies or aliens or whatever with one of his vile friends. But since he arrived home after
Encounters last night, he hasn't ventured out of his room. In any
other child, such a sudden change in behaviour would be a sign
of abuse, but she's learnt her lesson on that score, as Duvenhage
has not so subtly pointed out. Stephen is off playing golf with his
gang of lawyer buddies – 'networking' – but she's relieved that he's
not here. Lately she's finding his company increasingly odious. If
it wasn't for Baby Tommy she doesn't know how she would have
got through yesterday evening. She'd felt intensely uneasy after
her meeting with Duvenhage; unwelcome memories from those last
few weeks at Raymond Scheider had come flooding back.

'Martin,' she calls up the stairs. 'Do you want something to eat?'

No answer. She'll take him some ice cream. That'll do.

The kitchen smells rank, the counter tops littered with
grease-spotted pizza boxes and take-out Thai food containers sitting
in sticky puddles of leaked soy sauce. A line of black ants marches

around the edge of the sink and down towards the overflowing bin. No one's emptied the dishwasher and the week's breakfast bowls and coffee mugs are piled up in the sink. Tara knows she should really clean it up, especially as Olivia will be here later. She can just imagine the sneer on Olivia's face when she sees the smear of dried ketchup on the fridge door, the blackened pot that's still sitting on top of the dishwasher.

She digs in the freezer, unearths a tub of soft serve. It's crystallised, but what the hell. She hacks it into a bowl, chucks the tub on top of the crusty bowls in the sink and heads up to his room.

She knocks on the door, nudges it open. It's gloomy inside; he's pulled the curtains. 'Hey,' she says. 'Brought you some ice cream.'

He shifts under his duvet. 'Thanks.'

She places the bowl on his side table, sits down on the edge of his bed. 'Your father's really worried about you, Martin.'

'I know.'

'*I'm* really worried about you.'

He shrugs.

'If there's anything you want to tell me, you know I can keep a secret.'

He shakes his head. 'I'm cool.'

'Are you?' She reaches out to stroke his brow, is surprised when he doesn't flinch away from her touch. His skin feels clammy, but she doesn't think he has a temperature.

'Are you sure all you saw at the house was a snake?'

He shakes his head. 'No. I saw... something else.'

'You did? Why didn't you want to tell your father?'

He sighs, sounding way older than his years. 'He wouldn't understand.'

'Can you tell me what it was?'

He shakes his head.

'Could you draw it?'

He blinks at her in surprise. 'I... I guess.'

Tara scrabbles in his desk, finds a piece of paper and a pencil, places it on the side table next to the ice cream. 'Here.'

'I'm tired. Can I do it in a bit?'

'Sure,' Tara says. 'Whenever you're ready.'

'Tara? You didn't say anything to Dad about me...' He points towards the washing basket.

'No. Of course not.'

He sighs again, this time in relief and sits up and reaches over for the ice cream. She spies something on his upper arm, just below the edge of his T-shirt's sleeve. A smeared black line. 'Hey. What's that?'

'It's nothing.'

'You been drawing on yourself?'

He shrugs.

Oh well, she thinks. At least he's not cutting himself or taking meth or whatever the latest drug fad is. She decides not to push him further – after all, Baby Tommy is calling.

Tara skips downstairs to the kitchen, Baby Tommy's head cradled in her arms. She's worked straight through the afternoon, and after she's set this layer of paint, all she has to do is root the few strands of his hair, a job she's looking forward to, attach his limbs to his body and then tackle the part she's not so sure about: applying the thread to his mouth and eyes. But to be honest, for some reason she's not dreading this as much as she thought she would. She's become so used to Baby Tommy's photograph that she actually can't imagine him without this gruesome feature. Humming to herself, she digs out a baking tray, presses a piece of greaseproof paper on its base and gently places the head on top of it. Careful not to smudge the paint, she tenderly kisses his forehead and slides the tray into the oven.

Tara knows she'll have to prepare herself to let Baby Tommy go. If she really can't bear it, worst-case scenario she can always give the money back, can't she? She hasn't actually spent any of it. There's no law that says she has to hand Baby Tommy over, is there?

Buoyed by this thought, she digs out the vacuum cleaner and skips into the lounge. While she waits for the paint to set, she'll have time to clear the place up a bit. If she hustles, she might even have time for a shower before Olivia arrives.

The front door clicks open, and Tara hears Stephen calling her name. She checks the time. Five thirty. He's back early. She heads out into the hallway, pauses when she sees the strained expression on his face.

'What is it?'

'Olivia's here,' he says.

'What? Already? I thought you said she was coming later this evening?'

'She caught an earlier flight. I picked her up from the airport.'

'Why didn't you call me?'

Before he can answer, Olivia steps into the house, dragging her Louis Vuitton case behind her. Tara has to admit that she looks good – better than good. Her hair is squeezed into a bun at her neck; her charcoal suit looks freshly dry-cleaned. Tara reckons she could easily fit in with the Mother Tribe these days. She's lost the dowdy, harassed air she had when Tara first met her. (Probably because she palms Martin off on Stephen as often as she can.) Tara riffles her hands through her hair, realises that her T-shirt is spattered with paint, sees Stephen looking at her with faint distaste.

She tries to catch his eye. The least he could do is *try* to show a united front to Olivia, but his gaze slinks away from hers.

Olivia peers into the lounge. 'Where's Martin?'

'He should be in his room,' Tara says. Goddammit. She hasn't checked on him for hours.

'Martin!' Stephen yells up the stairs. 'Martin! Your mother's here.'

'I can go up,' Olivia says.

'No, let him come down,' Stephen says. 'He was fine this morning. No reason to treat him like an invalid.'

Olivia's eyes narrow. The last thing Tara feels like is being caught in the middle of a Stephen–Olivia bout. When the two of them are together she always feels oddly like an intruder, or at best an awkward teenager.

'Can I get you something to drink, Olivia?' Tara asks.

Olivia turns her mascaraed gaze on her as if she's only just realised she's there. 'No thank you, Tara. What I *would* like to know is what's going on with my son.'

'Didn't Stephen tell you?'

'He said he's having some emotional issues.'

Stephen snorts. 'He's fine. I told you there was no reason for you to come racing back here.'

'He's my son too, Stephen.'

'Martin!' Stephen yells again. 'Get down here *now*!'

Olivia sighs. 'Really, I expected better than this, Stephen.' She pushes past Tara, thumps up the stairs.

Stephen shoots another exasperated glance in Tara's direction and hares after her.

What now? Tara thinks. She supposes she ought to go too. At least show that she's concerned about Martin.

She follows Stephen up and onto the landing, sees Olivia poking her head into their bedroom, calling for Martin. If he's not in his room, locked in the bathroom or in the other two bedrooms, there's only one place he could be.

She races towards her sanctuary, tries the door. Goddammit. She must have forgotten to lock it. She peers inside, sees Martin sitting at her desk. Heart in her throat, she glances round the room, relieved that Baby Tommy's limbs are still neatly laid out where she left them. Thank God – the pre-Encounters Martin would have had a field day in here doing God knows what to them. 'Martin, what are you doing in here?'

He hands her a piece of paper. 'I did what you said, Tara. I drew it.'

Tara can't make sense of it immediately. It seems to depict the hunched figure of a man, looking over its shoulder, its eyes scrawled black circles, its head lumpy and misshapen.

'*This* is what you saw?'

Martin nods. 'The bogeyman,' he whispers.

'Oh, Martin,' she breathes.

He stands up and throws his arms around her waist. Tara is so taken aback, she only notices that Olivia and Stephen have entered the room when Olivia speaks.

'Martin?' Olivia says. 'Mommy's here.' Martin makes no move to disentangle himself and Tara can't help the surge of triumph she feels. '*Martin!*'

He finally looks up. 'Hi, Mom.'

Tara watches Olivia's expression of aggrieved concern turn to disgust as she stares at the collage of Baby Tommy. 'Jesus Christ, Stephen. What the hell is this? No wonder Martin's having psychological problems.'

But Stephen isn't listening. He sniffs noisily. 'I can smell burning. Tara? Are you cooking something?'

'No. I'm—' Tara's stomach plummets. Oh God – Baby Tommy! She wriggles out of Martin's embrace, pushes roughly past Olivia, races downstairs on numb legs, flies into the kitchen. Sees a drift of black smoke curling out of the oven. Pulls the door open and reaches inside, ignoring the heat searing her unprotected hands. When the pain gets too much she finally lets the blackened ruin of Baby Tommy's head drop onto the tiles.

She slumps to her knees. She can't believe what she's done. How could she forget him like that? Her Tommy...

She reaches out to touch him, his little pursed mouth now a melted snarl. She looks down at her right palm, where a blister is already forming.

She doesn't lift her head, even when she hears the bark of Olivia's laughter behind her.

Chapter 15

PENTER

Penter picks another ready bean and places it on her tongue, enjoying the tickle of its furry skin. As she chews it slowly, encouraging its juices, she watches the new brown – 'Ryan' – mixing the soil and spraying water on the shoots. Ryan doesn't seem to care about consuming, or that his hands and body are muddied with sweat and soil. How can he bear to look so abnormal? A few of the browns she has seen on the documents look as if they have undergone the browns' primitive modifications, but this one seems proud to be unsightly.

Apart from that educator, the only brown Penter has been in close proximity to is Danish, and Ryan is very different from him, not only in appearance. Whereas Danish's eyes are passive, there is something more active lurking in Ryan's. His eyes follow Jane in a different way from the way he looks at her, or even Danish. She raised this with Father at dinnertime.

'He is a primo specimen,' Father said. 'Much impairment there.'

'Why doesn't the upside just recycle deviant browns like him?'

'Perhaps they serve the system in some way we cannot understand,' was Father's response. 'They allow them to loiter.'

If Penter were a character in one of those boring and predictable movies, she would fall in love with the brown – they would find a connection across the divide. Imagine choosing someone as unsightly as the brown over someone as scenic as Father. The thought makes her embarrassed – yet another of the barrage of emotions evoked by the thought-seep – and she laughs.

Ryan looks up at her and scrimps his face. Is she meant to converse with him again? She's not sure what is expected. She has played her part, she has given him work as Father requested, she has completed her duty.

She wants to go back into the house. Ryan, like that educator, smells of bleeding meat, of that amber liquid he imbibes, of decay. He reeks like that karking yogurt. She can't stand close to him for long without covering her mouth, even out here in the ether. The *Manual of Upside Contrivances* explains that browns do not have a bag. Instead, they dribble their waste out like the pregrowns in the vats who have no control over their bodily functions. It's disquieting. No, worse; it's repellent. Father disagrees with her; he tells her that the ablution booths the browns so favour have become quite fashionable among senior members of the Administration. Penter will believe this when she sees it. At a stretch, she might imagine people abluting into a puddle in a chair in the lower levels of the Malls or the CCOs' Apartments, but not in the Tower, surely.

Swallowing the last of the bean, she turns her back on Ryan, makes her way into the house. She has things to do. It is not long now before they must depart. Danish is already starting to dismantle the precinct, hauling the set and the facades away. She has wondered many times if she will miss the upside, but, after encountering SKY, she has no strong desire to stay here, even with the beans and the sun and the love movies. No, what she will miss is her growing connection to Father. She knows it will be severed when they return home and have their penetrations renewed. Will she be glad when she no longer feels these inappropriate emotions? When the thought-seep is gone? She will be glad to have her clarity restored, but at the same time, perhaps she'll miss something about this lifestyle. One thing's for certain: she will be glad not to be Mother any more. It is an unsatisfying role; she's nothing more than a karking victual servant.

She walks through the house, listening for sounds that Father is near. He has been in his study all day, and she finds herself anxious, looking for him, waiting for him, wanting that ache in her entrails when she sees him. She feels like the little browns on the screen, as if someone is recording everything she does.

She creeps upstairs to his study door. It is disregardful, she knows, but she cannot stop herself from knocking. 'Father?'

The door clicks open. There he is. Her chest clutches in disappointment when she sees his face. He looks disconcerted, impatient. 'Mother? What is it?'

She invents a reason for disturbing him. 'Have you informed the Ministry about the trespassing brown?' she asks.

'I am awaiting a response from them.'

His gelphone trembles in his hand. He looks down at it, grimaces. 'I must report,' he says. She retreats and closes the door behind her.

She shouldn't have gone in there; she feels foolish. She walks to Father's sleeping quarters, pauses, then opens the door. It smells of the luscious oil he uses on his hair. She kneels down next to his bed and presses her face against it, inhaling his odour. How different and refreshing it is after that brown's stink! She knows she's being absurd. She tries to remind herself who she is. I am Penter Ulliel, Deputy Node Liaison for the Ministry of Upside Relations. If she were watching herself in a movie, she'd be appalled. But it's not a movie and she can't help recalling the way he touched her, the weight of his hand on her shoulder. It makes her shiver. She runs her hands over the blanket, pauses when her fingers brush against a lump. She ferrets under the cover and pulls out a book. She looks at it, uncomprehending. There's a picture of an unsightly brown female on the front, with the words 'BabyEx Mothercare Catalogue' above its head.

Mothercare? Did he obtain and secrete this for her? Does he love her after all?

She turns the pages, expecting to see mimeographs of Mothers sitting around tables with yogurt, perhaps Fathers bringing them convenience foods, but all she sees are pictures of disturbingly small browns – pages and pages of them. Penter feels a cold gasp of air tickling the back of her neck, just below her shunt hole.

This is disregardful in the extreme.

She has encountered halfpint browns in the documents, of course, and there was that one that the educator brought, but the ones in this book are way too small to be out of their vats. She has seen some in the advertisements, but cannot understand what browns do with such things. They look feeble, inadept. How can they work or consume? What do they do? In most of the mimeographs they are attached to small chairs, their toothless mouths open as if they are normals advertising gum-shine.

Father has made notes on some of the mimeographs: 'Why so unsightly?' 'Do they not choose?' 'Why vat free?' and 'Punishment?'

Penter has heard the stories of brown birth that circulate like some Player's bad dream and simply does not believe them. But sure enough, here are also pages of female browns with distended stomachs. Can the stories be true? Parasitic pregrown halfpints pushing their way out of a gash in the Mother's body? The thought makes her bilious. It is worse than SKY. It is even worse than Jane's favourite movies.

She pushes the book back under the cover and stands up, dizzy from the obscene images.

What else is Father hiding? She will need to inspect his study on her own. The shunt hole tingles at the back of her neck, protesting against the enormity of her disregard, but she continues to make her plans. It is her duty, as the Deputy Node Liaison for the Ministry of Upside Relations, to investigate the potential of such a massive breach of regard. He will leave soon to harvest the primary viable, and she will be free to explore.

If he is a Player, if he is purloining artefacts that are nothing to do with the purview of their project, then she knows what she must do. She touches the bony nodule fused above her heart, presses down on it. 'Heartbreak,' she whispers. That's what browns call it when blissful love is flushed.

Chapter 16

RYAN

Most of the grounds consist of the clotted red soil and concrete dust of a perpetual building site, but the vegetable patch is a well-tended oasis in the corner of the large garden. There are neat rows of spinach and corn and tomatoes, and beans grow healthily up canes. Ryan wonders who has tended this garden, since he is apparently the first casual labourer the woman, Mother, has hired. The family doesn't seem to mind living in half-built clutter, but they tend their vegetable patch like it's a Zen garden.

Ryan feels his tension melting as he works the patch, trimming back tendrils and cleaning up fallen leaves, turning the soil. Thoughts of all the needful girls and the angry men outside these walls recede into the back of his head, a head that hasn't felt this clear, this mollified, for ages. That's what he should do, he decides: go somewhere into the country, work on a farm. Or even join a monastery, safe and quiet behind high walls he'll never be forced to leave. The octopus-headed Adonises and hook-handed Shivas studded through the gardens look on beneficently, blessing his plan.

It had been a disappointment on Friday when he'd got to the post office at the shopping centre and had seen the parking lot bristling with police cars. He shouldn't have been surprised. A creep like Duvenhage wouldn't have got where he has with perversions like his without being canny, careful, self-protective. He wasn't going to lose this battle with a two-bit blackmailer like Ryan that easily.

Ryan just walked past, scanning the cars in the lot, trying to get a glimpse of Duvenhage, but he didn't find him. He hurried back up to Excelsior Avenue, taking the side routes, glancing over his shoulder, but nobody seemed to be following him. He lay down on his cot in his windowless room. He knew he should go and find Mother and do the work he'd been paid to do, but he just wanted to rest for five minutes, breathe, regain his equilibrium, calm his nerves.

He must have fallen asleep because he was startled awake from a dream, the burning pale eyes in the girl's face the only scrap remaining. He shook the image and reoriented himself. He needed to pee, and didn't want to piss in the basin again.

He turned left out of his room. He tried the first open door in the passage, but behind it was only a pile of four dust-coated water heaters. The next room was similar to his: bare white tiles and an unused cot against one wall. The corridor, which up to this point was illuminated weakly by the light coming from the garage at the far end, now jerked around an odd angle into dusky greyness. There were no doors on either side of this segment of passage, and it curved one way and then the next for several metres before straightening out again into a huge white room. This one was decked with white-painted parquet and was empty apart from a massive fireplace flanged by dressed stone against one wall. A series of neoclassical embassy-style French windows lined another side, and from there Ryan saw a landscaped green lawn with a kidney-shaped swimming pool indented into it. This must have been the living room and garden of the original house. The sight of this middle-class normality – and of generous quantities of natural light – relieved Ryan after the odd angles and bareness of the confusingly constructed new wing he'd walked through.

But still no place to pee.

The fireplace room had no exits other than the one he'd come through so he backtracked through the serpentine corridor. Or so he thought. He passed the two doors he had looked into and came back to his room. Only now it wasn't his room. The space was much the same size, but instead of containing his bed and backpack, this one housed a stack of loose floor tiles and a collection of concrete statues. Set into the far wall was a green door.

Jesus, he should have brought breadcrumbs to drop behind him. And the need to piss was becoming urgent.

Through the opaque-paned door was a warm expanse of terracotta floor tiles and black granite and hard-oak kitchen shelving. It looked like a kitchen in a catalogue, an impression compounded by the fact that the windows were all sealed over with wood-veneered chipboard. And it was vast, bigger than any dream kitchen he'd ever seen. These people were probably expecting to have the extended family – an entire clan of moles by the look of it – round when the building work was completed. If this was the house of a mafia boss, how many hits and takeovers would it take to finish the construction? The counter tops were lined with coffee makers, interspersed with sandwich toasters, industrial-sized hot-water urns, mounted can openers, sandwich presses, rice steamers, blenders. The further he walked inside, the more it looked like a kitchen showroom.

Of course! Import-export. That would explain everything. It was the perfect business for recent immigrants and would explain the half-finished opulence. Keeping the warehouse at home would help keep the business off the taxman's radar, and it would serve as a neat front for the more illicit business he imagined the mysterious 'Father' practised.

Ryan heard a noise and turned around, straight into Mother. His forearm swiped her side and scraped against something hard and knobbled under the lacy material of her bodysuit.

'I'm sorry, I…' he said, trying his hardest not to wipe traces of her off his arm.

She looked at him curiously. 'Can I assist?'

'I… Sorry… I was just wondering where the toilet is.'

'Toilet? That… Yes. You do not have a bag,' Her face twisted in an expression he couldn't read. 'There is a convenience that is suitable for upside citizens in the hallway. I will show you.' She led him out of the kitchen through a lounge area that was overstuffed with furnishings like another department of the showroom. The room was rank with the petroleum odour of plastic still clinging to it, but just underneath that, a smell of wet soil. Mother noticed him looking at the clutter and she smiled her skew smile at him. 'We have not been here long, so have not converted the entire abode. Primo, is it not? We are attempting to decorate just in the local style as we have seen in the facsimiles.'

'Yes, uh… it's very nice.'

She opened the door of the guest bathroom near the front door; Ryan tried to brand the exact location on his mental map of the house. 'Here is the convenience.'

As he pissed, he took in the pictures framed on the bathroom walls. Pictures of cows and trees and kittens in baskets, as if they'd been cut haphazardly from *Women's Monthly Magazine of Cheap and Generic Kitsch*.

'You will find next door in the closet the implements for your labour,' Mother said to him through the door. 'You may start in the greenery patch, then sweep the dust. Walk where you will, but remember not to transgress on the upper level. That is for the family only.'

'Sure,' he muttered. You don't have to repeat yourself.

He rinsed his hands and dried them on his jeans. When he came out of the bathroom, Mother was gone.

After a few hours of digging and hoeing, he had completely shucked off the disappointment of the morning's excursion. He was relieved, in fact. Petty theft aside, he was not cut out to be a criminal, to live in paranoid fear of the enemies he'd make. Sure, a hundred grand would have made his life easier, but if he was honest with himself, he knew he'd never get it. He's always been the sort of man who likes to work for his money, and now, bending his back and pushing his shoulders, sweating into the soil, he felt like he was earning an honest wage, not like that menial, meaning-less, computerised crap he had done back when he had a full-time job. Besides, he didn't want to add a man like Duvenhage to his growing list of enemies. He was a sick pervert, and he should be exposed. Ryan still had the files, and he'd think of some way to get them to the police without involving himself. In the meantime he was safe here, and was earning good money to do good work. That's the way he should have lived his life all along.

Around five that afternoon, he heard a metallic clang and rattle and peered through the bushes to see a station wagon pushing through the gates. Instead of parking in the garages where he'd slept the night before, the car drove on up to the side of the house and the man with the cane and the big head got out of the driver's side, limped round and opened the back door. The girl got out and, like a radar, swivelled her head to where Ryan was standing up in the higher terraces of the garden. She made him out through the bushes, stared at him for a moment, then bared her teeth. She might have been smiling, but despite himself, Ryan thought it was a signal of rage or desperation or – God help him – passion, or all three compounded.

The girl lifted her hand halfway, then went into the house. The driver limped back to shut the gates. That must be Danish. What did Mother call him? The 'tame brown'? What the hell did that mean? He was a pitiful figure, but although he had some sort of crippling disease that made him skewed and lopsided, and though his head was swollen to double the normal size, in some way he was more recognisable and less strange than the woman and the girl. Maybe he was South African; that might explain it.

After his day's work Ryan grabbed the loaf of bread and tin of jam from his makeshift nightstand and headed through into the kitchen, pleased to remember the route. He was quickly finding his bearings in the house. It was beginning to feel, if not like home, like a plush furnished apartment hotel. Space, privacy and comfort. And a wad of hundreds stashed in his backpack. After all the shit of the last week, he'd landed with his bum in the butter, to be honest. A song came into his head. *I gotta feelin'* something something.

He tapped out the tune on the counter top as he slotted two pieces of bread into a toaster and pushed the slide down. It didn't seem to respond so he followed the power cord out of the machine and crouched down under the counter to trace it to an electrical socket.

That tonight's gonna be a something something.

He was hungry. He was looking forward to his toast. He realised he hadn't eaten anything since the morning.

He was still searching for a socket when he heard the click of heels entering the kitchen.

'Hello, Mother,' he said, and then looked up as she approached. It wasn't Mother; it was the girl. He'd never seen her out of her school uniform and she was dressed in a discomforting outfit of vintage dress and high heels that were both too big for her, and a straw hat, as if she was in one of those old French paintings of riverside picnickers. She was dressed like a small copy of a picture of a woman.

In this get-up, another girl perhaps would just be playing the fool, expecting to be laughed at, but this girl was not playing. That milk-pale skin was flawless and her grey eyes burnt through him. He was hot where her stare landed.

'Hello, mister,' she said and he realised he'd never heard her voice before. It was deep and rich and sombre, not the voice a young girl should be using. The spacious, hard-surfaced kitchen was the perfect auditorium and the space between them vibrated with the sound. It grabbed his guts. 'I am Jane. How're *you* doin'?' She held out her hand like her mother had. A strange little girl playing at being grown-up? Or what?

'I'm Ryan,' he said, emerging at last from under the counter and standing up straight. His heart was beating in his groin. He couldn't drag his eyes away from hers. The toast limpened in the disconnected machine and Ryan pressed his hands to his brow. A thundering pain was starting up in his head.

'Danish took me scouting this afternoon,' she said. 'Do you want to see what I got?'

Ryan glanced around him. 'Uh, okay.'

She raised her left hand, which she'd been holding clamped to her side, extended it to him and opened it slowly, proudly.

There was some sort of insectoid mess smeared over her palm, spiky shards and yellow-green entrails trickling over her pale wrist. A very meaty locust, probably, which she had crushed in her eager grasp.

'It's a burd,' she said, pronouncing the word like a foreign term.

'No, it's a—'

'It flies in the sky.' She stretched her smudged palm to the ceiling, looked up to it and grinned – that same animal snarl baring miskept teeth, but this close he could see the unguarded delight in her face.

'It's pretty,' he said.

As soon as he got back to his room he had tried Karin again. This time, instead of flicking off, it went to voicemail. He thought quickly. 'Listen, Karin. I'm in the hospital. I... I had an accident. Please tell Alice that I'm okay and that I love her. That's all I wanted to say.' He thought he'd sounded convincing. A critically injured man trying to make amends. He needed Alice to call him, and if a little white lie was going to make that happen, it was all for a good cause.

But now it's Sunday afternoon and she hasn't called, and neither has Karin phoned back. Either Karin didn't buy his lie, or she just doesn't care. He doesn't give a shit about her either. But what about Alice? Did Karin even tell her? And if she did, what does it mean? Could it really be over with Alice?

For the tenth time today, Ryan feels eyes on his back. Jane's down there, he knows. As he hauled the cleaning equipment out of the store this morning, she trailed him ten metres back, slipping between columns and behind bushes, just as she has since Friday afternoon, as if she's playing some private game of spies. He looks down over his shoulder and, yes, there she is, gazing up at him from a slashed thicket, as still as one of the concrete statues. Her grey eyes burn into him and his skull pounds.

It's not right, her being left to wander this building site all alone. The way she mooches about after him reminds Ryan of Alice when she was much younger, maybe four or five, testing her independence but at the same time always safe in the orbit of her father, glancing across every now and then for acknowledgment that she was protected and loved.

He's seen just how isolated and alone Jane feels at the school among those rich and cliquey kids; he's seen the void she drags around with her, but it makes him sad that here in her house, which can only feel like a hotel to her – a temporary stop, not a real, loving home – she looks just as alone and lost. What is it with these people who have kids and don't even love them? You need a fucking aptitude test to open a bank account or buy a cellphone, but you need no qualifications to prove that you can love a child. It's just wrong.

Wouldn't it be equally wrong for him to just leave her here, without at least showing her that she deserves love?

He's managed to ignore her plight so far, as much as he loathes doing so. He'd love to show her that there's good in the world, but he's been mindful all weekend of how his rashness with Tess forced him to move before he was ready.

It would be a mistake, another part of him mentions quietly through the screaming in his brain. He should just go.

Jane looks up at him curiously from within a bower of peach trees, and he imagines he sees pleading in her icy eyes. He remembers how she fingered his blood when it dropped on her head last week at school, how he thought about a stabbed animal. He shouldn't have anything to do with her. He should just leave.

Sometimes she disappears. At these times he gets the sense that she's vanished into the entrails of the house. Her paleness makes him think of a subterranean creature, like the mole-people her parents must be intending to entertain in the windowless new wing. In all the occupied rooms there's that plastic smell underlaid by a pervasive dank smell of earth as if this is all a facade for show while the family lives in a hole in the ground somewhere. When she's not out trailing him in the garden, he can imagine the girl huddling in the dark underneath the couches, hiding her pale body in a fort before the exposure of her next week at school.

But she always reappears, materialising like a flash of danger in his peripheral vision just as he's feeling at ease, sending a warm spike into his guts. The ripping pulse she causes behind his eyes has become familiar.

Now she half raises her hand again and yells, 'Let's get outta here!'

He can survive this. He mustn't do anything stupid.

His phone trills in his pocket. It's such an unfamiliar sound to him that at first he thinks it's a bird until it kicks into the full rendition of Britney Spears' first hit, something Alice chose for him.

He puts the phone to his ear, glancing towards where he saw the girl. She's gone, and he's relieved. For some reason, he can't keep his daughter and the new girl in his mind at the same time.

'Daddy?'

'Alice, sweetheart.' Ryan remembers to keep his voice down, to sound injured. He walks deeper into the thicket, finds a dark place out of sight.

'Are you all right, Daddy?'

'I'm okay, love. Thanks for calling.'

'Where are you?'

'I...'

'Are you going to get better?'

'I think so... Yes. I'll be fine.'

'Mom didn't tell me until now. She doesn't believe you. She says—'

A hadeda ibis clatters out of the undergrowth and blares away, squawking to its companion.

Silence.

'Alice?'

'I can't fucking believe it, Daddy! *You are lying!* You're not in the hospital!'

'Wait. It's... I'm... There's a garden here.'

'She was right. You're lying!'

The call ends.

Ryan slumps down against a tree trunk, scraping his back as he goes. That was his last play, and he's fucked it up completely. Goddamn fucking hadedas.

He searches his phone for the last number received but it's listed as unknown.

An SMS comes in. <You lieing bastard. I'm gld she knows now. O yes your neighbour and his daughter send there regards. Its over this time>

<What do u mean?> he texts back.

<The girls fathers pressed charges. somth i shudve done. u will never see Alice again>

Ryan switches off his phone and pulls out the SIM card. Even if it was a trap, they won't have been able to trace his location from that short call, surely. He thinks of the police crawling around Bedford Centre. He's safer here than anywhere else for now. He'll hide right here in the house until he can make a plan. The appliances here, for one thing, are worth something. He wouldn't be able to carry much, but what if he steals Danish's car? Come to think of it, these people won't have a bank account. Whatever business they're in, they'll have plenty of cash on the premises. 'Heed the notices,' Mother warned him. Of course. Upstairs. They must keep it all there.

He rushes towards the house, but is halted by a deep instinct of self-preservation. *Wait! Think!* You do *not* want to be caught stealing from the home of a Serbian mafia leader.

He forces himself to stop, breathe. Tomorrow's Monday. Danish will take the girl to school. He'll have to wait until the right time, act normal until then. He does not want to get caught.

Chapter 17

TARA

Tara awoke yesterday morning so weighted down with loss that she found it hard to breathe. She refused the mug of rooibos and honey Stephen brought her, blocked out his voice when he tried to convince her she was overreacting; that Baby Tommy was nothing more than vinyl and paint, just a doll – a thing that could easily be replaced. She numbly let him attend to her blistered palm, glad of the sting when he smothered it in Betadine and bandaged it up. She deserved to suffer. How could she have been so stupid?

She spent the rest of Sunday cocooned in their bedroom, the curtains drawn, drifting in and out of a sweaty, troubled sleep. That evening, ignoring Stephen's entreaties to join him in the lounge, she slipped into the kitchen and fished Baby Tommy's warped head out of the kitchen bin where Stephen had carelessly thrown it. She wrapped it in tissue paper, slunk upstairs to her sanctuary and carefully placed it in Baby Paul's drawer, unsure what else to do with it.

This morning – Monday – she's feeling slightly better. Stronger. Even feels a smidgen of shame. Really, why is she taking this so hard? It's almost as if she's mourning the loss of a child – as if Baby

Tommy was actually a living breathing entity. She has to snap out of it. Stephen's right. All Tommy is — *was* — is a doll. A thing. A nothing. A commodity.

Yet the memory of his little melted head plopping onto the kitchen tiles still makes her ache. She's read several articles discussing the psychology behind Reborning, but she's never thought of herself as one of those women who yearn so desperately for a baby that they start treating their Reborns as living beings. Women who take their dolls out for walks in strollers, burp them, dress them in fresh clothes and nappies every day, even go so far as to buy devices to insert in their chests that ape the sound of a heartbeat.

She pictures Stephen and Martin standing around a tiny grave in the back yard behind the plunge pool while she sobs next to them in a black lace dress and veil. Jesus, she thinks. Maybe she has finally lost it, after all.

Her phone beeps again. Yesterday evening she finally sent a message to Batiss: <I'm really sorry but there's been a problem with your baby. Unable to deliver> She received a slew of replies but in her grief-stricken state she hadn't mustered the energy to read them. But she can't ignore Batiss forever. She snatches the phone from the side table, scrolls through the messages.

<what problem? this is disquieting>

<delivery date confirmed and contracted. penalty for non-delivery still in effect>

<converse with direct effect please. we r waiting for your reply>

<your silence is a matter for disquiet>

<we repeat: awaiting reply>

And then, simply: <☹>

Fuck this, Tara thinks. She doesn't need this. Not after the week she's had. Not after all that business with Martin, her concerns about Jane, and Duvenhage's bombshell about Raymond Scheider Primary. Sure, she needs the cash, but what can she do? She can hardly deliver Baby Tommy as is, can she? Not even an eccentric like Batiss will want a baby with a charred, misshapen head. She sends back: <send me your bank account details and I'll return the money> She's married to a lawyer, after all. If Batiss causes any trouble, she can always hand the matter over to Stephen. And if he finds out that she lied about the amount she's been paid, well, she'll cross that bridge when she comes to it. Not that she really cares what Stephen thinks. Not any more.

The phone beeps again, and Tara turns it off without reading the message.

There's a light tap on the door and Martin enters the room. She couldn't believe it when Stephen told her he'd decided not to return home with his mother. She's spent months listening to Martin boast that everything from the food to the furniture is better at Olivia's house.

The pre-Encounters Martin, that is.

Martin carefully places a steaming mug next to her phone. 'Brought you a cup of coffee, Tara.'

Add that to the list of things she never thought she'd see Martin doing. Incredible. She sits up, takes a sip. Just the right amount of sugar. How does he know how she has her coffee? She makes herself smile. 'Morning.'

'I'm sorry about your baby,' he says.

Tara takes another sip of coffee to hide her expression. 'Thanks. Hey, why didn't you want to go home with Olivia?'

Martin shrugs. 'Just didn't.' He still looks tired, the rims of his eyes are red, the skin on his face is looser as if he's losing weight. He scuffs a foot over the carpet. 'Tara, it's Encounters tonight. Please can I go?'

Ah, Tara thinks. So there is a motive behind this behaviour, after all. 'It's not up to me, Martin. What does your dad say?'

Martin scowls. 'He says I can go if Mom says it's okay.'

Typical Stephen, Tara thinks. Passing the buck. 'Did you ask her?'

'Ja. She says she'll think about it. Please, Tara,' Martin whines. 'Can you talk to Dad? They're going to install one of us tonight and—'

'Hang on, they're going to *what*?' He must mean induct or something, got the word wrong.

'Please Tara. Everyone else is going. It isn't fair if I don't go.'

'What's all this?' Stephen says from the doorway in a forced cheery voice. 'Family conference?'

'Can I go to Encounters tonight, Dad?'

'Sorry, my boy. Your mother said no.'

'She said she'd think about it.'

'Just spoken to her. The answer's no.'

'Aw *please*, Dad. I can stay in aftercare till it's time to go.'

He's thought of everything, Tara realises. She's really curious now. What the hell can possibly go on at these meetings?

'Sorry, my boy. I won't be able to pick you up anyway. I have a late meeting again.'

'I can fetch him,' Tara finds herself saying.

'Really? But I thought you said Encounters was—'

'It's fine.' If she arrives a few minutes early to pick him up, then she'll be able to see for herself what it's all about. And she's not immune to the satisfying prospect of defying Olivia.

Martin slumps with relief. 'Thanks, Tara.'

'Go get your stuff together,' Stephen says. 'We're leaving in five minutes.'

Martin whoops and races out.

Stephen frowns down at her. 'What the hell was that about? I thought you said that Encounters stuff was what set Martin off in the first place?'

She shrugs. 'Maybe I was wrong.'

'How's your hand this morning?'

'I'll live.' Which is more than can be said for Baby Tommy. The thought makes her crumple inside again. 'You want me to call the school, tell them you won't be in today?'

Tara thinks about spending the day alone with the ruins of Baby Tommy's head. Can't face it. 'No. I want to go,' Tara says. 'Do me good to be out of the house.' The library will distract her. Besides, she wants to see how Jane is today. And if Duvenhage has told Clara about what happened at Raymond Scheider, well, so what?

'That's my baby.' Stephen reaches out to stroke her hair.

She pushes his hand away. 'Don't call me baby. You haven't called me that in months. Why start now?'

Stephen recoils, frowns down at her, opens his mouth to say something, then thinks better of it. He's trying, Tara knows. But far as she's concerned, it's too little too late.

She's half an hour late for volunteer duty. She decided to make an effort, have a shower, shave her legs, blow-dry her hair and apply make-up in an attempt to put on a brave front, but this had taken longer than she thought it would. She couldn't bring herself to rush this morning.

She spots Clara emerging from Duvenhage's office as she heads down the corridor towards the library. She ducks her head, prays in vain that Clara won't spot her.

'Oh, good morning, Mrs Marais,' Clara calls.

Tara turns around and slaps what she hopes is a convincing smile on her face. 'Morning. Sorry I'm late.'

Clara's beady eyes flick to Tara's bandaged hand. 'What have you done to your hand?'

Oh, this? I burnt it on a baby's head. It would almost be worth saying it out loud just to see the expression on Clara's face. 'I was... cooking steak, burnt it on the grill.'

'Shame.'

'I'd better get on,' Tara says, scurrying away before Clara has a chance to say anything else.

She pushes through the library doors. Malika is sitting with the quiet-time kids, smothering a yawn, but the second she spots Tara she leaps up excitedly and waves her over. Tara smiles back at her, but doesn't approach. The last thing she feels like right now is listening to whatever snippet of gossip Malika's clearly dying to tell her.

Tara looks around for Jane, but can't see her anywhere. The other members of Jane's reading class are here – she's already spied Skye kneeling next to the Enid Blyton shelf.

'Tara!' Malika hisses.

'Hang on a minute,' she mouths back, before hustling over to Skye. 'Hey, Skye. You seen Jane?'

He looks up and rubs his eyes. 'Huh? Who, miss?'

'The new girl. Come on, Skye, you know who I mean.'

'Oh, *her*. No. She's off sick.'

'What's wrong with her?'

'I dunno.'

Tara drops to her knees next to him. 'Skye, when you all lined up during the fire drill, why didn't you want to hold her hand?'

'I just didn't.'

'Has she ever said anything to you about her family?'

'No, miss. She… she doesn't usually say anything.' He starts picking his nose and Tara has to stop herself from slapping his hand away. 'She just watches us, miss.'

'What do you mean, watches you?'

'She just stares at us all the time. It's creepy. And she smells funny.'

'That's not very nice.'

'You asked me, miss.'

'It's hard being different, Skye.'

Skye gives her a 'no shit, lady' look, and she decides to stop pressing him.

'Tara!' Malika calls again, not bothering to keep her voice down this time.

Unable to ignore her any longer, Tara sighs and makes her way over. 'What's up?'

Malika waves her into the corner of the room, her lips pressed together in suppressed excitement. 'Oh my God, Tara. You are not going to believe what Sybil told me this morning.'

'What is it?'

'It's that new guy. That janitor guy. Ryan what's-his-name. You know the guy I mean. I swear to *God* I knew there was something shifty about him.'

'What are you talking about?'

'The cops were here first thing this morning. Sybil says they're asking questions about him.'

'What's he done?'

Malika leans in closer, licks her lips. 'I shouldn't really say... Sybil asked me to keep it quiet.'

Brilliant job so far, Tara thinks. But she's curious all the same. 'You know it won't go any further.'

This is all the encouragement Malika needs. 'Well, they're looking for him. One of his neighbours has accused him of... *doing things* to his daughter.'

Tara recoils, swamped with mixed emotions. Horror, of course, but also a sense of relief that her instincts were right about him. Hard to forget the intense way he stared at Jane when they were out on the quad during the fire drill. 'And? Have they caught him?'

'They can't find him. He's run away. Stole some school equipment, went into hiding. Sybil says that his ex-wife accused him of... interfering with his *own* daughter as well. And Julie is just hysterical.'

'Julie?'

'She volunteers at the tuck shop. You know her, Artemis's mom. Apparently she'd asked Ryan to do some handyman stuff around the house. God, when I think what she must be going through, knowing that she actually invited a monster like that into her own *home*. With her husband away all the time.'

'That's awful.'

'It's worse than awful, Tara. I mean, he's been rubbing shoulders with our kids, hasn't he? When I think he's been around Ruby and Sienna... A pervert like that? God, it makes my blood run cold just thinking about it. Seriously, if anyone did anything like that to my girls, well, Jase would just shoot them.' She pauses. Tara catches her staring at her hand, waits for her to ask about it. 'You look nice today, Tara,' Malika says, without mentioning the bandage.

'Thanks.'

'So what do you think we should do about it?'

'What do you mean?'

'Well, I think everyone should know, don't you? I mean, for all we know he could have been doing anything, interfering with kids here.' Malika shudders dramatically.

'I'm sure the cops know what they're doing.'

Malika gives her a look of disgust. 'Sheesh, how long have you *been* in this country, Tara?'

Clara enters the library, shoots them an enquiring glance. 'Better get back to it,' Tara says.

'Yeah.' Malika nods, obviously disappointed with Tara's lack-lustre reaction.

Tara helps Skye choose a starter text, and tries to lose herself in the tale of *Brian the Bullying Bunny*. Being one of Duvenhage's books, it doesn't end on a happy note (Brian winds up being baked in a pie and eaten by the bunnies he previously teased).

The bell rings for break and the children quietly put their books away and file into the corridor. Malika sighs with relief and reapplies her lip gloss. 'Best head off to Woolies before I fetch Sienna and Ruby for their tennis lesson. So you really think I should keep it quiet?'

'I'm not sure what to do, Malika,' Tara says. She, more than anyone, is aware of the consequences of starting a witch-hunt. She should also think about heading home, but she's dreading the hours she'll have to kill before it's time to collect Martin. 'Hey, is Sienna going to that Encounters group again this afternoon?'

'Oh, absolutely.'

'You haven't noticed any... I don't know... weird behaviour from her? I mean after she came back from the first meeting?'

'Are you kidding? She's like a different kid, thank God.' Malika leans in closer. 'You know she's been in therapy?'

'Has she?'

'Ja.' Malika rolls her eyes. 'You hear about what happened last year?'

'I don't know the details,' Tara says, assuming that Malika must be referring to the Facebook bullying scandal her daughter was embroiled in.

'It was all blown out of proportion, of course. But Jason said she should get help. Speak to a child psychologist. Said she was becoming too bolshy, uncontrollable. He's paranoid that she'll end up some bratty teen who's only interested in make-up and boys.' Well, you can't fight genetics, Tara thinks uncharitably. 'Four hundred rand-plus an hour down the pan. But since she started going to Encounters she seems to have calmed down. Hasn't used any bad language, actually cleaned her room without being asked. It's like she's a different child.'

Yeah, Tara thinks, uncomfortable with how closely this account mirrors Martin's transformation – a Stepford child. 'You know what goes on at these meetings?'

Malika shrugs. 'They sit around and talk about their feelings, as far as I can tell.'

'So you're not worried about it?'

'Worried? Christ, no. It's a godsend if you ask me.' She hooks her bag over her shoulder. 'Whatever they're doing at those meetings, it's working. So what do you think?'

'About what?'

'About the pervert, of course. Should I let the other parents know?'

'Like I said, you're asking the wrong person.'

'Ja. I think I'll just mention it on Facebook, just in case. See you.' With that, she clacks her way out of the library, leaving Tara alone with her thoughts.

Tara jerks awake, wipes drool from her mouth. Suddenly panicked that she's slept the whole of the afternoon away, she checks the time. 4.45 p.m. Thank God. If she leaves now, she'll have more than enough time to see what the hell goes on in those Encounters meetings. She hopes she's not over the limit. She'll just have to take it easy; it's unlikely that there will be any roadblocks this close to rush hour.

Still aching from Baby Tommy's demise, the first thing Tara did when she returned home after library duty was pour herself a slug of Stephen's Johnnie Walker Black. She's not much of a drinker, and the alcohol made her gag as she knocked it back, but she needed something to get through the rest of the day. The second shot went down easier, as did the third. Numb and blurry, she spent the rest of the afternoon slumped in Stephen's La-Z-Boy, flicking through the DStv channels and dozing.

She doesn't feel inebriated, although her mouth tastes as if she's been licking the toilet bowl. She should really brush her teeth, but she can't be bothered to slog upstairs to the bathroom. She stands up and stretches, stumbling slightly. She's light-headed, but she reckons that's probably because she hasn't eaten today. She didn't have *that* much to drink.

Her phone buzzes. Strange, she doesn't remember turning it back on. She digs it out of her bag, checks her inbox. Surprise, surprise, it's another message from the tenacious Batiss.

<today delivery eastgate mall lower female ablutions 6 pm>

Tara sighs. What part of 'no' does this freak not understand? She taps in a response. <I TOLD you job is off. Send bank details for a refund>

<not acceptable. needababy. Delivery or contract breach. Input option>

Clearly Batiss is not going to give up. Does she really want to be hounded by this weirdo day and night? What should she do? *Could* she start again? Create another Tommy? The thought makes her sick inside – you can't just replace a child, can you? She taps in: <Send bank details. Job is off>

She's expecting a flurry of beeps, but there's no response.

She grabs her bag, finds herself hesitating next to the drinks cabinet. One last shot won't hurt. She'll still be fine to drive, won't she?

She's about to turn into the school gates, even goes so far as to flick on her indicator, then finds herself driving straight past. Doesn't dare second-guess herself as she cruises up to Jane's house, marvelling again at the outrageousness of that exterior wall. She pulls up on the verge on the opposite side of the road, just outside the entrance of a townhouse complex. The complex's guard steps out of his cubicle, eyes her suspiciously, fingers the walkie-talkie on his belt. She waves at him, smiles reassuringly. He nods and disappears back inside.

Why is she here at all? She's not responsible for Jane, is she? So what now? If she wants to check on Jane, then her only choice is to knock on the door and ask to see her. But is she really up to facing Jane's freakish mother again?

Then again, there's nothing wrong with being concerned about Jane's welfare, is there? She'll make it quick, check Jane's okay, then race back to the school, insist on being allowed to sit in on the Encounters meeting. Decision made, she slides out of the car, stumbling over the curb. She's not drunk exactly, but she's definitely slightly unsteady, and the alcohol is adding an aura of unreality to the afternoon light.

She crosses the road, pushes through the gates, straightens her back as if she has every right to be there. Glances at the dark mouth of the garage next to the house, suddenly hit with an image of Martin's drawing. The bogeyman, he'd called it. For an instant, she's sure she can see something moving in its shadows and she feels an overwhelming compulsion to flee back to the car.

A door slams. She sighs in relief when she sees Jane waving at her. She isn't wearing her school uniform – in fact, she's dressed like a mini Barbie in high-heeled plastic shoes and a pink dress that's several sizes too large for her.

'Hi, Jane.'

Jane totters towards her. She doesn't look at all surprised to see Tara standing in her driveway.

'I heard you weren't at school today. Are you sick?'

'Sick?'

'I mean, have you been ill?'

Jane smiles. 'No, miss.' Jane moves closer to Tara, sniffs the air. 'You smell funny, like he does.'

'Like who does?'

'The brown.'

Tara sighs. Not more of this shit, she thinks. 'So why weren't you at school?'

'I've been watching Ryan, miss.'

Oh shit, Tara thinks. She swallows, hit with a sudden wave of nausea. 'Who's Ryan?'

'The brown, of course. He tends the garden, miss.'

It can't be the Ryan the cops are looking for – what would he be doing at Jane's house? But she needs to be sure. 'Jane. This Ryan. Is he the one who used to work at the school?'

'Yes, miss.'

'Listen to me. You need to stay away from him. I think he might want to…' Might want to what? Just how in the hell is she going to explain the concept of molestation to this child? 'Has he ever tried to… touch you, Jane?'

Jane smiles again. 'Yes, miss.'

Tara fumbles for her phone, realises she's left it and her bag in the car. *Goddammit*. 'I need to speak to your mother, Jane. Right away.'

'She's not available, miss.'

'And where is Ryan?'

'He's with the beans, miss.'

She must mean the garden. The last thing Tara wants to do is spook him, or even worse, confront him. He could be dangerous. There's no knowing what he'll do if he's cornered.

But she can't leave Jane here alone with him, can she? 'I think you should come with me, Jane.'

'Where to, miss?'

'Um… It's not safe for you here, Jane. Not alone with that… with Ryan.'

'Oh. I'm not alone, miss. Danish is here.'

'Can I talk to this Danish, Jane?'

'I don't know, miss. Can you?'

Jesus. 'Can you fetch him for me?'

'No, miss. He's helping.'

'Can you take me to him?'

'No, miss.' She laughs as if she's just thought of a private joke. 'Today's forespecial. Trespassers will be corrected.'

Tara weighs up her options, aware that thanks to the whisky she's battling to think clearly. Decides that the only thing to do is to run to her car and fetch her cellphone. Call the cops and wait here with Jane till they arrive.

'I'm just going to fetch something from the car. Wait here, okay?'

Jane laughs her shrill laugh again. 'See you later alligator in a while crocodile.'

Tara slips through the gate, crosses the road, dives into her car, her fingers trembling as she fumbles in her bag for her phone. Where the hell is it? She roots through her stuff, resorts to tipping it out onto the passenger seat. Nothing. It's not here! Goddammit! Did she leave it in the house after she received that last message from Batiss?

'Fuck!' she yells.

She looks up, sees the security guard watching her distrustfully again.

She slams her car door, hurries over to him. 'Hi. I need help. Do you have a phone I can use?'

'A phone, madam?'

'A cellphone.' She grabs twenty rand out of her pocket, thrusts it in his direction. 'Please. Can you call the cops?'

'Why, madam?'

'I have reason to believe there's a very dangerous man staying at that house.'

His eyes flick towards the gate of Jane's house.

'Please. Will you just do that for me? Tell them that Ryan...' Shit, what's his surname? 'The maintenance man who used to work at Crossley College is hiding out in that house. They'll know who you mean.' At least Tara hopes they will. Surely there must be some sort of APB or whatever they call it in this country out on him.

The guard looks her up and down, then nods. 'Which police station?'

Tara's about to say, *Just call 911, stupid*, but stops herself just in time. If there is a national emergency number in South Africa, she doesn't know it. 'I don't know. The closest one. Please. A child could be in danger.'

The guard nods again and steps back into his cubicle. Tara hopes to God he'll do as she asks.

She hustles back across the road, pushes against the gates. They don't budge. That can't be right. She didn't see anyone locking them behind her. 'Jane?' she calls. 'Jane?'

She peers through the gap between the gates. The sandy area in front of the house is deserted. Jane must have gone back inside. And – *goddammit* – without her phone she can't let Martin know she might be late, or call Stephen and ask him to collect his son. It must almost be time to pick him up now.

What the hell should she do?

It will only take a few minutes to collect Martin, then she could head straight back here. By then the cops should have arrived. And then what? Hopefully child services will have the good sense to take Jane away from that horrendous family. She can only hope that nothing will happen to the girl while she's gone.

She jumps into the driver's seat, guns the engine and pulls out into the traffic without looking in her side mirror for oncoming cars. A black Mercedes swerves past her, narrowly avoids swiping her car. Ignoring the scream of a car horn and shouted abuse from the furious driver, she puts her foot down. She cuts through the side streets, taking chances. In her haste she takes a wrong turn and ends up in a cul de sac, has to backtrack to the main road, aware that she's losing valuable minutes. Her shirt is damp with perspiration when she finally pulls through the school gates. She's in time to see Malika driving away, makes out the shape of Sienna's head slumped against the passenger side window.

The parking lot is empty – Martin must still be inside. Where

has the time gone? The clock in her car is faulty, she has no clue how late she is. She jumps out of the car and jogs towards the front door, sees Mr Duma, the head maintenance man, about to secure the security gate.

'Mr Duma!'

He turns around. 'Ja?'

She pants up next to him, and he recoils slightly. She realises she must reek of stale whisky and sweat. 'I'm here to fetch my step-son. I think he must still be inside.'

He shrugs. 'I'm sorry, madam, but there is no one else inside. They have all gone.'

'But… that can't be right. He's not out here. Where do they hold the meetings?'

'In the school hall, madam.'

'Can I go look?' Before Mr Duma has a chance to answer, she pushes past him, feet skidding over the laminate flooring as she thumps towards the hall. She shoulders the doors open, darts inside. It's empty.

'Martin?' Her voice echoes through the space. 'Martin?' She spots something on the floor next to the base of the stage.

She races towards it. It's a phone – an iPhone.

Hands shaking with adrenaline, she bends to pick it up, feels her legs turn to water when she recognises the Jay-Z sticker on its back.

It's Martin's.

Chapter 18

PENTER

After what she's seen in Father's study, Penter feels a nauseous turmoil she's never experienced before. She needs to calm down or she will projectile over the carpet, which would be wasteful.

She's not sure what she expected to find, but it wasn't *that*.

She paces through the top floor of the house, past her bedroom then back again. Her skin itches as if she's grimed with the filth of this upside world. The diseases the Ministry's manuals describe are the least of it. It's the smut they pump into the air, the violence they celebrate on the television, the things they do to each other on SKY. It all makes her feel heavy inside and coated in dirt. She hears the whoosh of water flowing through the pipes. The brown, abluting again. The thought of it makes her want to purge, to stand under the water of the shower for hours until she is scrubbed clean.

'Mother?'

She turns and sees Jane, who takes her hand, leads her down the corridor. Penter covers her mouth and nose with her hand as they pass the brown's room.

Jane pulls her into one of the few rooms with unobscured windows. 'Look,' she says, pointing at the glass.

Penter looks out into the precinct and sees the educator trespassing through the gate. 'What does it want, Jane? Did you invite it here? Did... did Father ask you to contact it again?'

'No, Mother. Shall I go and talk to it?'

As the Mother, Penter should be the one to go downstairs and oust it from the precinct, but right now she can't deal with it. 'Thank you, Jane. Please tell it that I am not available.'

Jane smiles. 'Of course. Today,' she says brightly, 'trespassers will be corrected!'

Penter watches as Jane exits the room, listens to her light footfalls, then makes her way down into the kitchen. Danish is there, packing up the appliances and the other props. When his back is turned, she removes a mimeograph of Father from its frame and slips it up her sleeve. Why? He is a Player with warped predilections, baser even than a brown, but for some reason she wants to keep this picture, as if it will remind her of the time before she saw his... collection.

She steps into the hallway. She can hear Jane conversing with the woman, but cannot make out the words. She will give Jane a primo recommendation.

'Danish,' she calls. He scuttles towards her. 'Wait for the brown to leave and then lock the gates. Ask Jane to meet me in the garden.'

Danish nods, shivers. His hands are trembling, his eyes are dull in his skull. After he has completed his duties here, he will be sent straight to the Terminal Ward for recycling, although Penter cannot imagine that he'd have any viable parts.

She walks outside, pauses next to the swimming pool. There is a depreciated thing floating in the water, its belly bloated and white, its eyes opaque. She sighs. All the life up here that is left to rot away in the sun. She picks up a stick, drags the creature to the edge, scoops it out with her hand. She places it in the grass, watches as an army of ants quickly surrounds it. She enjoys watching them work together in the kitchen and in the garden. Nothing distracts them from their duty.

And nothing must distract her.

Jane is already in the garden when she arrives, playing with another of the pets that Danish has scouted for her, a black thing with too many legs that's running over and through her fingers. Each time it tries to skitter away, Jane catches it in her cupped hands. She does not seem to tire of the game.

'Will you miss the upside, Jane?'

'No, Mother,' Jane says.

'Not even the sun?'

'No. Not even the motherfucking sun.'

'What about your chum? That educator? Will you miss her?'

'Oh, her. No.' Jane laughs, almost like a real brown. Jane does not incite the same gut-turning emotions in her as Father does – *did* – but Penter's still pleased that Jane holds so little regard for the educator. 'She said that Ryan was dangerous. That he wanted to touch me.'

Penter laughs with her, feeling lighter. So that was all it was. 'She thought we didn't know?'

Jane smiles at her and clenches her fist, squishing the pet between her fingers. 'I told her that today is forespecial and that trespassers will be corrected.'

'Goody good,' Penter answers, although her levity is strained by nerves. She herself has trespassed inside Father's study. She doesn't know if she's doing the right thing; what the right thing is.

She wonders how Jane will evaluate her. 'Jane, do you think I was a good Mother?'

'Yes. You were primo.'

'Should I have shown more... love?' She watches Jane's expression. Does she even know about love?

Jane smiles as she drops the depreciated pet onto the ground, touches her hand. 'No, Mother. That would be obtuse. Laters.'

Penter watches as Jane slips back through the garden and into the house, leaving her alone with her karking thoughts.

Penter spends a moment saying goodbye to the garden. She feels lucky not to have had to leave the precinct. She may not be delicate, but she is pleased she didn't have to see first-hand how the browns deface the surface of their world; the pictures of the unsightly mess on TV are bad enough. She looks up at the sun for one last time; it makes her eyes water.

She picks a handful of ready beans. She'll petition the Ministry and Management to let her grow a tame bean plant in her Apartment. She has done well. She has been a good Mother, a good home-maker, and they will credit her for this.

They would also credit her if she told them that Father is collecting upside artefacts for his personal use.

Father *is* a Player after all. After what she has seen, there is no doubt. How can such a scenic man have such unnatural preferences?

She takes the mimeograph out of her sleeve, traces the shape of his face with her finger. She tries the words in her head, the only safe place to do so. *I love you, Father.*

But first, she thinks, watching Ryan move the ladder to clean the top-floor windows, there is one piece of unfinished business that she and Father must conclude together.

Chapter 19

RYAN

Ryan's up a ladder again, this time cleaning windows that are opaque with red soil and concrete dust. From this vantage point he watched Danish take Jane out in the car at lunchtime. He hoped he'd come back and take Mother out somewhere too, but when he returned half an hour later, Jane was still with him.

He has to wait until they are all away from the house before he can go and explore upstairs, but meanwhile he can case the upper rooms as he washes the windows. Up to now, he's seen nothing remarkable, just vacant rooms, their fitted carpets stripped back and rolled to the side, the once-white lacquer paint on the built-in cupboards yellow with age, nothing on the walls but outlines of departed picture frames, peeled pockmarks where posters were once hung.

Now he's hauled the ladder around to the back of the house. He turns away, dunks the sponge into the soapy bucket, sluices it onto the pane. Making things clean, repairing loose ends, has always been calming to him. He rubs away the dirt, causing the glass to squeak and shine. He thinks of Tess, her sad little hideout in the bushes. He thinks of Alice and Karin, growing out of his reach.

He rubs at the window until he can see inside. Again there's nothing in it, but unlike the other rooms this one is carpeted with an expanse of new, earth-brown plush and the walls are painted dove grey.

When he goes down the ladder with the bucket, he automatically checks for Jane, but she's either inside or out of sight. He shifts the ladder to the next window and brings up the loppers and the saw to hack back the gnarled wattle boughs that obscure it. He makes sure the ladder's stable and harnesses himself to it, stretching a little too much to get at the branches. He's done this enough to know how far is too far, he figures, but when a pigeon flaps out in front of him and the ladder almost tips, he has to grasp at the downpipe to keep from falling and cuts his right palm again.

The sharp pain in his palm clears his head, and he goes down to the garden tap to rinse his hand. The cut's not too deep this time; he blots it on his jeans and it soon stops bleeding. He prepares a fresh bucket of soapy water for the next window, scanning the garden for Jane as he climbs up again.

This window looks into a study, Ryan sees as he gradually clears the grime. It's dark inside, with a heavy wooden desk laden with neat piles of papers and old-fashioned ledgers in leather bindings, an olive-green rotary-dial telephone and a rolodex. There are two straight-backed wooden chairs on the brown carpet and, as Ryan rubs, he can make out a grey steel filing cabinet against one wall, a calendar, a cork pinboard with lists of numbers... Hang on...

Ryan rubs too hurriedly, smudging the clean glass again with the sediment from the filthy section. He dunks and rinses the sponge again, wipes. Yes, next to the pinboard is a series of pictures... photos...

Ryan remembers vomiting into the waste bin in Sybil Fontein's office.

They can't be, his mind objects, but Ryan knows they're the same pictures as Duvenhage's. He can see the shape of the children laid out on their gurneys. It's not so much the pastel colours of their skin – pale blues and purples and pinks and greys – it's those dark lines scrawled on the bodies that convince him. They have to be the same pictures.

What the hell are they doing hanging on the wall in this house?

He hurries down the ladder, hoping this time that the girl's not watching him. He washes his hands and arms under the garden tap with a good squeeze of washing-up liquid. He heads to his room, piles his few belongings into his backpack.

He should just go, he knows. Now. Don't ask questions. Isn't what he's seen proof enough that Duvenhage has something to do with these people? That it's some elaborate trap?

Evidently it's not enough, because now he's creeping through the lounge, expecting to find Jane hiding somewhere. But there's nothing, nobody... The house is dead quiet. This deep into it, he can't even hear birdsong from outside. The world is muffled.

Up the stairs, also carpeted in earth brown, that same smell of must and soil pervading everything. Instead of up, he feels like he's going into a cave. The landing has no lights on and all the doors are closed. The passageway is like a dark tunnel. The thick carpet absorbs the sound of his footsteps. The loudest sound is his breath.

Ryan gets to the rooms on the south side. There are signs up on each of the doors in this row. *Heed the notices*, she said.

'No admittance to unauthorised personnel. Trespassers will be corrected.'

Ryan maps the windows he's just cleaned. Which door will lead to the study?

He tries the door on the far right.

Good choice.

The dark contents of the study seem to flinch away from the yellow afternoon sunlight coming through the window, as if someone has just shone a floodlight into a night creature's burrow. A flurry of dust motes rides the beam of sunlight as Ryan peers in and then enters, closing the door quietly behind him.

He goes straight to the gallery of bodies on the wall. He knew it, but the confirmation still kicks him in the gut. These are the same fucking photos. Ryan can't help scanning them again, although what he should do is turn and go. Printed out like this the children look so much more like children, and so much more vulnerable, their nakedness much more vivid.

The churning in Ryan's gut is compounded by the fact that this family has something to do with Duvenhage. It can't be a coincidence. They must have lured him here deliberately somehow. But why haven't they done anything yet? They've let him come and go as he pleased, they've let him leave to get food at the shops. He could have escaped any time he liked. What sort of game are they playing?

The neat header above the gallery of portraits reads 'Edification Hub 1:307:561/h Exemplar Viability Assessment Mark-Up'. That's something like the label of the directory on Duvenhage's disk. The children's skin is uniformly pale, but on the high-definition prints he can see the detail on their bodies, the sort of bruises and scars and minor wounds that kids get. Some of them still have small dressings or healed scars on their faces. The children lie with their eyes closed, in a deep sleep.

Ryan can't bring himself to believe they're not asleep.

And here, half obscured by a list of figures, is a portrait of a black-haired girl wearing the Crossley uniform, and fuck, she's got pale grey eyes and high cheekbones. It's Jane. There's no doubt about it, Jane is looking back at him, twisting his gut with her eyes just like the real girl does.

Ryan shifts out of the light from the window and crouches to look closer at the photo. Jane's eyebrows are straw pale. The black hair must be a dye job or a wig. Why? It covers her ears, and there may be a bandage pressing the lower lobes to her head. Maybe. He can't make out that much detail in the postcard-sized photo, but there's something there under her ears. What have they done to her? What are they doing to all these kids?

Moving across to the desk, Ryan grabs the first leather-covered ledger, but it's just filled in with hand-written numbers. There's a blue-card folder placed squarely to one side of the pristine desk blotter. It's marked 'Encounters Pilot: Crossley College, Node 2:34:731/s'. He opens it, scans a list of names and numbers he can't make sense of.

Node 2:34:731/s Battery 1.3 - Encounters/Crossley College

Learner	est. inculc.	aptitude	est. viable lb	est. deprec.	rate
Brawn, P.	0503	98	121.3	0708	w
Da Gama, Z.	0702	87	98.3	1305	e
Dlamini, S.	1901	76	124.2	1404	x
Khumalo, F.	0802	95	134.9	1306	h
Hallock, J.	0901	85	96.2	1909	e
Hofstadter, E.	1302	89	131.7	2708	e
Marais, M.	0503	107	137.8	2906	h
Molope, H.	0103	76	110.7	0407	e
Pollard, V.	2802	99	154.2	2303	x
Ponzi, S.	1902	103	103.2	2205	h
White, K.	0303	92	112	0807	w
Xaba, K.	3001	89	107.2	2705	e

He flips the page, there's a letter beneath.

Headmaster _KENNETH DUVENHAGE_,

    It is with pleasure that we confirm our
transfer arrangements for the pilot exercise
of the Encounters scouting programme which you
have kindly agreed to allow us to run at your
Institution. In payment for the lease of _CROSSLEY
COLLEGE_ premises and access to _TWELVE (12)_
selected learners for purposes of assessment for
donor viability or operational aptitude, we confirm
payment of 67% balance of _ZAR 1,892,146.72_
towards _BSA_ account number _564-324-099_ on
period pay run date stipulated in Ministry of
Energy Contractors' Guidelines section 16.3.7.

    We thank you for facilitating the assimilation
of the pilot project's Viability Scout _JANE
SMITH_ into your Institution. The pilot has been a
great success and has identified prime candidates
and we look forward to rolling out the project in
several Institutions in the node in the periods
to come. The Ministry of Upside Relations has
reissued its Codes of Engagement, which are
enclosed herewith.

Yours in continued respect and cooperation,

Varder Batiss,
Senior Liaison, Ministry of Upside Relations

  Whatever this means, the massive amount of money changing
hands catches Ryan's eye. Duvenhage is in on something even

more crooked than kiddie porn. It all makes a twisted sort of sense. He can't shake the feeling that he should make Duvenhage pay, but he's got to come up with a better plan than a petty blackmail scheme. If only he had more of a criminal mind.

And what is this about Jane? What does 'Viability Scout' mean? Is it a foreign-exchange programme for Girl Guides or something? If Jane is a Girl Guide, it'd be just another reason for the brats at Crossley to shun her. The poor girl is most definitely not being assimilated properly.

'Assessment for donor viability' for a shitload of money? What does it mean? 'Rolling out the project in several Institutions'? Is it some sort of trafficking ring? And would child traffickers keep such careful written records? Wouldn't they want to cover their tracks? Ryan can't make sense of it. Then again, he supposes, the Nazis left behind a huge paper trail, didn't they?

Whatever it is, there's something not right going on here, but who can he tell? Who would believe him? Who would be able to do anything about it? He's not about to go to the cops about this. They'd just look at him blankly, then arrest him for whatever Tess's father thinks he did to her. Persecuted for showing a girl some tenderness; it's ironic.

Ziggy? He's a lawyer in some NGO, isn't he? He deals with stuff like this, doesn't he? Maybe that's his best bet. He can't just leave things like this. He's got to help these kids, expose this thing.

He uses his phone to take a photo of the letter and of the lists on the pinboard and of the photo collection. Then he takes one for himself of the picture of Jane with her black hair.

He types out a message to Ziggy. <Ziggy. Something illegal going on at Crossley. Money for kids or something. Abuse? Trafficking? Sending docs now. Check Duvenhage. Ryan>

Come to think of it, that library volunteer woman was here the other day with Jane. Could she be in on it? What the fuck was her name? Oh, yes... Tara something. He remembers because it's the name of that psychiatric hospital and he thought she could probably fit in well there.

<Also check library volunteer, Tara someone. She's in on it too. Thanks>

He presses send. He's pleased with himself – Ziggy will really help, maybe stop this happening to these kids. He's done a good thing here.

He closes the Crossley folder and places it to the side of the blotter, where it was when he came in. He's making for the study door when he hears a thump in the passage outside. He scans the room; there's a built-in cupboard where he can hide and he ducks inside and closes the door behind him.

It's dark in the closet but he feels space around him, can smell perfume and paint thinner, more of that wet-clay odour. As his eyes adjust, he notices that he's in a large space like a walk-in closet, lined with shelves. His phone beeps. It's a reply from Ziggy.

<You're sick, Ryan. The girl's father showed us the pictures, and the police. Turn yourself in, now. That's the last advice you're getting from me.>

The pictures? Which pic— Oh, fuck... Duvenhage's drive. Fransie must have made a copy. Christ, they think they're his. The pictures of the kids' bodies...

Oh, God, what must they think of him? Has Alice seen them? They'd never show them to Alice, would they?

But he's not sure. Karin could use them as the ultimate poison against him. They'd never believe a word he said.

He grabs his forehead with his hands and slumps back against the wall inside the cupboard. A light comes on and dazzles him for a moment.

At first he's not sure what he's seeing. The shelves are lined with transparent plastic boxes. There should be shoes or jewellery on display, but in each one is a dead baby.

Ryan tries to pull his eyes away; his mind wills his body to get

out, to face whatever's outside the study door, but his hand is rais-
ing the lid of the first coffin, his fingers are trailing over the first
baby's blue skin. It smells of cotton wool and dust, of perfume and
vinegar. Its skin is as warm as the room, and smooth but slightly
tacky. He presses his fingertips into its cheek and the flesh gives
slightly.

He can see the veins underneath its skin, can feel the softness
of its eyelashes and eyebrows. There's a fluff of peach down on
its lip, on its jawline under its ear. She's dressed in a pink-striped
babygrow with a smiley face and 'Be Juicy' printed across it.

The baby is dead. The baby is fucking *dead*.

He looks up and away from this little girl, drops the coffin lid
and backs away.

He doesn't want to count them; he doesn't want to see any more.

He just wants to go home.

He backs out of the closet and opens the study door.

Jane's on the landing, standing in the dark, looking at him.
'Come and see,' she says. 'It's gonna be legen... Wait for it...' She
stands there holding up one finger.

This is all too much. Ryan must get his things and go. His head
is eating itself from the inside.

'Come and see,' she says again. She walks a few steps down the
corridor to the next closed room. The same sign on the door: 'Trespassers will be corrected.'

'No. I should go,' says Ryan, but Jane opens the door and goes
inside. This is the bare room he saw from the window. A shape of
light falls across the brown carpet.

'This is my bedroom,' Jane says.

'But there's nothing in it,' Ryan says. Apart from, he now notices,
rows of jars stacked underneath the windowsill. Oh, fuck... Jars full
of insects and the stiff body of a rat.

'See?' She opens the door of a closet. Hangers with identical school dresses, the shelves stacked with neat piles of white blouses, navy cardigans and tan skirts. 'I can go in here,' she says, crouching down below the dresses.

She sleeps in the closet? Jesus Christ.

She doesn't come out, and Ryan ducks down to look for her. She's gone.

He notices a darker space in the back of the closet. It's a tunnel or a room. A panel's been shifted away beside it; she's gone through there. He crawls into the closet and peers into the darkness.

'I know what you do,' she says, her voice further away than it should be. 'I've seen you. It makes me... interested.'

It's time to go, Ryan.

He shuffles on his hands and knees into the dark. There's the feel of dry brick dust on his hands, a damp, earthy odour; the sound of scraping.

Scuffling. Is it Jane crawling further down the tunnel, or something else? He's crawled into the tunnel now, perhaps three metres in. He hears his own breathing, nothing else.

'Jane?' he says softly. 'Where are you?'

He hears a noise behind him, out in the room. He looks over his shoulder at the rich copper light from the room. A shape falls across it. The light goes out.

Jesus. Someone's locked him in here. The tunnel's too narrow to turn in so he backtracks on his hands and knees. 'Jane. Where are you?'

It's dark. He's scrabbling backwards and the dust tunnel turns to smooth melamine. He's back in the closet. The doors are closed; he kicks at them.

'Hello, mister?' Mother's voice.

'Let me out. What the—'

'Why are you in here, mister? I did instruct you not to transgress on this level.'

'I was invited in. By, by...' He points into the closet. All he sees is the closet's white back panel. The tunnel's been closed up.

'By what?'

'By...' Fuck it. *And what were you doing following my daughter into a closet?* 'Sorry. I got lost. I didn't know where I was.'

'Come. Look at this.' This is a new voice, a man's voice, powerful, but somehow false, like it's been amplified electronically. The door opens and Ryan looks up, from where he's kneeling beneath the dresses, at Mother and the man. This must be Father, the gangster, the foreign minister, whatever the fuck he is. The man who keeps pictures of children's corpses and a collection of dead babies. He's wearing a navy three-piece suit, black trainers and a grey tie. He has a massive lantern jaw and a tiny pinched nose, unreal somehow, like a Ken doll. His little eyes squint at Ryan myopically and emotionlessly. 'Come,' he repeats.

Ryan has no choice but to follow him out of Jane's room and back along the passage.

'What is this?' the man asks, pointing to the door to the study.

'I'm sorry, I can't see,' Ryan says.

'Here,' says the man, pointing at the doorknob. It's too dark, but Ryan can see enough. *Shit.* He looks at his hand where the blood from the cut has made a muddy paste with the brick dust. Even in this light Ryan can see that the brass doorknob is stained.

'You saw the notification?'

'Yes, I'm sorry. I... I'm sorry. Let me just go. I've appreciated the work but can accept responsibility. You've been kind. I should go.'

'You do not "go",' Mother says. 'Jane has chosen you wisely. She knows that you can educate.'

'Educate? Educate who? I don't teach...'

'Jane says you are forespecial with halfpints. You have no place to "go". You will come with us. You will educate,' Mother says. 'You are in our debt.'

'What? I've worked for the money you've paid me. I don't need this. Just let me go.'

'You purloined from my associate,' the man says. 'Mr Doowenharger.'

Ryan feels faint and he has to lean against the wall to avoid falling.

'You have trespassed against notifications, you have purloined,' the man says. 'You have been chosen. You will come with us.'

Ryan weighs up the chance that the man has a gun against his desperate need to run, and running seems like a good idea. He takes off down the corridor and when he gets to the stairs without being shot he thinks he's made it.

But Jane is standing in the hallway at the bottom of the stairs and touches him with something. All his muscles stop working at the same time in mid-stride and he clatters to the floor, face and elbows and chest and shins first. He skids along, leaving drool and blood in his wake.

Jane crouches over him and for a moment he sees her touching her fingertips to the cut on his hand. She looks at the blood with that same curiosity he saw all that time ago, sniffs it, rubs it on her white school blouse.

That's the first time she's touched me, Ryan thinks, before everything goes quiet inside. Her fingers are cold.

Chapter 20

TARA

Tara hasn't felt this level of anxiety since... well, since it all blew up back in Jersey. Her palms are clammy, her clothes feel as if they're two sizes too small, and she can't dislodge the feeling that whatever has happened to Martin is somehow her fault. If only she'd made it to the school five minutes earlier, if she hadn't left her phone back at the house, Martin might now be safely up in his room or sitting slouched in the lounge playing *Diablo VII*.

Stephen's holding onto the hope that Martin's just run away, that he's decided to give them all a fright, but in her gut Tara knows this isn't the case.

Despite the things she's heard about the South African Police Service, so far she's been impressed by how efficiently Martin's disappearance has been handled. She has no way of knowing if this is how the SAPS usually reacts to a missing child, or if it's because Stephen's pulled all the strings at his disposal. For the last hour, Superintendent Molefi, a beautiful, apparently unflappable woman with tired eyes and French-manicured nails, has been trying to inject some calm into the atmosphere with practical, solid questions. It's not working. Both Olivia and Stephen have responded snappishly, as if they blame the policewoman for Martin's disappearance.

'Mrs Marais.' The policewoman turns her attention to Tara. 'When you dropped Martin off at school yesterday morning, did you notice anything unusual about his behaviour?'

'We went through all this last night!' Olivia interrupts. 'How many more times? Martin is a good white boy from a good home, it's not as if he's some common street kid addicted to drugs. Why won't you people listen? He has *not* run away!'

Superintendent Molefi doesn't lose her composure at this outburst. 'We are doing everything we can to find your son, Ms Marais—'

'It's *Mrs,* can't you even get that right?'

'My apologies. It can be confusing as there are two of you here with the same name.'

Stephen rolls his eyes. 'No wonder this country is such a fuck-up if you can't even get that straight.'

Ignoring Stephen's comment, the policewoman fixes her gaze on Tara again. 'Mrs Marais?'

Tara clears her throat, glances at Olivia, who's squinting at her through the smoke wafting out of her mouth. The coffee cup she's using as an ashtray is brimming with butts – she's been chain-smoking ever since she showed up last night and the air is hazy with smoke. 'Well... he has been acting differently lately. More subdued than usual.'

'Don't listen to her,' Olivia snaps. 'What does she know?'

'Have you spoken to that bloody arsehole Duvenhage yet?' Stephen jumps in. 'About those bloody meetings?'

'Martin should never have been there in the first place,' Olivia says, shooting another hate-filled glare at Tara.

Superintendent Molefi sighs. 'I assure you, we are doing everything in our power to get to the bottom of this.'

Stephen snorts. 'What about the other kids? The other kids who were at the meeting. Have you spoken to them?'

'Yes, Mr Marais. As I said before, they insist that Martin left the meeting when they did.'

'Well, someone must have seen something. What about the bloody people who were running the group?'

For the first time since she arrived, a flicker of uncertainty dances over the policewoman's features. 'We are trying to contact them, sir.'

'Well, you're not trying hard enough.'

The policewoman stands up, gathers her belongings together. 'Thank you for your cooperation.'

'That's it?'

'Yes, sir. I'll be in touch if I need to speak to you again.'

Olivia sighs. 'Bloody typical,' she mutters, angrily stubbing out her latest cigarette.

Tara follows the policewoman out of the room. 'What about that maintenance man? That Ryan guy?' she asks, keeping her voice low so that Stephen and Olivia won't overhear. 'Have you found him?'

Superintendent Molefi sighs. 'Not as yet, Mrs Marais.'

'Could he have anything to do with this?' Although, to be fair, if what Jane told her yesterday afternoon – that he was there at the time, tending the garden – was correct, Tara can't see how he would have managed to leave the house in time to abduct Martin. He could hardly have been in two places at once. But it's not just Martin who's concerning her. If the allegations about Ryan are true, then Jane could still be in danger.

'We are looking into it, Mrs Marais.'

'And what about that house? Jane's house. She said Ryan was working there.'

'We've been to the house, Mrs Marais. It's deserted.'

'It can't be! They were there yesterday.'

'I understand that you are upset, but I assure you, there is no one in that house.'

'What house?' Stephen asks from the doorway. 'And who's Ryan?'

Shit, Tara thinks. She'll have no choice but to tell him now. She's not looking forward to the consequences. Stephen and Olivia will be furious that she didn't mention this last night. 'A guy working at the school. Apparently he has some sort of criminal past.'

'What kind of criminal past, Tara?'

'Interfering with children.'

'*What?*' Olivia shrieks.

Stephen rounds on Superintendent Molefi. 'For fuck's sake. And this pervert was working at my son's school? What's *wrong* with you people?'

'Mr Marais. There is no connection between this man and the disappearance of your son, I assure you.' Stephen opens his mouth to speak again but she holds up a hand to forestall him. 'Now, if you want me to continue my investigation, I must leave. Please, contact me immediately if Martin gets in touch with you.'

Stephen grudgingly unlocks the security gate, and Superintendent Molefi heads out into the morning.

'And you knew about this, Tara?' This from Olivia. 'How could you know something like this and only tell us now?'

'I only found out yesterday.'

Olivia jabs a newly lit cigarette in Tara's direction. 'This is all your fault. I told Martin he shouldn't go back to that group. But you blatantly ignored my wishes.'

'Calm down, Olivia,' Stephen says.

'Don't you fucking tell me to calm down.'

'It's not Tara's fault. Although why she didn't tell us about this—'

'You see, Stephen? You see what sort of a woman you married? I hope you're happy now.'

Trying to block out Olivia's shrill accusations, Tara races up the stairs to her sanctuary, slams the door behind her. She paces around the room, stares up at the Baby Tommy collage above her desk, feels the tears sliding down her cheeks.

Her phone beeps. She snatches it out of her pocket, praying that it's Martin, remembering too late that she found his iPhone on the floor of the hall. Surprise, surprise, it's another message from Batiss. <ur in breach node agent en route>

<leave me alone>

<no can do. latrs xx>

'Fuck you,' she mutters.

She glances up at the Baby Tommy photo again, slides open Baby Paul's drawer and takes out Tommy's little charred head. For some reason, holding it comforts her. She wipes away her tears, breathes in deeply.

Was that policewoman telling the truth about Jane's house? How could they have all disappeared so quickly? If anything's happened to Jane, Tara knows she won't be able to live with herself. Bad enough that she destroyed Baby Tommy, that she wasn't there for Martin when he needed her.

No. She needs to see for herself.

She hurries downstairs. Stephen and Olivia are still screaming at each other in the lounge, and she prays they won't hear the click of the security gate as she slips out.

She climbs into the Pajero, glad that she parked it in the street in front of their small front garden rather than in the garage. As she executes a swift three-point turn, she sees Stephen stomping down the driveway towards her, face distorted with fury. She turns up the radio so that she can't hear whatever it is that he's yelling at her, accelerates away, forcing him to jump out of her path. She puts her foot down, scraping the side of her car on the edge of the intercom stand as she shoots into the main road.

The house's gates are slightly ajar. If she wanted to, she could easily slip inside.

But she doesn't go in immediately. She spends several minutes sitting outside the house in her car, watching, waiting. She isn't certain what she's expecting to see. A couple of police cars doing surveillance maybe, like in the movies. But there's no sign of any police presence, and today there doesn't appear to be anyone on duty in the security booth of the complex across the road. The lack of sleep is catching up with her. Her eyes feel gritty, her empty stomach churns. She opens her bag, looks down at Baby Tommy's head. She's still not sure why she brought him with her. Some sort of talisman, she supposes. She rubs off some of the soot, again regretting that she'll never get the chance to see what he'd look like whole.

Steeling herself, she slings her bag over her shoulder and climbs out of the car. Walks slowly towards the gates and slips between them. She turns to double-check that no one has seen her trespassing, feels a stab of jealously as a series of luxury cars zip past on the road, their drivers oblivious to how she's feeling, all of them on course for just another ordinary day.

The house's facade casts a long shadow across her path, and she shields her eyes and peers up at the cracked statues staring down at her. The grimacing cherubs and other horrors seem to be laughing at her. Suddenly overcome by the feeling that she's being watched, she hurries towards the front door, bangs her fist on the wood. 'Hello?'

She knocks again. Tries the handle. It opens smoothly. She steps into the hallway. It's gloomy inside, the daylight floating through the front door doing little to banish the shadows. The sound of the traffic on Excelsior Avenue seems to fade away, as if the place sits in its own vacuum. She stands absolutely still, listens for any sign of life. Nothing. It's almost *too* quiet. The last thing she feels like doing is heading up the stairs that end in solid blackness. No, she'll try the kitchen first. Leaving the arched doorway open so that the hallway's meagre light leaches through, she fumbles on the wall for the light switch. Unable to find it, she digs out her phone and clicks on the torch app she's never had reason to use before.

'Hello? Jane?'

The first thing she notices as she sweeps the light around the room is that the appliances are all gone; the countertops are clear of clutter. The room smells musty, unused, like a house that's been allowed to decay for decades. But how can this be? She saw Jane here only yesterday.

She should leave right now. What if that Ryan guy is still hiding out here, waiting to pounce? It's a huge property, must be loads of nooks and crannies in which someone could avoid detection. No one knows she's here. Anything could happen to her.

Ignoring her instincts, which are begging her to flee back into the sunlight, she finds herself making for the green door at the far end of the kitchen. It opens onto some sort of dusty, plastered corridor that appears to bend and weave through the house. Using the phone's glow to light her way, she follows it, stumbling occasionally on the uneven floor. Taking a narrow stairwell to her left, she walks up numbly, trying in vain to get a handle on the house's odd layout. It leads to another anonymous corridor, this one lined with cheap plasterboard doors. She opens them at random: a small tiled area containing nothing but a rusty bed frame; a couple of empty bedrooms; a room stacked with rusty water heaters and a leaking bag of cement. The last door in the passageway is slightly ajar. She pauses outside it, her hand caught halfway to the jamb, flooded with the overwhelming impression that there's something behind it, waiting to jump out at her.

'Hello?' she calls, her voice cracking. Hand trembling, she turns the handle, opens the door quickly before she loses her nerve.

There's no furniture in the room – a dingy, brown-carpeted space – but there's a row of jars on the shelf below the cardboard-blinded window. She walks forward, stops dead when she realises the jars each contain an insect of some type. Most appear to be spiders – including the curled corpse of a baboon spider, but there are also a couple of scorpions, several grasshoppers and a hulking Parktown prawn. She gasps in disgust when she spots a large coffee jar at the far edge of the collection, the headless body of a giant rat squashed into its base.

She holds her breath, listening again for any sign that she's not alone. Thinks she hears something scrape in the bowels of the house.

She backtracks in panic, her soggy breath loud in her ears. Disorientated, she takes a turning at random. Is this the way she came? She whirls around, starts running, almost tumbles down the stairs at the end of the corridor. Runs blindly on, ends up face to face with a door. Is it the one that leads to the kitchen? She turns the handle, steps inside the room, blinking as bright light sears her eyes. What in the hell? The lights glare down at her from the ceiling; while she's been rambling around the house, someone has been here, turned them on. And that's not all. There's a brief-case on the counter next to the sink. She's positive it wasn't here before.

Move! she screams to herself, lunging towards the arched doorway that leads into the hallway and freedom. She's only a metre away when it opens. She backs up against the counter as a man walks through it, pushing an old-fashioned fedora back on his head.

He smiles broadly at her. His features are regular and instantly forgettable. His tweed suit looks too heavy for the weather. 'Tara Elizabeth Marais? Thrilled to parts to encounter you. I've been out in the wilderness investigating.'

She nods, tries to catch her breath. 'Who are you?' She's relieved it isn't Ryan, but how could this stranger know her name? 'You a cop?' That must be it.

'Pardon?'

'A policeman? Are you from the police?'

'Ah,' he chuckles. 'An upside law-enforcer? I am not, but thank you for the tribute.' He shuffles to the sink and turns on the tap. 'Hygiene first.'

As he washes his hands, she notices that he's missing three fingers on his left hand. The remaining digits – his thumb and ring finger – give it the look of a fleshy crab claw. She tries not to shudder.

'Then who are you? And how did you know my name?'

'Excuse me for being discourteous. I am Node Agent Rosen. On option for Varder Batiss.'

'Varder Batiss?' Tara whispers.

'Yes. This is his former node residence.'

'Varder Batiss lives *here*?' How can that be? Is the man who commissioned her to make Baby Tommy embroiled somehow with Ryan? Could Batiss be Jane's father? And it can't be a coincidence that Jane and Martin have both disappeared. Tara struggles to piece it together. The only conclusion she can reach is that Ryan, Batiss, and possibly whoever has been running Encounters are involved in some kind of child abduction racket. Christ...

Usually I would not be conducting these matters, but Varder Batiss's sub-assistant has recently... depreciated.'

Guts churning, Tara struggles to keep calm. 'Oh. I'm sorry to hear that.'

'Don't be apologetic. Happens to everyone, does it not? Varder Batiss personally approved his recycling.'

What the hell does that mean? 'Did you follow me here?' She's not sure what else to ask, what to say. If these people are involved in something as serious as child abduction, she needs to tread carefully.

'Oh yes. I have been tracking you since you reneged on your agreement. Renege – that is the correct parlance, is it not?' He chuckles again. 'I'm working on my pronunciation.'

'I explained to your boss that I can't provide the baby. There was a mishap with him.'

'A mishap?'

Tara digs in her bag, removes Baby Tommy's burnt head. 'This.'

He peers down at it, doesn't seem surprised that she's just pulled a charred baby's head out of her bag. He clucks his tongue. 'Oopsie doopsie. What a karking mess.' He reaches for his brief-case, clicks it open. 'I usually do shortfall insurance collections, viables and the like, but lucky for you I was in this exact upside node location dealing with a matter that is now resolved.' He chuckles. 'I don't think I need share that contracts are my reason for subsisting.'

'Why does Batiss want this baby?'

'Want?' He chuckles again. 'He doesn't *want*.'

'But what was he going to do with him?'

'Mrs Tara Marais, I do not know the answer to that question. I am not here to question why, only to deal with the repercussions of a breach. Now. I believe you embarked on a signalled contract. Not a primo method, but Varder Batiss felt you were a... trustworthy br— upside citizen. I am assured that in the law of this node, signals – electronic messages, you call them? – are as acceptable as triplicate contracts, so I won't waste your time with dilly-dallying. The penalty you have been assured of, have you not?'

'What is this penalty?'

He waves his claw-hand vaguely. 'Oh dotting the eyes and tutting the tees.'

'I don't understand. I've said that I'll return the money.'

He actually laughs. 'Money? You mean brown currency? Oh no.'

'What do you want with me?' There's something in his hand; it's blocky and shiny – a gun? She needs to get out of here, she needs to run. But her legs feel heavy, as if her shoes are glued to the floor.

'Don't concern yourself, Mrs Marais,' he says, darting forward. 'This won't hurt a bit.'

Chapter 21

PENTER

Father was wrong. The karking upside halfpint *was* missed and dust
was kicked up. But all should be primo now. Penter has read and
initialled Node Agent Rosen's report on his dealings with the School
Principal Duvenhage. There were no complications. The sweep is
complete. Dispatching a node agent was one of Father's tasks, but
Penter has found it remarkably unchallenging to discharge his duties.

Or should she say Varder Batiss's duties, for she now knows his
real name. She's tried to think of him as Varder Batiss, but the name
doesn't sit easily. He will always be Father to her.

She paces through her living quarters. She has filed her reports,
she has done her duty, so why does she feel so karking stale? Is she
still poisoned by blissful love? Or is the thought-seep still muddy-
ing her mind? Her penetration is renewed every second Moneyday
at Dead Shift, which makes it just two shifts to go. The thought
calms her, but she hasn't received the confirmation signal from the
clinic yet, which she should have received a shift ago. Just a cleri-
cal error, she hopes.

She fingers the last of the ready beans she smuggled back from
the precinct, several of which are now limp and decaying. They

do not taste the same at home as they did in the precinct. And she is not as comfortable in her quiet pod as she used to be. She's too used to hearing the whir of the machines outside the precinct gate, the bang and shriek of Jane's documents, the chatter of the birds and the scratching of Jane's pets. Here there is only the hum of the great wheel in the Bowels.

It is too quiet.

She opens her locker, retrieves the mimeograph of Father she purloined from the precinct kitchen. She wonders what form his punishment will take. He has many periods of service left before his scheduled depreciation, so perhaps the Ministry will be lenient. He has played, there is no doubt, but he is efficient. Does he blame her for doing her duty and reporting his disregard to the Ministry? Does he even think of her at all?

She hears a cough, turns to see Bakewell Klot, one of Management's Security Agents, lurking in her doorway. She fumbles the mimeograph back into the locker, hopes that he will not ask her what she is doing.

'Penter Ulliel,' he says. 'First Minister Cardineal Phelgm requests your presence in the Ministry Boardroom.'

Penter gasps. In all her periods she has only once been called to the boardroom – when she was notified of her lifework assignment and installed. Why would someone as senior as Cardineal Phelgm want to see *her*?

Could it be a matter regarding Jane? It was, after all, Jane who invited the brown educator into the precinct on Father's orders. Penter is also concerned about Jane's dealings with that purloined brown – Ryan – although Manestream Lygoate, one of Penter's immediate superiors, told her that Jane's experiment has been authorised. Penter has high regard for Jane, feels a sense of protectiveness for her – a feeling that she knows will disappear when she undergoes her penetration renewal.

'Thank you, Bakewell Klot,' she manages to respond. 'I will hurry.'

She checks to make sure her uniform is pristine, then follows Bakewell Klot towards the lifts.

She clasps her shaking hands behind her back as they glide up to the Ministry levels. The lift doors slide open and Klot bids her farewell as she exits onto an unnumbered floor in the upper domain.

One of Cardineal Phelgm's underlings rushes forward and bares his stripped gums at her. She can tell by his primo bodily modifications, which include facial and limb amputations, that Cardineal Phelgm must hold this underling in high regard.

'Penter Ulliel,' he says, 'I am First Underling Janus Stoat. Please, come this way.'

He guides her across the greeting area towards the towering boardroom doors. Flakes of gold in the floor tiles twinkle beneath her feet, and she scans the portraits of past Ministry officials that line the walls. They are hallowed faces in the annals of the Administration, and she can name every one. Her hands are no longer shaking. The upper domain is impressive, but it is not as overawing as she remembers from her installation. She was still a halfpint then, scared and impressionable.

She follows him through the doors and into the boardroom itself. Cardineal Phelgm is squatting at his desk at the far end, a cloud of lesser and senior underlings chained discreetly to a flotilla of desks in front of him. Underling Stoat ushers her forward.

She has heard rumours that Cardineal Phelgm is fused to his desk because he is fearful of upstarts grasping his position. As far as Penter is aware, he has never left the boardroom since he was invested, receives even his penetration renewals, periodic modifications and victuals connected to his chair. She feels a stirring of distaste at the sight of his greenish-white skin and bloated jowls. He reminds her of the depreciated thing she saw floating in the precinct pool, but she knows that his stripped veins and amputations are of the most opulent quality and should be esteemed. She needs to watch her words very carefully. In this room, she needs even to watch her thoughts.

'Penter Ulliel,' he says, gazing at her through his single modified eye. 'May I commend you on your catalogue performance. The viable has been successfully integrated.' Penter nods, feeling the warmth of regard flushing her veins.

Cardineal Phelgm grunts and waves one of his stumps at Underling Stoat. 'You may proceed.'

Underling Stoat plucks a file from the towering stack of papers piled around Cardineal Phelgm's head. Penter recognises it as the report she made on Father.

'Is this the entirety of the matter, Penter Ulliel?' Cardineal Phelgm grunts.

'Yes, your Superiority,' she says.

Cardineal Phelgm rolls his eye. 'Truly, it is almost as if this Varder Batiss is *asking* to be recycled.' He makes a rumbling sound in his throat and the underlings laugh along with him.

Penter does not laugh. The bile is rising in her stomach. Is Father to be terminated? She cannot help but speak. 'Your Superiority?' she says, her entrails cramping at her temerity. 'May I enquire as to Father – to Varder Batiss's – punishment?'

'You may not,' Cardineal Phelgm barks, and the room falls silent. 'It is not in your purview. But for your information, Penter Ulliel...' – he sneers, or smiles, she's not sure which – 'this is by no means the only transgression of Varder Batiss.'

He leans forward, uses the microtech pincers fused to his other stump to push a sheaf of papers towards her.

She looks down at the file, which she has not seen before. It is from Node Agent Rosen, the same agent she dispatched to deal with that man Duvenhage.

She reads it in disbelief, can barely keep her features neutral.

This was not authorised. This was not discussed. The extent of Father's playing is disregardful in the extreme. It seems that Ryan is not the only brown that Father has scouted unauthorised.

'Penter Ulliel,' Cardineal Phelgm grumbles, 'you can resolve this?'

She nods.

'You must decide how to dispose of this unauthorised brown. If you wish to terminate it, you will have the full cooperation of the Terminal Ward.'

He sinks back in his chair, closes his eye. She is dismissed.

She exits the boardroom, intent on undergoing her penetration renewal immediately. It can't be healthy to feel this way.

But when she reaches the lifts she does not press the button for Level H. Instead, almost as if her hand is following a command of its own, she chooses one that will glide her down to the senior Ministry Apartments.

To where Father keeps his private quarters.

Chapter 22

RYAN

Ryan stands up groggily and wipes the blood off his chin. That upsized Number Two was heavy going, but he knows that now he'll be nourished for the next several shifts. He vacuums the rest of his SugarGas and, even though he's full, crams a last fistful of Starchsticks into his mouth. They're like popcorn. He elbows his way through the throng of Shoppers and Customer Care Officers cluttering the entrance to McColon's and hurries back to the elevator bank. There are just a few moments until his next class.

He scans his ID token over the pad marked 'Academy Only' and the lift doors glide open. He steps inside and they close again; he leans against the mirrored back wall and the lift starts moving. As they ascend – or descend; he's not sure – the lift plays a panpipe rendition of a tune he's heard before. The shunt hole at the base of his skull beneath his ear throbs as he tries to recall the title. This information is not directly relevant to today's syllabus but it's not completely obliterated either. He's very lucky to have been deployed as a tutor and he knows it's all Jane's doing. She likes him.

He spoke to a brown who worked somewhere in the Mall – at Nondegradable Polymer Playthings or Lonly Books – a couple of shifts ago. He'd just clicked out for victuals so was able to tell him how the shunt works on retail CCOs. Their scope is narrowed entirely to making sales and serving customers, especially Shoppers. As a tutor of Upside Relations classes, the breadth of Ryan's upside experience contributes to the lessons, so his scope is set far wider.

But he still can't remember the title of this damn song.

Not to worry. The lift doors slide open and he scans past the administration desk and into his class where the halfpints are waiting.

When he taught his first lesson, a few shifts ago – time doesn't really work the same down here – he experienced a shock of recognition when he saw the faces staring back at him. Their skin was mottled and pale, undertones of green and purple blushing through, scars from recent modifications still healing. He realised that he was looking at the same sort of kids who were arrayed in Duvenhage's photographs; they weren't dead or beaten, they were merely modified and marked up as examples for the upside scouting project. They were never harmed. In retrospect, after his job had been explained to him by the Assimilation Agent, he felt like such a fool for jumping to conclusions.

These are not abused kids or victims of anything; far from it. This is an elite group of halfpints which has been up-streamed to the Ministry of Upside Relations. After their courses, they'll be assigned to special projects or to Node Agent mentorships.

He starts his speech with the script that's been uploaded. 'Halfpints, my name is Ryan Devlin.' There are titters from the back of the class. 'As you know from your previous modules, key to successful operations in the upside is assimilation and evasion. You must blend in and keep your covert activities covert.'

A hand shoots up at the back of the class. The child – Ryan's not sure whether it is a boy or a girl, since the features are both delicate and hairy – asks, 'Why?'

'Why what…' – Ryan scans his class seating plan – 'Argent?'

'What would you – they – do to us if they caught us?'

'It depends, but you might get arrested by the police force and jailed. They would ask you many questions and might even eventually uncover the nature of the relationship between the upside and the downside. You know from your previous modules that most upsiders are not even aware of the existence of your people, your world. To have this reality suddenly uncovered would be suboptimal. Upsiders, browns, forgive my language' – there are more titters from the back of the class – 'tend to react violently to surprises.'

'We're not afraid of browns,' yells a fattened, crooked girl from the back row. 'We'll stun your cortex and hand-recycle you!'

'Hand-semi-recycle you and watch you try to crawl,' adds a boy with a neck brace.

'Now, now, halfpints. The central ethos of all Upside Relations protocol is to avoid ostentatious confrontation at all costs. While you are indeed far more capable than most of the halfpints upside, they vastly outnumber you. So—'

'Hand-recycle them!'

'So,' Ryan says firmly, 'on to today's lesson. Making invisible ink from lemon juice in the field. Firstly, we'll need lemons. The Academy has kindly supplied us with two very valuable lemons for the demonstration.'

'Stun their cortices!'

When his shift is over, Jane is waiting for him outside the Victuals R Us market.

'Soup and bread okay again?' he asks her.

'Primo.' She smiles. Now that he's been here for several shifts, he can tell just how ordinary-looking she is compared to the rest of the people who live here. She was chosen for the Encounters project in part because of just how much she looks like upsiders, like normal people. The people around here are either freakishly huge or skeletal; and each of them has some deformation or mutation – an extra leg, a hump, spongiform bumps or weeping sores. Looking at Jane, he feels like he's looking at someone from home.

He doesn't feel the same way when he looks at her as he did. He has a vague memory of that uncomfortable pull inside, but what they did to him has neutralised that feeling. He rubs the back of his head. The wound is not quite healed and his fingers come away sticky. Now he feels at peace, a peace, he realises, he's been craving all his life. If only he'd felt like this all the time, he wouldn't have had the compulsions he had.

He smiles back at her and they enter the market through a broad glass door.

The market is held in a vast hall with white walls and white floors. The bays for each of the stalls are marked out in silver duct tape, and several of them are vacant. As he walks, he's aware of the dusty prints his shoes make on the floor, and of the narrow wheel-tracks of the barrows, the scrapes and shuffles of the customers' gait, and the spatter of various dirty liquids. A few barrows cluster in the middle of the hangar, filled with local produce: bread made from mildew flour, soups and stew mixtures made from reductions, root vegetables and a vast variety of mushrooms, anything that can grow or be husbanded underground, all of it coloured in a spectrum between dirty cream and dark earth brown. Inflamed cuts of unidentifiable meat lie on ice chips in a refrigerated case. The drone of a hurdy-gurdy and some sort of pipes played by a small band in the corner of the hall throbs beneath the hubbub of the customers milling about. The market smells of the clods the food was picked from, a musty, mouldy smell he's quickly become used to.

'Are you sure you don't just want a burger?'

She regards him quizzically. 'You know that convenience food is only subsidised on-shift. We haven't got the tokens to consume it off-shift. Besides, fresh produce is hygienic for your passages.'

Ryan shrugs. He doesn't mind cooking.

Jane selects a punnet of grey-blue mouldy something and sniffs it. 'Primo fungus. This will go well with cheese-and-extract soup.'

'You can put it on the side. I'm not having any of that.'

She shakes her head and drops it in his sack. 'You're such a brown, Mr Ryan.'

Despite the medieval feeling of the market, a bright neon sign reading 'FORFEIT' indicates a row of electronic check-out counters. As they make their way over to it, they come across a melee at a crate on the patch of floor marked 'Exotic Fresh Produce'.

'Ooh, new imports,' says Jane and joins the throng of downsiders snarling and drooling and moaning at each other as they jockey to get the best of the produce. Jane circles around the crowd, but she's too small to get into the thick of the throng so Ryan puts down his basket and pushes up behind her, jostling and elbowing a path between them. Effluent from the downsiders' sores and scars smears his sleeves as he goes, and he feels the gristly lumps under their clothes but he continues to shove through.

'Kark off, brown,' somebody hisses, 'and take your abnormal halfpint with you.'

'Kark you,' he snaps back, his shunt hole tingling.

Soon, a narrow way is cleared for Ryan and Jane, almost as if the locals are too disgusted by them to offer much physical resistance, and they peer down into the box as other, braver drones dig around among the produce.

The import crate contains plump apricots, green apples, bunches of model bananas, but there – there – is something he wants, a small package of green beans. There's a two-fingered claw gripped around them but he bends one talon back, ignoring the outraged cry from the woman it's attached to until she drops it. He tucks it under his arm and grabs two apricots for good measure before bulldozing his way out again, gently ushering Jane ahead of him.

'Oh, Mr Ryan, you got beans!' Jane is ecstatic, and an unbidden flash of a younger Alice's laughing face flits through Ryan's mind again. Then Jane's expression falls. 'But we'll never be able to afford them.'

Ryan's afraid she's right, but this is something he wants to do – something he needs to do. 'You never know. Let's see.'

They stand in the queue and bypass the temptations of SugarGas and Fatty Tissue, which appears to be a sort of nutritional supplement (*Accelerate your way to the Wards!*). At the counter, the CCO tots up their purchases: the apricots cost ten times more than the bread and soup and fungus combined, and the beans twice that again.

'I told you, Mr Ryan. There's a premium on upside greenery.'

Ryan's never seen Jane anywhere close to tears, but it looks as if she might cry now. He hands his tokens to the CCO. 'Have I got enough there?'

The CCO blows boredly over her newly lacquered finger stump and says, 'If you leave one of these.' She points at an apricot like it's a novelty dog turd. Clearly, the allure of exotic produce is lost on her. The finger stump has something like a rat's skull painted in precise miniature on the end of it.

'Okay. I'll leave that and take the rest.'

'No, Mr Ryan, you can't,' Jane says. 'That's all your tokens. What about apparel? What about entertainment? What about victuals for the rest of the week?'

He shrugs. 'I'll fill up on McColon's on-shift and besides, I'll be paid again next week. I want to do something nice for my... uh, for you.'

Jane looks at the beans and grins. She hugs him around the waist. 'Thank you, Mr Ryan.'

They drop their groceries into their root-fibre weave bag and head out of the shop towards the Apartments.

'You spent too many tokens, Mr Ryan.'

'It doesn't matter. It's worth it. Please, don't worry about it.' Ryan doesn't want to spoil Jane's treat, but he does feel he's been seriously ripped off. There's no reason these imports should be so expensive.

'It's not going to get you any closer to discharging your debt,' she says.

He wants to tell her not to worry again, but now that the euphoria of winning the sale is wearing off, he realises he has been stupid. He wants to pay off his debt and go home; he wants to see Alice.

Jane's blabbering away in excitement. 'You should see the sort of produce at special market days for Shoppers. They sell a wide range of colourful and fresh upside victuals, tip-top quality.'

One of the first things Ryan learnt about the Mall is this bizarre distinction between Shoppers and people with real jobs. 'What's the deal with the Shoppers?' he asks Jane. 'It's almost as if they want to pay as much as possible for things.'

Jane shrugs. 'They have to consume. If they don't consume enough, they get depreciated. That's the way it works.' Ryan can't understand some things down here, but others seem all too familiar. 'When I was in the Encounters project unit,' Jane continues, 'when I was upside, I felt like a Shopper for the duration. All that produce just hanging there. On produce trees! It was like a phantasm!'

They take the lifts up to their flat. Or is it down? Whenever Ryan gets into one of these lifts, he's completely disorientated, like that time he went to the Rand Show as a kid and they went into a gold-mining exhibit. A group of visitors would cram excitedly into the industrial lift, the doors would slam close. Lights would flicker and the lift would shake about. Doors on the opposite end of the lift would open, and there they'd be, underground, in a stuffy tunnel, hearing the blast and spray of the pneumatic rock drills. It didn't feel like any suburban lift he knew; it was more like they'd all gone for a ride in some magic time machine.

Then some older kid, a pimply and bored teen, mumbled, 'It's just a trick. We haven't gone anywhere. They just shook us around and opened the door to the other side of the room.'

Ryan couldn't believe it; he didn't believe it, until he saw the boy's mother glancing in his direction and nudging the boy in the ribs. 'Shhh.' Don't break the spell. Then he knew it was all some elaborate joke.

These lifts are something like that. They play music, they appear to move, and when they open, he and Jane are somewhere else. He reminds himself that there is only one set of doors here, so they must actually have moved somewhere – up or down, he can't tell. Unless there's a whole crew of stage hands who rush out as soon as the doors close and change the set outside? That would be too much, wouldn't it? Just for Ryan's benefit. Surely?

Of course that's not what's happening, Ryan tells himself. But he can't quite shake the feeling he's being toyed with in some intricate way.

'I'm very felicitous that the Administration agreed to lodge you with me in my Apartment,' says Jane, bumping Ryan out of his thoughts. That much is concretely true: he *is* here, standing with this strange girl in a strange lift. 'It's primo that such good chums should abide together.'

'Yes,' he says, trying to remember how he got here. He was working at the school, staying at a boarding house in Malvern. He remembers that clearly. He remembers talking to the girl next door – Tess, that was her name. She showed him something, a dark place. The rest is a bit fuzzy. He was hiding somewhere; he was in a garden. Cutting things? Climbing ladders? Or is he getting it confused with the work he did at the school? He has the feeling that he left that job, or lost that job, but can't exactly work out how.

Not remembering doesn't bother him as much as it should. He feels at peace, his mind is calm, and he knows that calmness like that is a state he's been after for a long time. Ever since he had to leave Alice and Karin. He misses Alice. The more distant the memories, the clearer they are, as if someone has smudged the last couple of weeks – days? months? – of his life. The thought of Alice is the only thing that spoils his peace, the only thing holding him to an unquiet past.

The lift door pings open and sure enough, they're up – down – on their floor. 'Welcome to the Apartments, Level F½' reads a sign decorated with a clown in a hot-air balloon, the sort you might see on the wall at a children's party or in a children's ward. Ryan shoulders the grocery sack and follows Jane along the corridor. The doors are not numbered and he has to rely on her to lead the way.

When they get to the right door, one of a row of identical grey doors on this level, she lets him in with a swipe of her gelphone and he unpacks the sack onto the kitchen table.

'Have you got butter here, Jane? Or olive oil? Tomatoes, onions? I'd like to prepare these beans the way my mother used to make them at home.'

'Prepare? Don't you just chew them? That's what I did in the upside precinct. They were appetising!'

'They're even tastier when you cook them. Trust me, I'd like to make a special meal for you.'

'I'm afraid I don't have any comestibles like that. You know that I can't afford luxury produce on a trainee's tokens.'

'Damn. I don't want to just eat them raw. It's not...' Ryan slumps against the table top. He wants to treat the girl. He feels something for her, something he didn't think he would, an almost maternal care. He's always wanted to care for the girls in his life, but right now he realises that he's gone about it all wrong. Care is about giving, not taking. What they did to him down here has made him realise that; he's a changed man.

And despite himself, he thinks about Alice. If he could prove to her – and to Karin – that he realises he got it wrong, and that he can love someone properly, maybe he'll get another chance. But Karin and Alice seem so far away; right now there's a child right here he could make happy, with a simple meal of beans.

'I'll go and ask the neighbours,' he says. 'Surely someone's going to have some ingredients.'

'That's not likely on this level,' says Jane. 'This level is designated for inferior Ministry drones. They won't have sufficient tokens for fresh produce.'

Ryan sighs.

'But,' adds the girl, 'I met a brown Shopper in the lobby the other day. She was so benevolent and sociable – she even smiled at me and spoke to me. Only a brown Shopper would do that, only a forespecial brown Shopper. Perhaps we can ask her for ingredients for the victuals.'

Ryan senses that Jane is trying to make him happy as much as he is trying to please her; she'd be just as pleased to munch the beans raw. 'Okay. It's worth a try.'

They take the lift up – down? – to Level U. The doors here are painted a variety of pastel colours and there's plush orange-and-purple carpeting through the corridors. Ryan feels like his grubby shoes are smearing the thick pile as he goes. The doors are spaced far apart along this stretch and numbered with engraved brass plaques. The light sconces that line the corridor are intricately whorled.

Jane hobbles rapidly along the passageway until they reach door number 401. She knocks timidly, then again, and at length the door opens.

'Yeah?' The woman is wearing a silky green mini-dress and gladiator-style high-heeled shoes. She has cropped hair and a huge, patchy scar running across one side of her face. It's a bizarre get-up, but compared to most of the people he's seen here, she looks comfortingly normal. An old part of him deep inside, the part that would stare at this woman's long legs and imagine seducing her, flickers briefly and then dies.

'Greetings, Madam Shopper. We met in the lobby six shifts ago.' Jane is clearly nervous, something Ryan has never seen in her before. She babbles on. 'You were kind enough to intercourse with me, and my friend here – he's also a brown – would like to prepare a victual with special ingredients, and I was—'

'Yeah, yeah, what do you want?' the woman barks.

'I'm sorry, ma'am. I was mistaken.' Jane turns to go, but Ryan notices a confused look pass over the woman's face. She rubs the back of her skull and shakes her head, as if shaking off sleep.

'No, I'm sorry. I do remember. Please come in.'

The woman ushers Ryan and Jane into her flat and neither of them can suppress their gasps. The open-plan living space is like a luxury hotel's lobby, designer furnishings littered across the marble floor. The ceilings are high and intricately moulded and the walls are painted in tasteful shades of cream. The woman leads Ryan and Jane through to the kitchen, her sharp heels clicking against the floor. The kitchen is an expanse of black marble tops and brushed-steel appliances, all gleaming as if they've never been used. The worktops are decorated with crystal vases of fresh flowers and ceramic bowls brimming with perfect, exotic fruit that just a while ago Ryan would have taken for granted: fat mangoes, unblemished bananas, taut-skinned kiwi fruits, and lemons, yellow like a photo in a catalogue.

'What do you need? I just had the Tower's Choice Homemakers' Pride Selection delivered so there's plenty to go around. They were on a double-price special, so you wouldn't believe the amount of tokens I knocked off with just this. I got them to throw in the Premium Imported Accoutrements package and asked them to deliver during Dead Shift so they charged extra. A primo deal if you ask me, and when they...' She trails off. 'Sorry, I'm babbling. What do you need?'

Ryan wants to tell her to box up the whole lot and get it delivered to the lower levels and order one for every flat there, but something stops him. 'Uh, just some olive oil, a few tomatoes, onions...'

The woman's riffling through the grocery cupboards as he talks and she loads the ingredients in a box. 'Red? White? Shallots? Spring onions?'

'Uh, red, thanks. You wouldn't have fresh parsley, would you?'

The woman walks to one of the three massive fridges and opens a drawer dedicated to fresh herbs. 'I would indeed,' she says, dropping a punnet of the herb into the box.

'Thank you, that's very kind,' Ryan says as he hefts the box under his arm.

'A pleasure to, to, uh...' she says, and a look of confusion passes her face again.

'Thank you, Madam Shopper,' Jane says, heading to the front door.

The woman follows them silently, as if she's lost, and watches them from the doorway as they walk to the lifts.

As the lift closes behind them and ushers them back to their level, Ryan asks, 'How do people live like this? How can the Shoppers have so much while the normal people have to fight for...' But Jane looks at him with such opacity, as if he's talking French to her, that he drops it. He doesn't want to be told 'that's the way it works' again.

Jane picks at her bean stew while watching a Ministry announcement on TV. 'It's toothsome,' she says, half-heartedly.

'I'm sorry,' Ryan says. 'I know you would have preferred to just eat them raw. I shouldn't have interfered.'

229

'No, no, Mr Ryan. It's toothsome.' She pushes her bowl away. 'I have phantasms about returning upside again on another project. There is abundance there. Perhaps Node Liaison Penter Ulliel will call on my services again. The Encounters project was a success and there is talk of more.'

'I wish I could go back too. I miss my daughter.'

'You are indebted,' she says. He remembers those words from some time in the blotted recent past. They make him afraid; they make him feel very far from home.

'I'm going to bed,' he says.

Jane stares at the TV screen with a blank face.

In the small bathroom, Ryan takes off his clothes and gets into the shower. He rubs the soap over his body with a blank sense of contentment. He remembers being troubled recently, but the fact that it's hard to recall, that it seems so far away, serves to amplify his calm.

The soap travels over his biceps, his chest, his stomach. As it goes, Ryan feels it sketching him out, mapping his body, reminding him of who he is and how he's changed. There is no tension in his thighs as he laves; his calf muscles are firm and pain-free. He works up a lather in his hands and cleans his buttocks and moves around to his crotch, feeling the absence there, the empty sack where his balls once hung.

He remembers it, like a film playing out, but he can't bring himself to feel anything. They cut his testicles out like a minor procedure. He was sitting in an office cubicle, like a client at a bank, and someone drilled a hole into the back of his head; he can't remember the person's face, just a shock of orange curls like a novelty wig. Then the person hooked his legs into metal stirrups on the sides of the cubicle and sliced into his scrotum. He wasn't wearing any pants.

He cleans under his limp penis, the back of his skull pulsing pleasant feelings through his body and calming his mind.

Chapter 23

TARA

Tara's vision is blurry, as if she's looking through a veil of thin gauze, but far as she can tell, she appears to be in a spacious white-walled room. A private hospital ward? No, it can't be – she's sitting slumped on a soft surface, some kind of couch upholstered in slippery, slightly greasy fabric, rather than lying on a gurney. She keeps absolutely still, listens for anything that could give her a clue as to her whereabouts. Hears nothing but a faint mechanical hum that seems to be emanating from beneath the floor. Fighting to keep the panic at bay, she tries to turn her head again. It feels too heavy for her neck; she can barely hold it up. And there's something wrong with the air in here – it's heavier, as if she's miles underground; there's a slight burn in her lungs as she struggles to draw in enough oxygen.

Just where in goddamned hell *is* she?

She needs to think back – stretches her mind to remember the last thing she did. Recalls some sort of altercation with Stephen and Olivia, followed by a desperate desire to go somewhere – *where*, though? – vaguely remembers driving. A car accident? The memory is out of her grasp. Can't quite catch it. She attempts to stand, gasps as her thigh muscles cramp, pain shooting down her legs, spiralling into her joints. She sinks back down.

Wherever she is, there's something wrong with her; she's groggy, feels detached, as if she's coming round from an anaesthetic. Is she hurt? *Has* she been in an accident? She runs her hands over her body, recognises the familiar cloth of her jeans and sweatshirt. Despite the shooting pains in her legs, she can't feel any obvious wounds, and the strap of her bag is still looped over her chest.

Her phone! Yes. She scrabbles in her bag, roots past her keys, a bunch of tissues, an old tube of lip-ice – finally feels the comforting shape of her BlackBerry. She pulls it out, presses the '1' key – the speed-dial to Stephen's number – hears the beep-beep-beep of the battery dying. Keeps trying anyway. Turns the phone off and on again. Nothing – it's dead.

Fuck. Not even enough life in it to send a text.

Blinking frantically helps. Her vision is still hazy, but gradually she begins to make out individual shapes and textures. It looks like she's in some sort of high-end apartment. The room is featureless, but the materials used to build it are expensive, top of the range. Marble counter tops, white stone floor, white walls, no paintings or decorations. Like a blank high-end showroom. And apart from the couch, there's no furniture in here except for a low glass coffee table, on which she spots the only flash of colour in the room. She leans forward, blinks again and her sight finally clears. Sees some kind of book or brochure – the source of the colour – and next to it... Is that...? It is! Baby Tommy's head! She reaches for him, willing her body to obey her. Jesus, everything aches. Her muscles, even her skin. She's sure she hasn't been beaten – she doesn't feel bruised or broken, more as if she's contracted a virulent strain of swine flu. She touches her forehead. Does she have a temperature? Her palms are clammy with nervous sweat; she can't tell if she's too hot or not.

She manages to grasp Baby Tommy's head. It calms her. She drops it on her lap and picks up the brochure. It's heavier than she was expecting, and she barely has the strength to hold it up in front of her eyes. There's a photograph of a generic mall aisle on the cover, gold, embossed script printed across the top of it. She loses focus again, squeezes her eyes shut, and when she opens them she's able to make out the title: 'You're Here Now, Upside Citizen, so Why PANIC? J'

What the hell? She flips the page, sees a double-spread of Comic Sans writing. It looks like a list – some kind of index, maybe? It takes all her concentration to stop the words distorting in front of her:

1) Welcome to the Wards! 6–7

2) Welcome to the Mall! 18–9

3) So you want to Factor, how do you apply? 25–16

4) Victuals and other Ablutions 26–30

5) Shopper Etiquette 19

6) Drone Management and Navigating Bureaucracy 34–277

7) Everything you wanted to know about Penetration but were afraid to ask 55–56

8) Getting Around: The Lift and Other Hazards 101

9) Hey! Don't Use the Stairs! 77–98 (includes bonus illustrations!!!!)

10) Ten Top Tips for Successful (and painless!) Recycling 88–89

11) The Meat Tree and Other Myths 1–5

12) Epilogue: The Policy of Leaving ⊗

'Mrs Tara Marais? May we converse with you?'

A figure steps into her line of sight – tall, skeletally thin. Bright red hair. Tara draws in another deep breath. Did she black out again? She has no memory of seeing the woman entering the room.

Don't panic!

Wait – she's seen this woman before… The girl, the new girl… Jane. This is Jane's mother. And then it hits her. The house. The statue house. She remembers a man – a man in the kitchen. A man in a hat – had some sort of deformed hand. Does this mean she's still in that house? One of the rooms in that awful house? She breathes in deeply again, sniffs the air. Detects some sort of chemical odour, cleaning fluid maybe? That place smelled musty. No. She's somewhere else.

'I know you,' Tara manages.

'Yes. We've conversed before. I am Penter Ulliel, Deputy Node Liaison for the Ministry of Upside Relations.' Another figure appears behind the woman – a man – stocky, a large square-shaped head. 'And this is Bakewell Klot, a Management Security Agent on secondment to the Ministry.'

Groggy she may be, but Tara's hit with an urge to giggle. What the hell is this? The man's attired as if he's about to go to a fancy-dress party in some kind of old-fashioned admiral's outfit, and he looks as if he's one step away from a major cardiac event; his skin is purple, wormy pink veins pulse in his forehead. The hysteria vanishes when she notices the pistol shoved in his belt. 'Charmed to meet you,' he says in a high, girlish voice.

'May I?' Jane's mother drags the brochure out of Tara's hands. 'Did you read it? One of our recent upside assimilants has drafted this guide for new intakes' edification. Was it helpful?'

Tara opens her mouth to speak – to say what, she's not sure – when she's swamped with a surge of dizziness. She presses the heels of her hands into her eyes, waits for the bright spots to die away. Opens her eyes again, sees Jane's mother – what did she say her name was? Petra? No, Penter – staring at her concernedly. 'What have you done to me? Am I drugged?'

'We've learnt that acclimatisation can be confusing. Your penetration shunt will help make this...' – Penter waves a hand around the room – '*experience* more palatable.'

'My what?'

Jane's mother frowns. 'Your shunt *has* been fitted, hasn't it?' She touches the back of her head, just below her ear.

Tara mirrors her gesture, runs her fingers over her own neck, touches some kind of scabbed hole below her own right ear. She presses it gingerly; the wound feels spongy, not like any kind of abrasion she's had before. Presses it again, expecting to feel a bright surge of pain, but it's oddly numb. Removes her fingers, notices, with clinical detachment, that they're bloody. Is this why her head feels like it's stuffed full of cement? Did that guy in the kitchen pistol whip her or something?

'We understand that you are still acclimatising,' Penter says. She points at Baby Tommy's head. 'But I would appreciate it if you can tell me what this is.'

Tara swallows. Her saliva tastes as if she's been drinking blood. She really wants to tell this woman to go to hell, but when she opens her mouth, she finds herself answering the question. 'Um... Baby Tommy. It's a baby. A Reborn. A... doll.'

'And Father – Varder Batiss – requested that you make this?'

That name. Varder Batiss. She knows that name. Tara fights once more to unjangle her thoughts, put them in some kind of order. Then, all at once, she gets it. They are all connected. Batiss. Encounters. That pervert, that maintenance man – Ryan. The house. Jane. And Martin. Yes! She was at the house looking for Jane after Martin disappeared when that guy in a hat did something to her. Knocked her out? Shot her, even? But apart from that abrasion on her neck she just feels sick rather than injured. Whatever this Penter woman says, they *must* have given her something. Drugged her. Poisoned her. 'Where am I?'

'Varder Batiss's private quarters.'

'Where?' The apartment, if that's what it is, looks, *feels*, expensive, high-end. Somewhere in Sandton, maybe? If she could only look out of a window, get her bearings. But there don't seem to be any windows. 'How did I get here?'

Penter sighs. 'Varder Batiss, Mrs Tara Marais, is a Player. You have been illegitimately purloined from the upside.' She shares a glance with the purple-faced freak. 'He instructed a node agent to transport you to the Wards for unauthorised recycling, charging you with contractual breach. But, of course, the contract was never authorised by our Ministry.'

Upside? Recycling? Ministry? What the hell is this woman talking about? That this Batiss person kidnapped her? And is Jane's mother in on it? Why, though? 'And Martin?'

Jane's mother frowns. 'Martin?'

'My stepson. He... he was at Encounters. He's missing.'

Penter relaxes, beams at her. 'Ah. The primo viable. We have good news for you, Mrs Tara Marais. The viable is already safely integrated into the system. Its penetration and deployment were a great success!'

Jesus, Tara thinks. These people are clearly deranged. 'Look, my husband is a lawyer. He's connected. He'll be looking for us, he won't stop. You have to let me go. Let Martin go.'

Penter and Purple Face share a chuckle. 'You are not a prisoner here, Mrs Tara Marais. You were brought here erroneously. You can exit at any time.'

'I... can?'

'Of course. Unless you choose to integrate, of course. There are several options for a—'

Tara waves her off and gets to her feet, trying not to scream as the pain in her thigh muscles intensifies. At least her head has cleared somewhat.

'Apologies for the discomfort,' Penter says. 'When you arrived at the Wards you were prepared for harvesting. The discomfort will fade. The shunt you have received will facilitate both your forgetfulness and your speedy recovery.'

Tara slams her fists on her legs, wills herself to take a step, just one. *Move.* She sweeps the room, sees a door three or four metres to her right. She stumbles forward. The soles of her feet are numb, but every movement sends fresh agony shooting through her muscles as if red-hot knitting needles are being skewered into her legs. She reaches the door, grasps the handle, waits for them to stop her, for that purple-faced freak to pull out his gun.

Neither Penter nor Purple Face move, but continue to watch her with blankly polite expressions. Are they torturing her? Playing with her? It can't be this easy. She turns the handle, expecting the door to be locked, but it opens smoothly onto a long, empty corridor as bland as the apartment itself. There's a bank of lifts at the end of it.

'But before you exit,' she hears Penter say behind her, 'may we ask for your cooperation?'

Tara hesitates, looks over her shoulder. 'My... what?'

'We are confused.'

Tara almost laughs again. '*You're* confused?'

'Yes.'

Tara battles again to clear her muddied thoughts. Recalls someone telling her – or maybe it's something she's read – that the best thing to do in a dangerous situation is agree and cooperate with the aggressor. Penter doesn't appear to be dangerous – although Tara's certain she is mentally ill – but she can't be sure about that freak of a man. And she can't forget about Martin. She needs to find Martin. This woman knows where he is. That's all she needs to concentrate on now. She'll make sense of all this other crazy shit later. 'If I... cooperate, will you take me to Martin?'

'That would be most irregular.' Purple Face chuckles.

'Indeed it would,' Penter says. 'But not unprecedented. It is possible that we can accelerate a special authorisation. Bakewell Klot, would you initiate the process?'

'You are certain, Liaison Ulliel?' Purple Face says in his weird squeaky voice.

'Yes.'

'I will.' He bows his head and shuffles towards the door. Tara steps away from it and cringes as he brushes past her, watches as he waddles down the corridor towards the lifts. Now it's just her and Penter. Could she overpower her? If only she didn't feel so goddamned woozy.

'Please,' Jane's mother says, gesturing towards an identical door on the opposite side of the room. 'I would most appreciate if you would enter through there.'

'And then you'll let me go? Take me to Martin?'

'Yes.'

What should she do? Christ. There's no way she can trust this woman, but what choice does she have? Martin. Martin has to be her priority. She hesitates, then hobbles towards the door, keeping an eye out for anything she might use as a weapon, but the counter tops and surfaces are free of clutter.

Penter holds the door open for her, waves her forward with a sweep of her hand. 'Please. I would be most appreciative.'

'What's through here? Hey, is Martin...?' She steps past Penter, voice dying away as she takes in the wholly unexpected sight in front of her. What the fuck is this now?

The room she's entered – which is half the size of the impersonal kitchen cum living room area – is stuffed full of vintage furniture and clutter, most of which appears to date from the fifties. Tara gradually realises that it's arranged in twee tableaus: a kitchen area complete with a Bakelite larder cabinet and Formica table, and a facsimile of a cosy lounge with a plastic-covered three-piece suite behind it. But that's the least of its bizarreness. Someone – the mysterious Varder Batiss, perhaps? – has posed a collection of mannequins, waxworks and several of those lifelike silicone sex dolls on and around the furniture. Swallowing a burble of hysteria, Tara stares at a waxwork figure of Princess Diana wearing a 'Kiss the Cook' apron; it's frozen in the act of serving a plate of plastic cupcakes to a tableful of busty blond sex dolls dressed in flowery dresses.

Tara shuffles further into the room, the throbbing in her legs momentarily forgotten, and claps her hand to her mouth to hold in another humourless giggle as she spots a male silicone sex doll, a pipe glued into its O-shaped mouth, leaning against a faux mantelpiece, apparently sharing a joke with the familiar-looking waxwork standing next to it... Jesus, is that George W. Bush? It's like being in the middle of a chaotic movie set or museum – Madame Tussauds for the insane.

She squeezes past the Dubya model, careful not to knock against it, aware that she's still unsteady on her feet. Several figures are lolling on the plastic-covered lounge suite – a poorly rendered Nelson Mandela waxwork flanked by a couple of maniacally grinning naked child mannequins – all of them staring straight ahead at an ancient television set.

Tara looks down, feels her breath stop in her throat.

Jesus.

Lying on the carpet in front of the set is a jumbled mass of limbs, heads and tiny bodies.

She's never seen so many Reborns in one place before. There must be at least thirty. Unlike the other figures, the baby dolls look as if they've been haphazardly thrown on the floor, as if whoever dumped them here did so in a hurry. And, as she looks closer, she realises with dawning disgust that each one has something... *wrong* with it. An ice-skinned baby with a spider-web tattoo over its face; another with... Jesus, are those tentacles for arms? A perfectly mottled Reborn with a smooth, featureless face; nothing where its eyes, nose and mouth should be.

Tara knows with sickening certainty what's missing from this scene: a baby with a sewn-up mouth and eyes. She shudders to think of Baby Tommy ending up in this room; is now almost glad that she ruined him.

She turns to Penter, who is staring in bemusement at a scuffed male mannequin dressed, for some reason, as Disney's Snow White. 'What the hell is this?'

Penter sighs. 'It is Varder Batiss's collection. We believe he has an unhealthy obsession with upside bodies, with anatomical facsimiles.' Penter points at the Reborn pile. 'Can you inform what these are for?'

'What do you mean?'

'Am I not clear? What do browns – forgive me, upside citizens – use these for? Why do you create them?'

Browns – she knows that word. Jane used that word. Who the hell *are* these people? 'They're just dolls. You can buy them on the internet.'

'Yes, but why?'

Tara tries to think of an answer for this, tries to push a clear thought through the fug in her mind. 'Um. Loneliness, I suppose. A... need to...' To what? Whatever they've given her is seriously screwing with her ability not only to think, but to speak straight. She tries again. 'A need to connect. Some people find it hard to... to... be with other people.'

Penter narrows her eyes. 'Loneliness? But there are so many of you. Why make facsimiles?'

'People want something to love, don't they? It's not always that easy.' She pauses as she's hit with another wave of regret for Baby

Tommy. 'Sometimes when people have lost... um, when they've lost a person they love, they want a reminder. Reborns can be... an outlet, I suppose.'

Penter sighs. 'Do you think Varder Batiss is lonely? That he needs outlets? That he is searching for love?'

'I don't know.' Tara feels a spurt of anger. It helps clear her mind. 'How would I know? I've never met him. I've answered your questions. Now take me to Martin.'

Penter nods. 'Yes, that was agreed. Please follow me.'

It's a relief to be out of that nightmare of a room. On her way out, Tara remembers to grab Baby Tommy's head from the coffee table, shoving him into her bag before joining Penter at the front door. She winces as she's hit with another muscle spasm.

'Do you need help, Mrs Tara Marais?' Penter asks, and for a second Tara's sure she is going to touch her. The thought fills her with revulsion.

'No!'

Tara can't make sense of what she's just seen. The best explanation she can muster is that these people are in some sort of strange cult or religion and Varder Batiss has transgressed one of their moral codes. But what has this got to do with her? With Martin?

She can't dwell on this now. She's in no condition to unpack this craziness. Her thoughts are still too sluggish. Still, she's grateful that although her leg muscles are throbbing, the shooting pain has faded, and she's able to make the long walk to the lifts without too much discomfort.

The door in the centre hisses open and Tara follows Penter in. She numbly registers that there don't appear to be any control buttons on its walls.

'Where are we going?' Tara asks. 'Where is Martin?'

'In the Factory, of course.'

'The *what*?'

Pan-piped musak drifts from the ceiling. She's not certain, but it sounds like 'Bang Bang (My Baby Shot Me Down)' by Cher.

It's too much. She leans against the lift's smooth metal wall, closes her eyes. It would be easy to give up, to collapse on the floor, curl up into a ball and wait for all of this to be over.

But she can't do that. Not with Martin waiting for her. She pictures bringing him home, turning up at the town house, Stephen and Olivia rushing out to greet them; imagines Stephen's outpouring of relief and love, Olivia's gratitude and grudging respect.

'Mrs Tara Marais?'

Tara jumps. She must have drifted off.

The lift pings, and its doors slide open onto a high-ceilinged empty space that resembles a disused warehouse. The walls are of face brick, the floor dusty and bare, but as Tara follows Penter across it, she makes out taped square areas on the floor, the words 'Butcher', 'Cleaner', 'Reader', and 'Lemons' printed on the concrete in faded black stencil.

'This is one of the old markets.' Penter tuts. 'The Players used it for some disregardful experiments and it was shut down. Sometimes I think they don't know they were even vatted, do you agree?'

Tara doesn't bother answering. It's clear, as her mother would say, that Penter is crazier than a junk-yard dog. And you have to be careful around crazy people. Who knows what they're capable of doing, what could set them off? She trails Penter around a corner, comes face to face with a wide brick wall, on which some inept artist has painted a gruesome mural of a clown riding a tiny motorbike, the words 'Brum Brum Welcome to the Factory!' snaking out of his mouth. There's a narrow door camouflaged in that awful painting, a sign on it reading: 'Warning: keep appendages closed at all times.'

Penter turns the handle, and Tara follows her straight into a cavernous area – the largest interior space she's ever seen. It has to be double the size of a football field at least, so expansive that she can't see where it ends. Awed by the scope of it, it takes her a few seconds to realise that it's crammed with row after row of old-fashioned school desks.

And not all of them are empty.

'Holy *fuck*,' Tara says, when she finally finds her voice. The figures sitting in earth-brown overalls with their backs to her are diminutive – so small, in fact, that she's almost certain they must be children. But that can't be right, can it? Didn't Penter say this was a factory? It certainly doesn't sound like any of the factories Tara's encountered before. Apart from the constant faint mechanical hum that she heard back in that apartment, the immense area is eerily quiet.

Penter beams at her. 'Yes. Isn't it *primo*?' She points at an empty desk. 'But look at all the vacancies. You can see why we have to scout, can't you?'

Tara half listens to her words, the ache in her legs now completely forgotten. The ceiling is so high she can barely see the criss-cross of its metal struts, and for some reason there's a complex web of tubes and wires hanging down from it. She drags her gaze down one of the tubes – a clear snake the diameter of a garden hose – realises that the end of it appears to be connected to one of the small hunched figures a few rows in front of her. No, not just connected... *fused* into the neck of the person she's looking at; she can make out a lump of what looks to be scar tissue surrounding it. Her stomach rolls over, she gags, swallows a mouthful of bile. That can't be right. Nuh-uh. No way. Is she hallucinating? Some by-product of the drugs they've given her? She pinches her arm. She's still feeling detached, but she's sure she's not that far gone.

She finds herself touching the spongy wound behind her ear. Presses it. Feels something pop deep inside her mind, followed by a sudden wash of calm as if she's just taken a trank. The nausea abates.

'Follow me.' Penter's voice floats towards her. 'And please, heed the warnings. Keep your appendages closed.'

Tara can't make her legs move. Can't tear her eyes away from the hunched figures dotted around the room. And the tubes attached to each one.

'Mrs Tara Marais?'

All Tara can think is *Martin* – she has to get to Martin. With a gargantuan effort, she makes herself walk forward. There's just enough space to squeeze past the desks. Her eyes graze over the figure closest to her; it's definitely a child. In its unrevealing overall, she can't tell if it's male or female. He or she is sitting hunched over, using some sort of soldering iron to weld steel shapes onto what looks horribly like a denture plate.

She reaches out, gently touches the child's back, trying not to stare at the wad of scar tissue sealed over the end of the tube inserted into his or her neck. 'Hey... are you okay?'

The child looks up and Tara gasps, recoils, bashes into one of the empty desks behind her. One side of the child's face is lumped and misshapen, a growth covering an eye. The child smiles, showing off red, toothless gums, then drops its head and continues to work.

Tara numbly follows Penter past row after row. Several are completely empty, but all of the children she passes seem to be deformed in some fashion. She takes in stumps where hands should be, an unfortunate whose back is so twisted and hunched its neck appears to be non-existent, and several with skin so translucent and fragile that she can make out blue veins pulsing beneath. Not one of them looks up at her curiously; all are concentrating on the work in front of them.

'Aren't they scenic?' Penter calls. 'Factors are allocated primo modification care, as you can see.'

Tara knows what this place is. Of course she does. She's seen sights similar to this on the news, exposés of wealthy design houses accused of exploiting Asian workforces to increase their profit margins. But she had no idea it was happening in South Africa. And on this scale! It's beyond sick. Why haven't the cops shut it down? Bribery? Must be. Jesus.

'Mrs Tara Marais?' Penter calls. 'I am sorry to hurry, but there are other... matters I must complete before the moist break.'

'What is this? Some sort of sweat shop?'

'There is no sweat here!'

'So just plain old slave labour then?'

'Slave? Oh no. I have read my upside history. These are not like the citizens you upsiders forced to work and pluck sugar. Look: they are content.' She taps one of the tubes hanging from the ceiling. Tara shudders. 'They have constant victuals, they are busy and are consuming, they are entertained. Plus, they get primo modification and lemons. What more does a body want out of life? Really,' Penter continues, 'if I were not so suited to upside liaison, I would wish for a placement here, too.'

'But these are *children!*'

Penter chuckles. 'Little appendages make for efficient workloads, everybody knows that!'

'And... and what are they making?'

'Various consumables. Tech and modes, mostly. Victuals too in some sectors.'

Tara passes a child who instantly reminds her of Jane. She has the same shock of odd-coloured hair and slight build. Except that the stumps of this child's arms appear to be fused – melted – onto a strange bulky machine that reminds Tara of a sewing machine. She waits for another surge of nausea. Feels nothing. Realises that she's now beyond shocked, is almost glad of the mind-numbing drugs they've given her.

'But... But how can you say they aren't slaves? They seem to be... attached to their work stations.'

'Factors are not stuck. They can petition for a work replacement if they wish. Few do, of course, but we still need to fill the vacancies and make up for the high attrition rate.'

'Attrition?'

'Most upside assimilants depreciate quickly, which is why we have chosen to scout halfpints now. It results in many more productive periods.'

Tara has to admit that the silent children don't look as if they are in obvious distress, their hideous deformities aside. Is this some kind of twisted disability scheme? Maybe their families send them here, thinking they're going to be gainfully employed. Maybe, she thinks with a surge of disgust, their families *sell* them to people like this woman. 'And... *Martin* is here?' She suddenly recalls something Olivia said to that policewoman, something racist about Martin coming from a good white home, that he will be missed; that he isn't some addicted street child with no choices.

'Yes. In row 79/f.5c, station 14. Tech production. It's a good posting.'

'But... why Martin? Why did you choose him? He comes from a good home. You must have known he would be missed.'

'Isn't it obvious? Because he was the primo viable we selected! I'm sure you agree that he had a surfeit of misdirected energy.' She smiles, and Tara gets the impression that there's a tinge of sadness to it. 'Father said his redirectable destructive capacity was in an extraordinarily high percentile range. Ah. We are close.'

With a jolt of recognition, Tara spots the back of Martin's head in the next row and, somehow, she finds the strength to run.

'Martin!' Tara drops to her knees next to his desk, throws her arms around him. 'Are you okay? Are you hurt?'

He slowly raises his head, gazes at her blankly. Jesus, they've drugged him, too. She looks down at the desk. His hands are moulding a pink gel substance; she can't tell what he's making.

'Can you stand, Martin? Come on, I'm going to get you out of here.' She glances at Penter, waits for her to disagree, pull out a weapon, threaten her. But she continues to smile at Tara in that infuriatingly benign fashion. 'Martin, come on.'

He doesn't budge. She grabs his arm. 'Please, Martin. We have to go home. Your dad is waiting for you.' When he still doesn't respond, she moves behind him, slides her arms under his armpits, tries to lift him. But it's like trying to heft dead weight. He may only be twelve, but he's large for his age, weighs almost the same as she does.

'Please... *please*, Martin. I can't do this by myself. You need to move. Think of all your stuff at home, your computer games. Come on, Martin. Let's go home.'

A dreamy smile now on his face, Martin continues to mould the plasticky mess in front of him.

'What have you done to him?' Tara yells at Penter.

'He is integrated, Mrs Tara Marais.' Penter smiles. 'He is content.'

Tara grabs Martin's arm again, attempts once more to yank him out of the chair. 'Martin, *please*.'

She looks up at the ceiling, that tube attached to his neck. There must be something in that tube, they must be feeding him some kind of drug. She grabs it in both hands, yanks upwards as hard as she can, and Martin lets out a high keening wail that doesn't sound human. She drops the tube instantly; it hasn't budged an inch from the matt of tissue healed around it. Fuck – has she hurt him? Has it been... surgically inserted like some kind of shunt or drain? Jesus.

'We must leave now,' Penter says, still with that infuriating smile. 'I have allowed you to see the viable.'

'I can't just leave him here!' Tara rounds on her. 'Please, you're a mother. You must understand.' Penter's smile drops, and for a second Tara thinks she's got to her. 'Please help me. I'll... I'll say that you helped me, that you did what you could. You won't get into trouble. Please—'

'You can integrate, if that is your desire, certainly,' Penter interrupts. 'I can petition the Ministry. Perhaps you could educate?'

What the fuck? 'Educate?'

'Yes. Instruct our halfpints on abnormal lifeskills, like the other brown. That one will be modified soon and—'

'Just shut the fuck up with all your brown shit!' Tara's reached the limit of her patience – and, she realises, her sanity. 'I have to take Martin with me! Help me, please.' Tears are falling freely now. The wash of calm she felt when she pressed the wound at the back of her head has entirely dissipated. She needs to appeal to this woman's maternal instinct. 'He needs to be home. I can't leave him here. As a mother – as a woman – can't you understand?'

For some reason Penter seems to find this amusing. 'Mrs Tara Marais, I will ask you again: if you wish to integrate, I can petition. Otherwise, we must leave immediately.'

She's getting nowhere. Tara weighs up the odds. If she tries to overpower Penter, there's no way that Martin will be able to help her in his condition, and what are her chances? She's sick, weak, barely has the energy to walk, never mind fight. The last thing she wants to do is leave Martin here, but if she does manage to leave – if this woman isn't lying to her and they are really going to let her go – then she could come back, bring the cops, get this whole place shut down. And if the cops are on the take, well, she'll go to the media. Stephen will know what to do.

And, she has to admit, she's desperate to get out of here for her own sake. If she looks too closely at the grossly deformed children around her again, she'll lose it for good.

Yes, that's what she'll do. Get out of here, come back with the cavalry. She tries to ignore the other, darker thought that's been nudging at the back of her mind. That maybe Martin might be getting just what he deserves. She shakes her head to erase the thought. How can she even think that? What's wrong with her?

Tara sinks to her haunches again, winces as her leg muscles spasm once more. 'Martin. Listen to me. I'll be back soon. I promise.'

No reaction.

She stands up. Rubs her eyes.

'Mrs Tara Marias?' Penter says. 'Shall we?' She gestures for Tara to walk in front of her, presumably back to the door through which they entered. Tara tries to keep her eyes straight ahead, doesn't allow them to skate over the horrors around her. Why would this woman just let her go after what she's seen? She knows what they're doing here. Icy sweat dribbles down her sides, and she sees, in horrible clarity, how it will all play out. Shoved in the boot of a car at gunpoint, hands and feet bound, the clunk of the lid closing on her, the bumpy drive to a rural mine dump, an abandoned quarry.

Her body never found.

Should she try to flee? She winces again as another jolt of pain shoots through her thigh muscles; the adrenaline coursing through her doesn't seem to be helping her situation.

She pictures a thick green poison sliding through her veins. Maybe that's why they haven't shot her yet. Maybe she's going to die anyway.

When she reaches the door, Tara turns to look once more at the back of Martin's head, but she's forgotten which row he's in, can't spot him. Just do as the woman says. Don't argue, don't panic. Yes, if she gets out of here alive, she can save all these kids.

Penter close behind her, Tara scuffs her away across the dusty market space, reaches the lifts. As before, the area is deserted. This is it, Tara thinks. This is where she's going to do it. No witnesses.

'Mrs Tara Marais?' Penter says softly behind her.

Tara turns her head, feels her bowels contract, knows for sure that Penter will be pointing a weapon in her face, almost can't believe it when she sees that the other woman is empty handed, seems to be indicating she should approach the lift at the far right of the row.

Penter smiles her benign, bright smile. 'Before you depart, may I thank you for your concern about Jane.'

Of course. Why didn't she think of this before? Jane could be a way to forge some kind of connection with this woman – make it harder for Penter to kill her. 'How... how is Jane?' she asks, feeling, for a fleeting, ridiculous second as if they are just two mothers shooting the shit in a shopping centre.

'She is primo. Catalogue, even.' Penter beams.

'When I was at the house... That man... that Ryan... I told Jane he was dangerous, that he—'

'Oh that!' Penter laughs.

'He's a paedophile. A predator.' Tara feels that she must make this woman understand, even if she is some sort of gangster running the world's largest and sickest sweatshop operation. Jane is still a child; she could be in danger. Tara is aware that this makes no sense. Her logic is fucked up. This woman has done something to Martin, possibly something irrevocable. Why should she bother to help her or her family? But she's desperate; she can't stop. 'Listen to me. Ryan... He is a monster.'

'Oh, we know what he is.'

The lift pings open. Tara steps inside it, expecting Penter to follow her. But she stays where she is. 'Goodbye, Mrs Tara Marais,' Penter says. 'Ignore the signs and please, live well.'

Before Tara can answer, the doors slide shut. Tara waits for the usual swoopy feeling of being inside a lift, but after only two or three seconds, the doors open again. She's expecting to see Penter still standing in front of her – maybe this time with a gun in her hand, a vicious smile on her lips (*You didn't think it would be that easy, did you, Mrs Tara Marais?*) – but instead, she sees a low-ceilinged corridor in front of her.

She hurries out, so overcome with relief that she sags against the wall, barely able to believe that she's made it. She hears the lift door shut behind her, then makes herself walk forward.

The passageway ends at a grey door, a rusty metal sign on it reading: 'Trespassers will be corrected.'

Ignore the signs.

She pushes through it, emerges at the bottom of a stairwell, the kind of dusty, piss-stinking space found in parking lots. Her muscles scream as she ascends the stairs, but she ignores the agony, keeps on going, loses count of the number of flights, is hyperventilating when she reaches a door at the top. Thank God. She's expecting to step out into sunlight, but instead she emerges into a low, brick-walled tunnel.

She's now so worn out that she doesn't even attempt to wipe away the exhausted tears and mucus soaking her face. She crawls through it, reaches yet another door. Scrambles to her feet, grabs a slippery brass handle, turns it, and stumbles out into a room.

This can't be.

She knows this room. Recognises the row of jars containing desiccated insects – the rat skeleton that's now swathed in a shroud of black ants. But... How can she be here? No. *No.* The last of her strength ebbs out of her legs. *This is it*, she thinks, as she collapses to her knees. She hears – but doesn't feel – the dull clunk of her head hitting the floor.

Chapter 24

PENTER

It's time.

Penter acknowledges the Terminal Ward drone's respectful greeting and walks towards the harvesting room. She looks through the round window behind which Father is strapped into the recycling chair, stabilising fluid pumping from a drip into his arm.

She touches the node at the back of her own head. The clinic has still not taken her for her penetration renewal. She has missed three cycles now, and the shunt hole is even beginning to seal over. When she woke today, she had a message from Cardineal Phelgm which informed her that she is to return upside; perhaps this is why a renewal is not deemed necessary for her. Penter takes it as a vote of confidence by senior Administration. They trust her enough to discharge her duties upside for extended periods and remain in regard even without the shunt.

Who knows? Perhaps she will not undergo another penetration renewal until she is recycled. Her new role as Head of Upside Scouting and Reconnaissance is a permanent position, now that the pilot phase has proved a success. Clone projects will be rolled out in several nodes and she will oversee the many family units that will be assigned to precincts in nodes all over the upside. Her fingers ache pleasurably from the hours she's spent initialling and signing the requisite documents and contracts, and every nerve ending in her skull is crackling with a new emotion: excitement.

She didn't hesitate when Cardineal Phelgm offered her the position, and somehow managed to hide her felicitation and surprise. As she stood to attention in front of his desk all thoughts of the troubling aspects of upside life – SKY, the concrete, the bloodletting, the dangerous vehicles – were forgotten. All she could think about was the taste of fresh ready beans on her tongue. She had not expected this – did not think that after Father was caught playing she would have been considered for another upside position, especially not a primo promotion! Perhaps it is because she dealt with that brown educator with such alacrity. Perhaps it is because she dealt with Father's indiscretions so efficiently.

As she requested, Jane has been assigned to her unit. She knows she can depend on Jane. She is a calm and adaptable halfpint, proven most recently by her primo relations with the damaged brown. If anyone can keep her composure for an extended period in the field without the aid of shunts and calming medications, it is Jane.

She has only one matter to conclude before she searches out a new precinct.

One final decision to make.

Father's eyes are shut, but as she gazes at him, they open and stare straight into hers. Something sighs deep inside her; she has forgotten how scenic he is. Blissful love, she thinks. According to the browns, it makes the world rotate.

Father has agreed to a corrective penetration which will smother his disregardful urges. But for how long? When it wears off, will he still want to play? Will he still want to collect facsimiles of brown carcasses? She is not sure. Why is it that even without a penetration renewal, she feels no need to play, to meddle, to collect unauthorised upside artefacts? Is playing a predisposition a person is vatted with? Some say that Players are rotten, that they are vatted suboptimally, with an irreparable urge to disrupt order. If this is true, then it is no wonder that Father was so enamoured with the upside and his karking collection. If Players were allowed their way, the world would become just like the upside, like a show on SKY.

She personally delivered his collection to the incinerator.

She steps into the harvesting room and approaches Father's recycling chair. If she wanted, she could reach out and stroke his skin.

'Father,' she says.

His gaze does not waver. 'Mother.'

'I am not Mother,' Penter says, remembering their first disregardful encounter in the television room back at the precinct. It feels far away, as if it happened many periods ago. 'Here, my name is Penter Ulliel, Head of Upside Scouting and Reconnaissance.'

He smiles. She is not sure if it is tender or mocking. 'Apologies, Penter Ulliel. Here, *I* am Varder Batiss.'

'Why did you collect those artefacts?' Penter blurts. She knows that her features betray her ongoing thought-seep.

He closes his eyes, shivers as a shot of fluid floods down the drip tube. When he opens them again, they are cool, distant. 'I was curious, Penter Ulliel. The anatomical fakery and… birth interested me.'

Penter's not satisfied. Curiosity is not an answer. She recalls the educator's words. 'Were you looking for… for an outlet, Varder Batiss?'

He barks a laugh. 'An outlet, Penter Ulliel? An outlet for what?'

Love, she thinks, but doesn't say. She turns away. She wonders how she would feel if he had said that it *was* love that he was searching for. That the facsimiles he collected were an outlet for this emotion, like that meddling educator had suggested.

She wonders how she would feel if he had asked *her* to be an outlet.

She wonders if she will listen to the ache in her chest, which is at war with her intellect.

If she relents, he will be Father again. Cardineal Phelgm made this clear. If she chooses to include him in the new project unit then he will be Father and she will be Mother. They'll be a nucleated family again.

And if she does not relent, he will be recycled.

It is up to her.

It is time to make her choice.

Chapter 25

RYAN

Ryan wakes up to a familiar sound: canned laughter and a tinny line of upbeat music. It's an American sitcom and for a moment he thinks he's back home. Really home, with Alice and Karin, and that time has somehow bounced backwards again to before the whole mess started.

But the potato-sack smell of the sheets and the dull artificial lighting hit him at the same time as the pain in the back of his head. He can't remember how long it's been since he's seen the sun. He's a Johannesburger, bred on sunlight, and anything more than two days of rain sends him into a deep depression. It's been longer than that down here.

The positivity and peace of the last few days – however long he's been here; what they call 'periods' down here, to avoid the natural, light-related connotations of circadian rhythms – have deserted him, he realises as he hauls his body over the edge of the bed. Then he remembers what has happened to him. He puts his hands to his devastated crotch and tries to shake himself awake from the nightmare, but he's already awake. He's sitting at the side of a bed in a room that's not his.

He begins to scream, and there's something satisfying about the rip in his body, and he screams some more.

A little girl comes through the bedroom door. She tilts her head and curls her lips at him. She doesn't pause, just comes straight up and presses something against his neck.

Ryan is eating porridge at the breakfast nook. His body feels a little bruised, his bones ache. He tries to stretch himself straight.

'Are you optimal, Mr Ryan?' Jane asks.

'I felt uncomfortable in the night. I didn't sleep well.'

'You had memories this morning,' she says.

'Really?' Ryan asks. 'About what? Did I tell you?'

'No, but you were shouting. I sedated you.'

'Thanks.'

'You are due for a penetration renewal today. That will solve your discomfort.'

'Okay,' he says. 'How do I arrange that?'

'Just go to the on-shift clinic at the Academy. Level H.'

'Okay.'

Ryan has the sense that something should be worrying him, but he can't place what it might be. Why look for things to worry about? he asks himself. If I'm feeling peaceful, why question it?

'Happy dispatch, Mr Ryan!' Jane announces. 'Penter Ulliel has invited me onto a new upside project. We will be repeating the Encounters operation in a new school. Penter Ulliel admired my role in the pilot project and has asked me to reprise it.'

She's as happy as Ryan's ever seen her and it warms him. 'Great. Well done,' he says. 'You'll have the chance to get fresh fruit and vegetables again. I'm sure you'll enjoy that.'

'Yes, and to look at the sky and the creatures,' she bubbles. Ryan can tell she's imagining a future full of travel. He feels proud.

But then her face falls.

'What's the matter?'

'I will regret you, Mr Ryan. If I am to join the unit permanently, I will not see you.'

'Oh, don't be silly,' he says. 'You must do what makes you happy. I'm not going to stand in your way. I'll be here when you come back... I suppose.'

'We can amble to the Academy together this shift,' Jane says, working up her cheer again. She gets up and goes to the bathroom and, as she walks away, something discomforting nudges at his mind. He looks at the shape of her body in the Academy uniform and the nudge pushes him harder.

He looks back down at his porridge, and then an older memory surfaces. Alice used to love instant oats, the peach-flavoured ones. The bits of fruit in it were actually flakes of dried apple saturated with peach flavour and dyed salmon pink. He didn't tell her.

He was dreaming about Alice last night, wasn't he? He misses her. Perhaps that memory is trying to talk to him. Maybe that's what this sense of dread is trying to communicate. The penetration renewal might make him peaceful, but what if it also makes him forget? He's willing to forget a lot, but not Alice.

'I'm not sure exactly how it works around here,' he starts when Jane returns, 'but what if...' He knows he's manipulating her, and he feels bad. He knows what she wants and he's going to use her needs to suit his own purposes. It comes so naturally to him. Is this who he's always been?

'Yes, Mr Ryan?'

'What if... Do I have to pay off my debt by tutoring? What if I came to work with Penter Ulliel. And you? Would that discharge my debt?'

'Mr Ryan! What a primo notion. I will ask her at our next meeting. She may be able to talk to the bond administrator.'

The poor girl doesn't realise that he's cheating her. Her friendship is his best chance – likely his only chance – of getting upside again. Once he's there, he'll just disappear. He'll go back to Alice, and they will never find him. Doesn't he teach that about the ethos of Upside Relations? They avoid conflict and detection at all costs.

The shunt hole in the back of his head is throbbing weakly, sending short sparks into his brain as he thinks this. It's nothing worse than the zaps he's had every time he's quit his mood-stabilising drugs. But he knows that whatever they've implanted there is trying to assert its control and is trying to reach in and shut down these seditious thoughts of his. It's essential not to get the penetration renewed: it's only because it's due that he's managed to conceive of this plan and, peace or no peace, he intends to see it through. He is going to return to his daughter.

When they get to the lifts, Jane scans them open. There are no buttons in this lift; it just takes them where they're scheduled to go. Which, for Ryan, is Level H.

'Felicitous renewal, Mr Ryan, and enjoy your shift,' Jane says. She waves in her tentative way, lifting her palm halfway and wriggling her fingers, like she's learning a foreign code. She is. People don't wave here, Ryan's noticed; it's an upside affectation.

The doors slide closed in front of her and Ryan gets the sudden sense that he's alone, that he's beyond help. The walls of the corridor seem to compress in on him and the lights seem to dim.

It's all in his head, he thinks, and the only answer is the grin of the ubiquitous institutional clown on the sign opposite the lift. 'Level H' is all the sign says. The corridor's carpet has a disorienting pattern of honeycombed hexagons in orange against burgundy, and Ryan is mesmerised as he watches the pattern writhe off like an optical illusion along the span. Again, he gets the discomforting feeling that this whole place is a stage set hurriedly slapped together just for his benefit. There's no listing of offices or departments, but still it's evident where Ryan is supposed to go. The clown points a bulbous gloved finger along the long corridor to Ryan's left, and unadorned arrows punctuate the wall as it disappears to the vanishing point.

If that's where he's going to get a drill stuck into his head and false thoughts loaded into it and his memories erased, that's the direction he won't be going, thank you very much. He scans his gel tag over the lift's call button, but it answers by glowing red and emitting a bloop of failure. An 'E' flashes briefly on the display in the middle of the button.

There has to be another way out of here. He walks down the corridor to the right. The corridor walls have no doors along them – it's just an unadorned tunnel in dove grey with a single mint-green stripe running along it. The colours clash nauseatingly with the carpeting. But unlike the stretch to the left, this corridor curves and switches and before long he's not sure which direction he's headed. He recalls the corridor in the new wing of Jane's house, all organic curves and apparently pointless twists. Organic... yes. In the close silence, Ryan can imagine himself walking through some giant creature's intestines, transgressing into a sanctum he should have no business seeing.

It's just your imagination, he tells himself.

But the silence is not quite as silent as it was.

He walks on, the corridor never branching, no junction to confuse his path: it's either the lift that won't let him in, the way to a penetration renewal, or this way.

The background hum gets louder and begins to resolve itself as he walks; a stale, cool breeze churns up from ahead of him. He can hear snuffling, a wet sound of phlegm in a giant throat, or is that just his own ragged breathing echoing against the walls?

He turns another switchback and his feet glide in something slippery, a puddle on the floor, which, without his noticing, has become slick, polished concrete. The walls are now unplastered face brick, crystalline deposits of salt growing out between them like fungus. Ryan recalls the rising damp in Duvenhage's office. It all seems so far away now, but the memory kindles a small knot of panic inside him, and as it grows he can feel the hole in his head throbbing harder, as if fighting off an infection. He knows it's too weak now to stop the memories and the fear. If he just turns back, gets the penetration renewed, he will feel calm and at peace again, just like in the garden.

The tide of panic flows on, unstoppable, and washed up in the debris he can see not only Duvenhage – is there something he needed to finish with him? – but Alice swirling past, reaching out for him, begging for him to pull her out.

He won't forget. He won't turn back.

The walls are lined with colour-coded pipes and conduits, and the noise has become louder, growing subtly like contagion, until it's become painful to his ears. There's a thump-thump-thump and shrill whine and an exhalation and the stale air has become a wind riffling his hair. Still, beneath the noise he can hear something else – voices. Shrieking? Crying? The hubbub of conversation.

He rounds another bend and sees a doorway, double doors with thick black rubber aprons. Broad silver-foil tubes arc across the ceiling here and the air-conditioner's motor, lodged in a large alcove, screams as it pushes to capacity. One of the tubes has come loose and it lashes like a gigantic spinning caterpillar as Ryan slides past it and opens the door.

He's in the Mall, opposite the food court, and he can find his way back from here.

'Was the penetration renewal optimal?' Jane asks him when she comes into the flat. There's a hardness to her tone, suspicion.

'Yes, no problem.'

'You didn't tutor your class.'

'Uh, yes, sorry. The waiting room was full. It took a while. You know how clinics are.'

She looks at him. 'You know you'll be docked for missed shifts?'

'Docked?' Ryan fights a spurt of adrenaline. He has to keep calm. If he'd had his penetration renewed, nothing would frighten him. 'You mean... pay?' he asks as nonchalantly as he can.

'Yes, I mean pay.' She walks towards him where he's sitting with a glass of water at the kitchen nook. 'What did you think I meant? Amputation?' She laughs, that whimper-grunt he's become used to. 'You're such a motherfucking brown, Mr Ryan. Amputation is a privilege, expensive. Sometimes tutors are given amputations as a long-service bonus. Disregard is not the way to earn amputations.'

'Okay. Well... as I say, I couldn't help it. The Academy Administration will understand, I'm sure.'

'Understand? There are rules and the shifts are designated quite clearly. If you're in breach, you're in breach. There's nothing to understand.' Her tone is making him nervous. What is this leading up to? For all this time he's fooled himself that she's just a normal girl, but she's not. She's one of them... She lives here, and here they do things in a fucked-up way. He's got to be careful, and at the same time pretend that everything's absolutely fine. Staying in her good books and getting upside with the project unit is his only chance of seeing Alice again.

He shrugs. 'Okay.' But he can feel the hot blood in his face.

'Oh, don't be upset, Mr Ryan. I'm just – what do they say on the documents? – yanking your train. I'm pretending with you!' She laughs again and Ryan is washed with relief. 'I have primo dispatch. I spoke with Penter Ulliel.'

'Yes?'

'She says you can come with us and discharge your debt that way. She was impressed with your efficiency when you laboured in the precinct. She likes browns; they're always so hard-working, she says. Except for the rat-breeding ones, of course. But you're not a rat-breeder. So kark the Academy and Academy Administration! You're on the Upside Relations Special Project team!'

'Yes!' He jumps from his seat and goes across to hug Jane, but something stops him before he does. The feeling that somehow it would be wrong to touch her... That she would be cold. 'Thank you,' he says. 'I won't disappoint you.'

'There is one stipulation, though.'

'Yes?'

'You know that incognito is part of the ethos of Upside Relations operations?'

'Yes.'

'Well, to that end, Liaison Penter needs you to be modified before you join the team so that you will remain incognito.'

'Modified? What does that involve?' Although somehow he knows what it involves.

'Oh, just a minor change to your physicals.' She makes a vague gesture around her face and Ryan slumps back against the wall. He needs to stay calm. 'The next Encounters project will be taking place near the same node as before, so there is a chance that you may be recognised. The modification will ensure that you are not.'

'Uh...'

'I see that you are concerned. Do not be concerned. Team members are regularly modified. I was modified before the pilot project, as were several of my colleagues. Father himself has been modified thirty-seven times and doesn't he appear primo?'

Ryan's mind is racing, and he concentrates on keeping his face passive. If this is the trade-off, a bit of plastic surgery, then he'll have to accept it. Otherwise he'll never see Alice again. Maybe it will be a good thing. He'll be able to face everyone from his past and they won't know who he is; he can start fresh.

He thinks of Father, how he looks like a soap star. It could be worse.

They've given him an injection of something and he can't move as he's pushed along the corridor in a wheelchair. Or it's more that he doesn't feel the need to move. He imagines that he could lift his arms, wiggle his feet, if he wanted to, but it's just right, just like this. His muscles are absolutely relaxed, like he's in the middle of a deep sleep. The knot of terror lodged in his sternum is wrapped up in cotton wool; he can feel it, but it's far away.

The orderly shunts him into an elevator. The doors close and it starts moving. In his inert state, Ryan can feel which direction they're travelling in. It's definitely down, and slowly. His body feels like a mould of jelly, rippling with the subtle shifts in gravity. A mould of jelly floating through the sky on a parachute; no, a jelly-fish drifting its way to the bottom. He giggles. The lift creaks and sighs. The orderly snorts back some mucus.

The doors open.

'Thank you, orderly, I'll take it from here.'

Ryan squints up at the woman's face, and is shocked by how normal she appears. She looks like she belongs at home. A regular South African woman with all her parts in the right places. She has a pleasant smile, not the rictus twitch he's become used to down here. She's wearing a shiny medallion around her neck. 'LOVER' it says.

'What are you doing here?' he asks.

She unclicks the wheelchair's brakes and starts pushing him along a straight corridor lined with shining wall tiles, her medallion clanking on its chain as she walks. 'My name is Nomsa Makgatho. I'll be your modifying agent for the shift. You're very lucky, you know, to have been accepted into an Upside Relations team. Up until recently, upside citizens have only been assimilated for labour or parts. Your diversion must be part of the new policy promulgated by the Administration in the last session. I must say you'd make a primo donor if you ever found yourself at a loose end.' She appraises him. The knot of fear burns hotter inside him.

They stop at a door with an ideograph of a man in a welding mask holding what looks like a large electric carving knife or a small chainsaw.

The nurse knocks at the door and calls, 'It's ready, Butcher.'

Behind the door there's a snuffle and clink. 'Okay. Bring it in,' a grouchy voice returns. The fear is starting to seep out of its package.

She starts to push him through the door and he halts her. 'Nurse? Nomsa?'

'Yes, Mr Devlin?'

'What does... what will the modification involve?'

'Oh, you know. Nothing to be nervous of. Just a nip and a tuck.'

Chapter 26

TARA

'Tara?' Stephen stands in the doorway, backlit by the entrance hall's light, dressed only in a pair of boxer shorts. He looks terrible, Tara thinks vaguely, before her legs buckle under her. He catches her under her armpits just in time, then wraps his arms around her, squeezing her so tight that for a second she's unable to breathe. 'Christ, I thought... Oh, Christ Jesus, baby! I thought you were dead!'

She leans against him, buries her face in his chest, shivers as his fingers stroke her hair, run over her face. She hears his breath hitch and he pulls back, gently turns her head to the side.

'Jesus, Tara. Who did that to you?' He pulls her against him again.

'Did what?'

'There's a cut – a wound – behind your ear. I can't tell if it's serious. We should get you to a hospital—'

'No!' She can't go anywhere. There's something very important she needs to tell Stephen. Something vital. If she could just...

'You might have other injuries. You might...' A muffled sob. 'Tara... have you been... were you raped?'

She wishes he'd shut up. She's almost got it. Then it comes in a flood. Martin... she's seen Martin. She needs to tell Stephen. She knows where he is, if she could only just... 'Stephen. Listen. Martin—'

'Shhh,' Stephen says. 'Shh. It's okay, baby. Where... where have you *been*?'

'I've...' Where *has* she been? Walking. She remembers walking. In the dark, all quiet. No traffic. She notices that Stephen's staring down at her left hand in confusion. She follows his gaze, realises that she's gripping Baby Tommy's head so hard that her fingers are aching.

'Let's get you inside.' Stephen snakes his arm behind her, steadies her as she shuffles through the hallway and into the lounge. She doesn't resist. She's aware that she's beyond exhaustion, the muscles in her legs are trembling, her head feels... mushy; she can barely keep her eyes open.

Stephen helps lower her onto the couch and her limbs sigh with relief. She sinks back against the cushions. Struggles up again. Ugh. Something smells bad.

He switches on the light and she blinks as it stings her eyes. Dropping Baby Tommy into her lap, she looks down at her hands – they're filthy, her nails chipped and ripped. And what did Stephen say about an injury? She touches the back of her head, just below her right ear. Feels a scab, about the size of a five-rand coin. Presses it. Mmmm. A pleasant buzzing sensation. Makes her feel woozy. Doesn't hurt. Presses it again, then looks down at the rest of her body. Her jeans are chafing her thighs – they're damp around the crotch. Has she wet herself? Is that the source of the bad smell?

All that doesn't matter now. Martin. He's... She knows where he is, she *knows* she does. She must tell Stephen. If she could just remember *exactly*...

Stephen paces in front of her, tugging at his thinning hair. He's unshaven, his eyes are bloodshot. She's never seen him looking so haggard. 'Shit. What should I do first? I'd better call the cops, let them know you're back.'

'Back?'

'They've been looking for you. Found your car out in Alex. Christ, baby. We didn't know... We thought you'd been hijacked. Christ, you didn't walk from there in the middle of the night, did you?'

Alex? Does he mean the township? But she left her car... Yes, that's it. She left her car outside Jane's house, didn't she? 'Stephen, listen to me. Martin... we have to go get him.' He shakes his head, scrubs his hands over his face. She needs to make him listen. Why won't he listen? '*Stephen!*'

'Oh, baby. You don't know? Jesus. You're really worrying me now, Tara.'

'Know what?'

'About that headmaster. That fucker. Baby, it's been in all the papers.'

'What has?'

'Wait. I need a drink for this.' She watches as he takes out two glass tumblers from the drinks cabinet, pours several fingers of Klipdrift into each one. His hands are shaking violently – she doesn't think the drink is his first of the night.

He pushes a glass into her hand. She takes a sip. The brandy burns her throat; she can feel it trickling all the way down to her empty stomach. Takes another. Jesus, she's so *thirsty*.

'This is not going to be easy to hear, Tara. After you left us... That day Olivia was here, remember?' Tara nods impatiently. Of course she remembers *that*. 'Well, the cops went to go interview Duvenhage again, about the Encounters group or whatever it's called. Couldn't find him. His wife said he was AWOL. Tracking company traced his car to the airport, and when they...' He swallows, and

Tara realises he's struggling to hold back a sob. 'And when they... when they looked inside it, the boot... it was... it was soaked in blood. Martin's blood, baby. They tested it for DNA. There's no doubt.'

Tara shakes her head. 'But I saw him, I saw Martin.' *Where* did she see Martin though? That house... that's where. Wasn't it? For some reason an image of a sewing machine pops into her mind. The brandy isn't helping. It's making her feel even fuzzier.

'You couldn't have, baby. They found too much blood, too much for him to have survived. There's no doubt. I know – I know what you must be feeling, you want to believe he's alive, but, Tara, he isn't. He couldn't be.'

'I...' She tries to make sense of what Stephen's telling her. Duvenhage, that prissy busybody, a murderer? 'They've... found him? Duvenhage, I mean?'

'No. The fucker's disappeared. They're looking. They'll find him. And it's not just that, baby. They think he's connected to that Ryan guy. That janitor.'

'What?'

'Ja. Some kind of kiddie porn racket. They found pictures, evidence that links the two of them.' Another smothered sob. 'We can only hope that Martin didn't suffer.'

'But... but when was this?' Did she see Martin before Duvenhage took him? No, it can't be. It feels as if she's only just seen Martin – hours ago, minutes, maybe. 'But when I left yesterday—'

'Tara,' Stephen interrupts, 'you've been gone for five days.'

'No. That's impossible.'

'Tara, baby, listen to me. We thought you were lost. I thought I'd lost you.'

She takes another sip, then drains the glass. Feels the brandy doing its work, clouding what's left of her thoughts. Opens her mouth to speak again, but can't muster the energy.

'Here, baby, lie down.' She allows Stephen to lift her legs up onto the couch.

She closes her eyes, and then, nothing.

'... think Duvenhage might have something to do with her disappearance?' Tara's groggily aware that Stephen's voice is floating into the lounge from the corridor.

'Unlikely, Mr Marais. His car was left at the airport before she disappeared. But we are not discounting anything at this stage.' A woman's voice. Well-modulated, deep. Familiar. But Tara can't quite place it.

'It's a coincidence though, isn't it? Her disappearing around the same time? What about that Ryan bastard?' Stephen again.

'We will have to wait to hear what she says. But there is no evidence to suggest that. The location where her car was found points to a hijacking, a robbery perhaps. Our only witness reports seeing a white male, early thirties, driving the car.' This time Tara manages to place the voice – Superintendent Molefi.

'That Ryan's white, isn't he?'

'Yes, Mr Marais, but he doesn't fit this man's description at all.'

'Last night... she was confused. A head injury of some sort. Think she might have amnesia?'

'Possibly post-traumatic shock, Mr Marais. She must go to a hospital to be checked out. You should have taken her last night.'

'I know, I know. I was just so relieved to see her. Christ knows where she's been. She's filthy, lost weight...' His voice fades away; they must have moved into the kitchen.

Tara sits up too quickly, the motion making her stomach lurch. She gags, tastes sour alcohol. Draws in a shuddering breath. Jesus, she feels like crap. Her head is throbbing, she's dehydrated, recognises the beginnings of a major hangover. She lifts her hand to touch the wound behind her ear, realises she's still clutching Baby

Tommy's head, her fingers stiff from cupping the curve of his scalp all night. She drops him on the coffee table, rubs her hands over her face. Tries to stand, wincing as her knees pop. Looks down, sees that she's dressed in her pyjamas. Her jeans and sweatshirt are bundled in a stinking ball at the base of the television stand. Stephen must have removed them last night, left her to sleep on the couch.

Her eye is drawn to a bunch of papers scattered on the side table next to Stephen's La-Z-Boy. She inches her way over to it, grabs one of the pages. It's a 'missing person' flyer, only the person missing is her: her black-and-white face grins back at her above the words 'Have You Seen This Woman?' She recognises the photograph, actually remembers the exact moment when Stephen took it. It was on their holiday to Cape Town, in the bar of the Mount Nelson, the day before she returned to that mall to buy her first Reborn – Baby Lulu.

She stretches her arms behind her head to rub her neck, grimacing as she's hit with a waft of stale sweat. Jesus. Was she really gone for five days? How can that be? Was she in that house for that long?

Ignoring the ache in her thighs, she shuffles into the hallway, hesitates outside the kitchen doorway.

'... nearer to finding him?' she hears Stephen asking.

'We're doing all we can,' Superintendent Molefi replies.

'You think he's gone overseas? What about his passport? Can't you trace it?'

'We found his South African passport in the safe in his office, Mr Marais. There's no sign of him. It is almost as if he's vanished off the face of the earth.'

Tara stumbles through the door. The superintendent looks up, slides off her stool, steps towards her. 'Ah, Mrs Marais. I am happy to see you're safe.'

Stephen gasps and runs around the breakfast counter. 'Sorry, my baby, I didn't know you were awake.' He guides her towards one of the stools, helps her onto it. She can't decide what's more confusing, Stephen treating her like she's made of glass, or the cotton wool that seems to have replaced her brain.

As she sits down, she's hit with a vague image of Martin smiling blankly at her. Sitting at a desk. *Where* though? At school?

'I know you're exhausted, Mrs Marais,' the superintendent says gently, 'but can you tell me what happened to you?'

'Can't we do this later?' Stephen says, with a trace of his usual irritability.

Superintendent Molefi ignores him, continues to fix her gaze on Tara. 'Mrs Marais? Are you up to talking to me?'

Tara nods. Steadies herself by gripping the counter top. Takes a grateful gulp of water out of the glass Stephen hands to her. 'A man... a man in a hat. I was looking for Martin, and he... did something to me.'

'Was it Duvenhage, baby?' Stephen jumps in.

Superintendent Molefi shoots him an exasperated glance. 'Was this while you were driving, Mrs Marais?'

'No.'

'You were parked? You were in your car?'

'I... I can't remember. I parked my car at the house...' That's it. She's getting warmer, she can feel it! 'He's in there somewhere. That house.'

'Which house, Mrs Marais?'

'You know which house. Jane's house.' She looks across at Stephen. 'Stephen, tell her. You know which house I mean. The one with the statues.'

'I don't, my baby.'

'The one I told you about... Where the pervert, Ryan, was hiding.'

'And what about it, Mrs Marais?'

'That's where he is!'

'Who? Ryan? The man who hurt you?'

'No! Martin! Martin's there.'

Stephen slumps. 'Tara... Martin's dead.'

She stands up. 'He's not. He's not. Let's go. Come on.' Stephen moves as if to take her in his arms, but she pushes him away. 'We might not have much time.'

'You need to get her to a hospital right away, Mr Marais,' Superintendent Molefi insists. 'She is not well.'

'I'm *fine*.'

'Tara. I know you feel guilty that you didn't connect with Martin when he was alive, but—'

Jesus! 'I know where Martin is. Why won't you listen?'

'Mrs Marais—'

'*Please*. I can show you. Please.'

Stephen sighs. 'If we go with you to the house, then will you go to the hospital?'

'I don't think this is a good idea, Mr Marais,' the policewoman says.

'Yes, yes, anything.' Tara jumps in. 'I swear, but please, let's *go*.'

Stephen glances at Superintendent Molefi, sighs again. 'Wait here, I'll get you some clothes.'

'This way,' Tara says, checking to make sure that Stephen and the policewoman are still following her.

The house smells even mustier than she remembers. The air is thick with dust motes, the paintwork appears to be flakier, shabbier, as if the house has given up, as if it's dying, crumbling in on itself.

Tara hurries down the corridor, opening doors at random. She knows the room has to be on this level, she's sure of that much.

'Tara,' Stephen says. 'Please, baby. Let's go back to the car.'

She ignores him, pushes open the door at the far end of the passageway. 'Here!' She's found it! The room with the jars. But...

but where is he? Where's Martin? She was sure he would be in here, but apart from that horrible insect collection, the room is empty.

'Christ,' Stephen mutters, glancing at the bottled rat at the end of the row. 'What the fuck is this shit?'

Tara's eyes dart around the room, fix on the cupboard. Yes, that's where he is. She knows it with a solid certainty. He's in there. She races over to it, yanks open the doors.

'Tara? What are you doing?'

A white wall stares back at her. 'This can't be—'

Has she got the wrong room? No. It's definitely this room. She remembers stumbling out into this space. *From where though?* And... It must be a false wall. Yeah, that's it. She bunches her fist and knocks against it, listening for a hollow rap like she's seen detectives do in the movies. All she hears is a dull thunk.

'Mr Marais?' she hears the policewoman saying. 'We must stop this now.'

'Tara, come on, baby,' Stephen pleads. 'We need to get you to the hospital.'

She ignores him, knocks on the wall, harder this time. Bunches her fist and punches. Again. And again.

She feels Stephen's arms wrapping around her waist, tries to twist out of his grip. 'Baby, what are you—'

'Martin!' she screeches. 'Martin!'

As Stephen and Superintendent Molefi finally manage to drag her away, the last thing she sees are the bloody smears her ragged knuckles have left on the paintwork.

Chapter 27

RYAN

Ryan buttons up the light-blue shirt and knots his tie. He can't remember the last time he wore a tie. A funeral probably, or maybe even when he got married to Karin. Could it have been that long ago?

The shirt is light and silky, the dye like a Tuscan sky. When he'd asked for smart clothes, pointing to a picture in a magazine, Penter had smiled. The next morning there was a box and a suit bag from A Camisa.

He tucks the shirt into the slacks and cinches them with a narrow leather belt, the type he would never have worn. But this evening he's dressing to impress.

He runs a slick of gel through his cropped hair and musses it, glances across at the mirror just long enough to check that the hair is okay. Deliberately avoiding, as he's quickly learnt, looking at his face.

It will be all right. He shrugs on the jacket. Its casual styling clashes with the rest of his smart outfit, but that can't be helped. He flips the hood over his head and leaves his room.

The new house is far more anonymous than the mansion the Encounters team squatted in last time. It's an old Kensington house that looks like any of the dozen others on the block: beige seven-foot wall topped by four perfunctory electric strands, a lavender bush by the front gate, red-tiled roof and blushed paint job. A far better way to blend in than that grotesque eyesore up on Excelsior Avenue.

Ryan tries to bring himself to care what will happen to the scouted children once they're taken, but he can't. That's not his business. He's not responsible for any of it. If you want to blame anyone, blame the school principals, just like Duvenhage, willing to sell their souls and their children for some seriously good money. Or blame the teachers, blame the parents, blame society. Blame fucking capitalism; you may as well bash your head against a brick wall. It's none of his business. Ryan was as good as dead, but he's made this arrangement to come back home for one reason only: to see Alice. Beyond that, nothing's important.

He runs his hand through his spiky hair one more time, feels the new contours of his cheeks. It will be okay; clothes maketh the man. He gets into the station wagon. He's collected Jane from school already and the rest of the afternoon and the evening is all his.

As he backs the Volvo out, he suppresses a wave of panic that he'll be stopped. But he never is. There's nothing preventing him from just leaving; they haven't even been renewing his shunt since he's been back up here. He's in total control of his mind; he has his free will back. There's nothing preventing him from taking the car and driving as far as he can. They've even arranged a new driver's licence to match his new face and his new name – follow the local laws, avoid conflict and detection at all costs. He could take a bundle of cash from Penter's desk and just go. But he always comes back. For now it suits him. He has a house to live in, he's protected, he has a job... He has a family, he laughs to himself. But after tonight, things might change.

He's not fooling himself; it might take a while to earn Alice's trust again, but once he's made a good impression tonight, that will be on course. And when the team packs up and goes back down, he has no intention of going with them. If Penter knew that, would she be so lax with him?

He shrugs off the question. It doesn't matter to him. One day at a time. That's how he's always lived.

He pulls into a rooftop parking spot at Bedford Centre, tugs the hood low over his head, locks the car and walks over to the entrance, concentrating on exuding confidence, walking as if he belongs here. He's a rich businessman from upstairs in the office tower, sauntering entitled through the mall. He looks at the shine on his crackling new Italian loafers as he walks. Rich businessmen have a free pass.

But when he looks up, a paunchy, scarred security guard at the roof entrance is looking at him rudely. He's just jealous, Ryan tells himself. Of course he's got an issue with rich people. He walks on, keeping his face down, the hood blinkering him.

A small child with a balloon skitters across his path, looks up at him and freezes. Ryan has to stop suddenly, the smooth-bottomed shoes sliding on the travertine, to avoid ploughing over him. The balloon is decorated with a clown advertising a pizza franchise. It slips from the boy's grasp. The boy looks into Ryan's eyes, his mouth widening, and then he flushes red and starts screaming.

Ryan shifts around the kid and hears his mother trotting up as he jinks right down another corridor. He doesn't look back.

Stay calm, he tells himself. It's just a kid and a security guard. It's not that bad. Surely. It will be okay. If he's in luck, Alice and Karin will be here soon.

He checks his wrist, but he's not wearing a watch. Come to think of it, he can't remember the last time he wore one. What happened to his watch?

He goes into a phone shop. There's a woman in a white blouse and black suit jacket sitting behind the counter. She's wearing a yellow scarflet around her neck like an air hostess. She's looking down at her keyboard.

'Hi. I wonder if you can tell me the time.'

She looks up at his face and gasps, but professionalism constrains her. He watches her frightened eyes scan the cut of his shirt, the weave of his tie and calculate his worth.

'It's... it's uh...' She swallows something down and checks her watch. 'It's twenty to six.'

'Thanks.' Ryan tries to smile his reassuring smile, but it doesn't work so well any more. If Karin and Alice are coming tonight, they'll be here soon. He turns to leave.

'Anything else I can...?' The sentence trails off behind him, the woman obviously relieved she won't need to finish it.

Ryan hurries down the escalator and takes up his place on the bench on the mezzanine level. An old wino clutching tiredly onto a bottle in a brown plastic bag shifts away from him unconsciously but doesn't look over at Ryan.

Ryan keeps his head down as more children and parents walk by and as security guards circulate, thinking only about the end of their twelve-hour shift. He peers at the escalators from under the lip of the hood until, at last, he sees Karin's thin form riding up to the top level. But where is Alice? Ryan lifts his head and scans the atrium, ignoring the double-takes and hastened steps of the passing shoppers who notice him.

He almost doesn't recognise Alice when she passes close by him, far behind Karin's wake. She's dressed all in tight and too-short black, her hair dyed darker than he's ever seen. She's carrying a single red rose. Worst of all, she's clutching the hand of a tall and pimply boy in faded black jeans and T-shirt. His mousy hair's in a failed coxcomb and he's walking slightly ahead of her with a confident swagger he simply has no reason for.

'Alice!' Ryan jumps up and follows them up the escalator,

elbowing a bag-laden woman aside, forgetting everything he's prepared. 'Alice!'

She turns around and her face curls in disgust. She stumbles at the top of the escalator and walks away, scanning ahead for her mother. The geek strides along with her.

'Alice, wait! It's—' He wanted to do this somewhere quieter, somewhere he could explain to her why his face has changed. She's almost running now. She glances back at him, not a hint of recognition in her eyes. He tries to catch up and she ups her pace.

'Mom? Mom?' she's saying, and now she pulls her hand out of the boy's. They've rushed into a corner between the bookshop, a jewellery shop and a pizzeria. She has to turn around.

Ryan holds his hands up. He stands still, tries to sound calm. 'Alice. It's me.'

The boy steps forward. 'Listen. Just leave her—' he squeaks, losing his nerve when he gets a good look at Ryan's face.

This boy was not part of the plan. 'Fuck off!' he hisses at the boy. The kid looks like he's about to wet himself. He takes two steps backwards, and Alice takes two towards him. Some space is better than none.

'It's me. Dad.'

She looks at him. Stares at his face longer than anyone has since he got it. She shakes her head, backs away, holding up the rose like a talisman, like a crucifix to a vampire.

'I promise, Alice. I've just... I've just had... I can explain. Can we sit somewhere?'

She's still shaking her head. She steps back to the boy and grabs his hand again. 'No. Leave me alone, you fucking freak,' she says.

'Alice. Come on. You know it's me.' Ryan walks towards her. He reaches out and takes her arm.

She drops the rose and Ryan steps on it as he advances, feeling the soft crush of the bud under his thin-soled shoe. 'Leave me alone!' she screams in a shrill yell. '*Mommeeeeeee!*' She sounds like a five-year-old. Ryan's never heard her so afraid. He lets go and turns, and walks straight into Karin, who knees him in the groin. It doesn't hurt Ryan, now he's been fixed, and he stumbles on, trying to get past her. Karin rakes a sharp shoe point down his shin, grabs a clawed handful of hood and face, and twists.

'You don't fucking touch my daughter!' she's yelling, high on adrenalin. He can see the sweat beading on her top lip. She has no idea who he is.

'Sorry, sorry,' he's saying as he shakes himself loose from her grip. He's trying to make for the exit when a weight smacks him from behind. He's hauled over and pepper spray jets into his eyes. Someone's sitting astride him, knees paralysing his arms. He can't bring his hands up to cover his face, and more of the stinging liquid is sprayed onto it. Someone else kicks him in the groin before he's hauled up. Ryan could almost laugh.

Later, after the security guards have made him wait in a sweat-smelling, windowless cubicle, have taken a photo of him and loaded it and the details they've found on his new driver's licence laboriously onto their computer system, they cut him loose.

'Nobody's pressing charges,' the scarred security man says. 'But you don't come back here.'

Ryan feels a magnetic pull back to the house, back to Jane. She never screams when she sees him. But it's almost too simple. The tang of predestiny – as if they knew all along he wouldn't stray far and that's why they don't care if he goes out – sparks a last little ember of rebellion in him. He doesn't go where people tell him to go, he tells himself, but it's a small voice, feeble and unconvincing. Maybe it's time to grow up, get real, make the best of his restricted circumstances. That's something he's avoided throughout his life. Maybe that's something only kids do, that constant kicking against authority. He's nearly forty, for fuck's sake, and he's still floating around in the world, completely untethered. Especially now. His last anchor, Alice, is gone. So maybe Jane's right. He belongs there; he has a job.

That last little voice of independence inside him turns the Volvo left at Sovereign Street instead of taking him straight across. He's going to try one final time to revisit his past, to regather those pieces of himself that he's lost.

He parks a few houses down from Ma Beccah's house and walks the rest of the way. The night air is cold now and he tugs the hood down over his head and pushes his hands deep into the pockets of his jacket. A shower of plane leaves falls around him as the breeze gusts.

As ever, the front door is unlocked. Ryan pushes through and goes down the passage and to his room at the back, hoping Ma Beccah won't see him. He tells himself that he's here because he just wants to collect the rest of his things, but somewhere else inside, he wants to be where he was – who he was – before this all started. If he had just kept his nose clean at the school, if he hadn't been so stupid as to get involved with the girl next door, if he hadn't—

But he stops himself. He knows it all started a long time before that.

He's so used to this dark path through to the small room, the floorboards creaking here and there as they always did, the smell of the tenants' cheap meals clinging to the air, that he's surprised when his door doesn't open. He instinctively pats his pockets for the keys before he remembers he's been gone for too long. He rattles the doorknob as if it will miraculously open.

'Out! Out!' Ma Beccah's standing in the doorway to the sitting room. Just like she protects her house, she protects herself without hard, aggressive metal, without locks and gates and guns, but through the sheer force of her will and righteousness.

'Ma Beccah,' he starts, then swallows the rest of his words. He draws the cowl over his head and retreats without another word or a glance.

'There's nothing here for you.' Ma Beccah's voice follows him.

The last strand of habit holding him here turns him right at the gate and along to Fransie's house. The light's on at the porch, but the old man's chair is empty. As his eyes grow accustomed to the darkness, he notices a slight movement in the shadows. The space beside the house has been cleared; Tess's fantasy castle, what she thought was her safe space, has been deleted. Nonetheless, the girl stands there in a dark fleece top, her arms folded close around her chest. Ryan remembers their previous encounter; she seemed light, charmed. Now she stands sullen and scrapes her shoe at something on the scrubby patch of lawn, unsmiling, disengaged. Some light has gone out in her. He could make her happy, couldn't he?

She looks up when she senses him standing on the pavement looking over the low wall and screams. It's a gut-ripping scream and before Ryan can process the shock, Fransie is running down the stairs with a bat in his hand. Ryan races up the road, away from the car, afraid to pass in front of Ma Beccah's house again, but soon Fransie has caught him. For the second time tonight he feels a wallop over his kidneys and he stumbles to the pavement, tearing the knees of the suit and skinning his palms. Fransie cracks him a blow over the skull and Ryan rolls into a foetal ball at the base of a wall.

Fransie hawks a throatful of phlegm and Ryan feels the weight of it spatter against the hood.

'I see you around here again, I'll kill you.' Another fat wad of mucus hits him. 'I promised my girl I'd never let anyone touch her again.' A half-hearted kick in the back and Fransie's gone.

Ryan waits a few minutes before hauling himself up and sneaking back to the car like a whipped dog.

The next day – he thinks it is, it doesn't matter any more – Ryan's tending the small vegetable patch in the new house's back yard, back in his ragged jeans and sweatshirt, his new face uncovered. He checks the carrot and beetroot seedlings and carefully replaces the protective mesh. At this time of the year a frost is unlikely, but one could strike without warning.

'Why are there no beanstalks?' Jane asks. She's standing in a square of sunlight, enjoying the warmth. It's not doing her skin any good, Ryan thinks, but he doesn't say so. He doesn't want to lecture her.

'It's the wrong season for beans,' he says. 'But there will be carrots and beetroots in two or three months.'

She pulls a face. 'If I wanted dirt produce, I could stay at home.' She crosses her arms and cocks a hip like a sulky pre-teen. She *is* a sulky pre-teen, Ryan reminds himself. That used to mean something different to him. He tries to remember what it was about her that so compelled him back at the school, but he can't feel it. He remembers it, but it's like watching someone else in a movie. Jane's just a little girl.

'It doesn't matter anyway,' he says. 'We won't be here long enough to reap anything. Nothing will be ready before we go back.'

'But there was living produce in the other abode,' she complains.

'That house had an existing vegetable patch. We're starting one from scratch here, despite the fact that...' He stops. It doesn't matter. When he was down there, he felt the uncomfortable pull from the hole in his head every time he thought to argue with the rules. Up here, there's just numbness. The shunt hasn't been renewed for weeks and the hole doesn't work on him any more. It doesn't matter. Nothing matters. This is what it is to let go. Let someone else tell him what to do, no matter how illogical. If you just stop fighting – stop trying to have an opinion – everything's just simpler, isn't it? It's not like he has any option. It's not like he has anywhere to go. Besides, he really likes planting vegetables. It makes him feel like a monk, like he did at the mansion, in peaceful, directed service in the eye of the storm.

He digs out another neat furrow with his trowel and sprinkles in new seeds. 'Are turnips any better?'

Jane twists her lips and turns back to the house.

For the third time today, Ryan sharpens the edge of the trowel with a stone, then pushes the point into the skin of his left palm. He watches curiously as the blood pools then seeps over his wrist and down his forearm. Again he wonders if he'll feel anything.

He twists the trowel's sharp point in the gash.

Nothing.

Chapter 28

TARA

Mindful that it's her last day before she goes on maternity leave, Tara takes extra care packing away the books, double-checking to ensure that the kids have correctly turned off the library's computers. She wishes she'd listened to this morning's weather forecast and worn something lighter. The back of her long-sleeved shirt is damp with sweat, and the summer heat isn't helping her swollen ankles or the morning sickness that's still taking her by surprise deep into her third trimester. Still, she thinks, gazing at the neatly ordered shelves – *her* neatly ordered shelves – what right has she got to complain? This is what she wanted. All her dreams coming true. A fairy-tale ending.

Sure, Kestrel Academy is still a private school – not quite the sort of needy institution to which she planned on applying when her permanent residency finally came through – and she's only part-time for now, but who knows? After she's finished breast-feeding, perhaps she will take up the offer to teach here full-time. And at least Kestrel Academy has a far more liberal approach to reading matter than Crossley College. Ms Traverso, the school's head – a woman so New Age granola that Tara wouldn't be surprised if she rocked up to assembly one morning dressed entirely in dreamcatchers – has given Tara free rein, only insisting that she not order any books that might contain 'hate speech' or 'anti-green' messages. Tara can't help smiling at the horror with which she imagines Clara van der Spuy would eye her collection of Harry Potter and Suzanne Collins novels. Not that Clara's in much of a position to do anything these days. According to Malika, who Tara occasionally runs into at the Eastgate Woolworths, Crossley's old librarian succumbed to a stroke shortly after the school went bust, and is stuck in some crummy institution on the East Rand. Shame, Tara thinks. She keeps meaning to visit her, but has never quite got round to it.

So it's an improvement, all right, but Tara's come to the conclusion that these places are all the same. It doesn't matter what ethos they hide behind, be it Crossley College's pseudo-Christian morality or Kestrel Academy's environmentally friendly New Age philosophy. As long as the kids get the grades promised on the websites, scandal is kept to a minimum and the parents keep shelling out the cash, the wheels keep turning. In fact, all the schools she's ever worked at are just different versions of the same machine, she thinks, wincing as an image of Martin pops into her head. She shrugs it away. She tries to keep thoughts and memories of Martin – along with Jane, Duvenhage and everything that happened during that terrible time – safely hidden behind a wall. She and Stephen never talk about Martin these days, especially now that Olivia's hysterical middle-of-the-night phone calls have stopped.

She concentrates on the faint screams and laughter of the children outside in the playground. Like she's always rationalised, she's here for the kids. She can make a difference to them. She's shown that already.

Thoughts of Martin safely stowed away, the rest of the day stretches pleasurably ahead of her. She'll spend the afternoon decorating the nursery – she can hardly recognise her sanctuary now that the walls have been painted in a soft eggshell blue and the cot and the changing table have been delivered.

She digs in her bag for her keys, feels the smooth curve of Baby Tommy's head pressing reassuringly against her palm as she does so. She carries him with her everywhere, has never dared probe too deeply into why she feels the need to keep him close to her. But why should she? Now that she's sold off her Reborn collection, has shut down her website, it seems only fair that she hold onto one small part of her old life.

The slam of a door in the hallway outside the library makes her jump. She pokes her head into the corridor, sees Busi Gwayise, the English department's HOD, storming out of the boys' bathroom, two pupils slinking after him. She recognises the kids immediately – Kavish Naidoo and Morgan Ebersohn – a pair of spoilt, ultra-privileged ten-year-olds who have caused disruption in her library classes more than once. Bullies, she thinks. Thugs in the making. She flinches as another forbidden image of Martin slides into her head.

Locking the library door behind her, Tara heads towards them. She's never seen Busi looking so irate. He's one of the more pragmatic members of staff, a mild-mannered, soft-spoken man who has no time for the rabidly vegan, fringe-skirted ethos that most of the other teachers embrace. Tara's guiltily aware that if she weren't pregnant and things weren't going so well with Stephen, he's the kind of guy she might have been tempted to flirt with.

'But, sir,' Tara hears Kavish whine. 'He's so—'

'I don't want to hear it. Both of you to Ms Traverso's office. Now!'

'But, sir, we didn't—'

'Just go!' Busi snaps. 'Your behaviour is entirely unacceptable. I'll make sure your parents are informed.'

Muttering, the two boys slump their way down the corridor.

'Everything okay, Busi?' Tara asks.

He smiles at her distractedly. 'Those two. Nothing but trouble.'

'What are they up to? Not another stink bomb, is it?'

'No. Taunting the new boy.'

'New boy?' That can't be right. How can there be a new pupil? It's nearly the end of the school year.

Busi smiles apologetically at her and disappears into the bathroom, emerges a few seconds later with his arm around the shoulder of a small, outlandishly dressed child Tara doesn't recognise. School uniform is optional at Kestrel Academy (to encourage the kids to exhibit their 'inner creative side', according to the website) and most do this by wearing pretty much the same shit – Ben 10 or My Little Pony shorts and tees. This kid looks like an uncool throwback to the seventies. He's dressed in fraying velvet flares and an ill-fitting long-sleeved dress shirt; his longish, tangled hair looks like it's been cut with garden shears.

Busi ruffles his hair. 'They won't bother you again. You going to be okay, Dick?'

The boy looks up at him, glances at Tara, holds her gaze as a strange smile creeps over his face. 'Thank you, sir,' he says. 'But I'm just *primo*.'

Tara bites her lip to stop herself from screaming, feels her right hand reaching up to touch the faded scar just behind her ear. Fights to keep her expression neutral as she watches the kid disappearing down the corridor.

Busi shakes his head. 'Poor kid. Magnet for bullies, that one. Shame, someone needs to talk to his mother about how she dresses him.' He sighs. 'You coming to the staff room, Tara?'

Tara manages to mumble something about having to get home to Stephen.

'You okay? You're looking a bit pale.'

I'm just *primo*, she almost says, bites it back just in time. Tries to swallow. 'I'm fine. Morning sickness, you know.'

'Shame. My wife was the same. Well, all the best. Hope to see you next term.' Busi smiles at her, slides his hands into his pockets and ambles towards the staff room, leaving Tara alone.

Martin, she thinks, her hand unconsciously toying with the scar on her neck again. *Martin.*

Uh-uh. *Don't go there.* She drifts down the corridor on numb legs, pauses outside Ms Traverso's office, ignores the two boys who are slumped sulkily on the bench outside it, waiting to be reprimanded.

The school secretary, a jangly-earringed version of Sybil Fontein, looks up from her computer. 'Can I help you, Mrs Marais?'

Tara breathes in. Plunges her hand into her bag and cups Baby Tommy's head. What does she think she's doing? She needs to go home. She's got things to do. 'No,' she says. 'Actually, I don't think you can.'

Barely acknowledging the secretary's good wishes for her maternity leave, she turns away, uses her staff card to swipe herself through the security gate and hurries towards the car park. She hesitates next to the bank of recycling bins, pulls Baby Tommy's head out of her bag. Drops it into the bin marked 'Plastic', slams the lid.

She can only breathe easy again when she's sitting in her car. Turning the radio to full blast to block out the dangerous thoughts, she guns the engine and drives away.

She doesn't look back.

Chapter 29

PENTER

Penter shuts the door on the last brown. Thank the ether they have all gone! The Mothers always ask the same question in their nasal tones: 'Your accent, it's so unusual, where are you from?' They talk like document mascots.

'Down under,' Penter has learnt to respond. According to Jane, that's a real upside location.

Some of them comment on her outfits and hair, saying things like, 'Oh, I just love this.' But she knows by now that these Mothers are lying. When they say they love something, they mean the opposite. It can be tiring. And the last Mother today wanted to chatter about being a 'single parent'. 'It must be hard on you not having Jane's father around,' it said, prating on and on.

'No,' Penter had replied. 'It's a karking relief.'

That had made the Mother close its yapping mouth!

Penter assesses the waste in the kitchen. Why are brown half-pints so messy? Her counter tops, the forespecial ones she chose from the catalogue, are littered with cupcake crumbs and smears. Ryan will have to clean it after he's finished in the garden. Still, this new scouting method she designed is very productive. Instead of the risk, expense and logistical complexity of harvesting at an institution, Jane scouts the viables at the school and invites them over for cupcakes and horror movies. Once they're gathered in the television room, Penter quickly assesses the most optimal viables, and she doesn't even need to leave the precinct to harvest them.

Yes. Things are progressing in a catalogue fashion. Cardineal Phelgm's office itself has sent signals of support.

Their current precinct is more scenic than the last one, although she is disappointed that there are not any ready beans to be had in the vegetable patch. She still hasn't been tempted to venture outside it. It's not that she's afraid of going out, it's just not necessary. Jane's quite the opposite, using any excuse to go out with Ryan, and bringing back tales of upside Malls and parks, which don't appeal in the least to Penter. They sound dirty and uncomfortable. No, she's content to stay behind the gates of the precinct. There is always much to be done: authorising contracts and dispatching node agents to manage the repercussions of the harvest.

Penter opens the fridge and collects a batch of ready beans that Ryan purchased yesterday from a marketplace. They don't taste as fresh and delicious as the ones that grow on the stalks, but Penter still prefers them to the frozen convenience victuals.

She finds Jane in the television room, looking out of the window, watching Ryan pulling stray grass from around the new shoots.

Every evening now, they watch a document before victuals. Today Jane has chosen something called *A Little Princess*, which she says reminds her of the tame brown, Ryan. Penter hopes there isn't any love in it. She's lost her interest in love documents, and it still embarrasses her that she went through all that turmoil about Father. She does not regret him in the least. Like the browns say, she must have been fucking mad.

Without turning around, Jane says, 'It's depreciating, Mother.'

Penter sighs. 'I know.'

It is inconvenient, but she'll have to think about recycling Ryan soon. A pity, as he has been most loyal, altogether stopped his wandering.

'When can we get a new one?'

'Soon, Jane.'

'Can I scout one? One like Ryan? I know how.'

'Of course.'

Jane turns abruptly and throws her arms around Penter's neck. 'I love you, Penter.'

Penter gasps as her chest is flooded by a warm wash of pleasure. It is nothing like the ragged anxiety she felt for Father. This feeling is deeper, *blissful*. The research was right after all.

She looks over at her daughter, and when she says the words, she now knows what they mean.

'I love you too.'